# The Sphere
*A Journey In Time*

by Michelle McBeth

*To my husband, Sean, who believed in a talent I never knew I had.*

# Chapter 1

My Thursday started much the same as every other Thursday for the past four months. The smell of meat cooking over an open fire wafted up the stairs with the promise of a bland yet hearty breakfast. I rolled out of my creaky bed onto the cold hardwood floor and immediately reached for my stockings. I dressed quickly, thankful that my low rank spared me the more lavish, complicated clothing options. I grabbed a candle and padded downstairs to see what I could do to help.

Mary was just pulling out a fresh loaf of bread. I snatched it from her and started slicing it while she tended to the meat. The fragrant steam wafting up from the recessed pockets of the crusty bread filled my nostrils as it singed my fingers. I spooned a dollop of fat from a crock on the fire where it warmed and spread it on the still piping hot bread. It was definitely delicious if exceedingly unhealthy, but I wasn't about to make waves by suggesting a healthier breakfast option. It had taken me over three weeks to convince Mary I was trustworthy enough for this maid's position before it fell vacant unexpectedly. Given the importance of the house's owner, she was always wary of young women trying to impress themselves upon him. Her suspicions were founded in the fact that this was exactly what she was trying to do. To that end, she now approached me with a handful of what looked like herbs and dirt. I raised my eyebrows in question.

"Magic," she said, and dropped it into a pot of boiling water with an excited look on her face.

I nodded. "Magic." My sigh filled with a well-practiced silence. Mary had schemed for the past 5 months, possibly since before I had arrived, to get her employer to fall in love with her. She believed it was the key not only to being settled for life, but immortality with a place in one of his plays. I never betrayed that I suspected she was already the inspiration for a character. I finished my piece of bread, grabbed a pail and an apron and set off to tend the fires. None of the house's residents had awoken yet, so I started in the common rooms, clearing out the previous day's ashes and loading in more wood from the small stack beside each one that Anthony had replenished late last night.

When I finished with the fireplaces on the first floor, I returned to Mary in the kitchen. She was prodding at the contents of her pot with a wooden spoon. "'This is the day, I declare. Today he will be mine!"

I began to prepare another piece of bread for myself. "Today indeed." My heart fluttered for a moment, and I dropped the bread. What was today? Mary gave me a questioning look as I excused myself for a moment and ran as quietly as possible back to my room. I removed the string from around my neck that held a small iron key as I approached the chest sitting on a table by the side of my bed. My heart sped as I opened the lock and pulled out a small daily journal I hid inside. Thursday. Thursday the 19th of November. Today was the day. Today he would write the Sonnet. Today I could ask him about it. And if all went well, today I could go home.

Not that I hadn't learned to enjoy Stratford. The countryside was lovely. I sometimes was allowed to go out for walks to the main square when the family was away from the house. The life was hard but mentally very simple, which I found relaxing, and being in the same house as one of the greatest literary minds in all of history was hard to beat in terms of company. But I missed so much from my own home. The small chest I had been allowed to bring contained items only necessary to my mission and a few things of a more practical nature that would go unnoticed. Mary dismissed my nightly disappearances, assuming I was going off on my own to pray, not to tend to personal matters like brushing my teeth. I replaced the journal and locked the chest again.

I went back down to the kitchen and, though the breakfast ham was ready, I was too nervous to eat any more. Mary admonished me briefly for not eating enough, took the bread from where I had dropped it and beckoned me over to the pot to smell her concoction. Though I felt a basic moral opposition to the idea of her trying to woo a married man with children, it wasn't in the nature of my station to express that displeasure. *Don't make waves*, I often reminded myself. Besides, as far as history knew, Mary would never be successful.

I picked up the first breakfast tray and took it to Susanna's room. She rolled over and gave a grunt of acknowledgement in my direction but did not make any move towards rising. I could not help but think to myself, *typical teenager*. I set the tray down on a small table and opened the curtains. As the soft light of dawn filled the room, another groan betrayed that she knew she must soon leave the warmth of her bed. I tended to the fireplace to make the room more cozy as she slipped on a dressing robe and shuffled over to her breakfast. I parted with a polite smile that she failed to notice as she poured her tea. I found the less I said to the residents of the house, the more likely they were to ignore me. I was fine with that state of affairs for all but one of the inhabitants.

The morning passed in a daze. My duties were largely routine, affording me time to concentrate on my plan for steering the upcoming conversation with the master of the house. William usually wrote in the mornings and spent the afternoons with his family, but the children's tutor had sent word he was ill, so Anne was taking the children out to the main square today to run some errands. That meant an afternoon without any distractions for him.

He liked to linger in the kitchens when he had nothing else to attend to. I wasn't sure if it was because he didn't feel the need to put up any pretense with us, or if he actually enjoyed Mary's simple mindedness and my quietness. Perhaps he did come up with character ideas from people he interacted with in his life. In the back of my mind, I scanned through the plays I knew, wondering if one of the characters could have been based on me. Mary was out in the garden digging up the last of the potato crop when he wandered in and sat on the stool across from me. I looked up from my work and almost blushed at his smile. Even after all these months, I was still star struck by him.

"Ale, sir?"

"Aye, Rachel." This much at least was routine. I needed to seem casual and normal. This was just any other day to him. I couldn't betray my excitement and nervousness.

I trotted down to the cellar and filled a mug with ale from his barrel. I paused for a moment to focus. "This is it," I said to myself. I gathered up my skirt in one hand and took the stairs at a measured pace, careful not to spill his drink. He was disinterestedly looking around the kitchen when I returned and placed the mug in front of him. I wiped my hands on my apron thinking it amazing that I hadn't yet contracted some horrible disease due to the lack of indoor plumbing and returned to the wood block where I had been chopping vegetables for stew that evening. I waited for him to speak as was proper at that point.

"Mary did attempt to poison me this morn."

My hand froze for a moment before I dropped the knife and covered my mouth to stifle a girlish giggle. He knew Mary's intentions but found her humorously harmless. I resumed my chopping with a sly smile on my face, trying to not betray my involvement in her benign witchcraft. We sat in personable silence for a few moments while he drank his ale. "What new works have you to show us this day, sir?"

"Ah Rachel, thou needst not feign interest for my sake." He smiled and sipped his ale again.

"Nay good sir, I do assure you, tis a genuine interest." I returned his smile, then looked down at my chopping. "The tradesmen in the square do show me a bit more respect than most methinks, thinking me well versed in the arts of the day. 'Tis not every maid in town can quote from 'Romeo and Juliet.'" The play by now was one of his most performed works. "'Course they would be more impressed to be sure, were I to summon a verse from Richard or Henry." My mind involuntarily shouted, "My kingdom for a horse!"

"Dull subject for a maid of thy age. Stick to the love stories," he raised his cup to me.

"Another love story is it then?"

"Love in a familiar manner. Tis yet another sonnet." He raised his eyebrows at me over the lip of his drink.

My pulse sped. This was it. "Another! What makes it now, sir, two and twenty?"

"Twenty."

"Twenty! 'Tis quite a feat, sir. I can barely imagine writing one meself. What manner of love story is this one?" I tried my best to sound nonchalant though my own mind detected every bit of pretense behind my words.

"Here, thou canst read it for thyself." With a flourish of his hand and slight bow from his seat, he produced a sheet of paper.

My body froze, knife still in hand. I tried to hide the deep breath I took as I casually put the knife down and wiped my hands on my apron. I reached for the sheet in his outstretched hand. I once again wished I could steal it back with me. Here in my hands was the first draft and perhaps only copy written in his own hand of William Shakespeare's 20th sonnet. My hands shook. I paced the room to hide the trembling of the paper behind my steps.

I knew it well of course, but focused on reading the lines slowly as though I had difficulty reading the words and understanding what they meant. The original wording was indeed a bit different from the versions found in the anthologies of my time, but the meaning was still the same. For some reason though, reading his works in his own hand, moved me much more than in print. You could almost see the emotion expressed in the cursive. It was elegant yet intense. The ink curled around the more vibrant adjectives, and the rhythm was evident in the varied boldness and spacing of each word.

"Whither didst thou learn thy letters and numbers? Women, for the most part, do not attempt such an undertaking. Tis at odds with the common way."

I was snapped out of my reverie instantly. *You have a part to play*, I reminded myself. "My father. He fancied a life more grand for me than that of a maid."

"Alas, I mourn to know thine existence is so heavy," he chided me.

I feigned embarrassment at his perceived insult, and thrust my hand up to cover my mouth as I let it gape open in shock. "Marry, nay! 'Tis not so. 'Tis a simple life, but a pleasant one. He only thought mayhap one day were I to labor with a merchant in a shop and have a place of mine own."

"Wouldst that be more to thy liking?"

"Than present?" I paused to smile, thinking that if I had to live this sort of life I would have wanted to live it here. "I have access each day to a most brilliant mind, an easy state, a warm, comfortable home in a beauteous land..." I trailed off. I realized I would indeed miss this place, eager as I was to go home. "'Tis a lovely life." I glanced down at the sonnet again. *Play your part*, I reminded myself again. Perhaps I was not the best person to choose for this mission after all. I was already far too invested in the outcome. "Who is he, sir?"

A sad smile crossed his lips again. "My son."

I tried to contain my surprise. All my research on this point had led me in a different direction. "Your son?" My shock was not entirely unjustified. Hamnet was never mentioned in the house. The pain that struck William's features was a clear indication of why. His marriage to Anne had been the equivalent of a shotgun wedding. Mary had mentioned that he lost patience with Susanna as she aged into adolescence, but the joy on his face when he spent time with Judith was hard to miss.

"He died but a few years ago. The twin of Judith. A brilliant lad. I had so many hopes and dreams for him. He would have been a great man were he given the chance." He paused, and the heartache of the memory was evident even in his bearing. He slumped on his stool as he looked through me, lost in some memory of his son. I felt a strong compulsion to reach out and cover his hand with mine, but that would have been a major breach of protocol. His face twitched, and he seemed to recover slightly as he looked up at me again. "Much as thy father wanted more for thee."

"I grieve for I ne'er knew him, sir." Was this enough? It had to be. For now, at least. Let others decide the validity of the evidence. At least it would refute one of the more compelling arguments in the matter. William looked down into his mug and sighed audibly again. The desire to stay and continue the conversation was overwhelming. I wanted to probe his mind further. We'd had a few conversations like this since my arrival. I had needed to win his trust, to show him I was a harmless outlet for his need to talk about his work, but this had been one of our most meaningful conversations to date. I wanted to ask more questions, find out more about his son. But we all knew the rules. Get out as soon as possible. With a great reluctance, I handed the paper back to him. "Beggin' your pardon, sir."

He nodded and drank from his mug as I gave a slight bow, wiped my hands on my apron and headed back to my room. Mary, I knew, was still outside in the gardens, and Anthony was out tending to the horses. I felt guilty abandoning William in the kitchen. With such a heavy heart, he could use some company and he would need a refill soon. Perhaps, I thought, I could wait till Mary came back in. No. No excuses. It was simpler to leave now without having to talk to her. She would want to know what I was up to.

I climbed the stairs slowly and soberly. My thoughts kept going back to William. I knew about his son's death, my research had told me as much, but no one talked much about his relationship with his children. People loved to sensationalize his life, but in the end, he was not much different from most fathers. I thought back to the various fictional depictions of him that I ran across in my studies. None of them had been remotely accurate, but then a devoted husband and family man didn't lend itself to a very sensational sort of movie or book. The truth rarely did.

I paused on the stairs. There was so much we still didn't know about him. I sighed and continued my trek upstairs. *It's not my job*, I chanted to myself with every step. To have such power and have such restrictions placed on oneself at the same time was sometimes painful. But then I counted myself lucky. I had just spent four months living with one of the greatest writers in history. It was an honor. It was enough. It had to be enough.

I got back to my room and surveyed my sleeping area. Nothing lying about was technically mine. I had purchased items upon arrival, but none of that would be coming back with me. I always wondered what happened after I left. What stories would they make up about my sudden disappearance? What would they do with the belongings I left behind? Perhaps given our last conversation, William would think I had left to make a better life for myself.

I knew better than to ask a planter what they might find out about events after my departure when they came back to deliver the evidence. The staff was right to keep us as segregated as possible. It kept things strictly business. Once I left here, that would be the end of my association with this place, and I couldn't request information from them.

I removed my apron, folded it gently, placed it on the bed and smoothed it out. I straightened the brush on my bedside table and stood back to look at my space. It was barren and familiar.

I removed the string from my neck for the very last time and unlocked the chest. I pulled out my journal, opened to the first clean page, dated it, and wrote simply, "It's Hamnet."

I replaced the journal and pen inside the chest and dropped the key on top of them. Then I dug past the few possessions towards the bottom. I pulled out a small, square, velvet box and released the clasp to open it. Inside was a small, silver sphere that I removed and placed on my bedspread. I replaced the box inside the chest and closed the lid. The chest was small enough that I could grasp it under my left arm and pick up the sphere with my right hand.

I took one last look at the room I had shared with Mary for the past four months. I inhaled deeply before flipping the top of the sphere open with my thumb. I barely noticed the faint glow of the button inside as I pushed it. No trace of me remained in the room.

# Chapter 2

"What is the date?" The voice echoed in my head.

The change was instantaneous. One second I had been in the maid's room in Stratford. Now I was here in this harsh, sterile room. We librarians referred to it as the White Box. The lights were blinding. I knew they were only slightly brighter than normal lights, but after spending months in a gloomy countryside in a candle lit house I was not used to the intensity of electricity any more. I dropped the chest and sphere on the floor and pitched forward. I managed to stay upright, a first, and leaned over to vomit. Don't fall into the vomit, I told myself. Perhaps I shouldn't have eaten at all today. No, it probably would not have mattered. Everyone vomits. Everyone struggles to stay upright. Everyone closes their eyes against the light. I fought against the urge to vomit again though the smell of bile and sweat was overwhelmingly nauseating.

The woman's voice came again, "What is the date?" It sounded like Jennifer, maybe. The first few minutes of a return were always a blur, and I didn't know the recovery team that well outside of this room. I thought back to pre-mission briefing. *What was the date? April something.* I should've checked before I left. I wrote it in my journal. Why did I never remember to check? I managed to croak, "April 10th?"

"What is the date?" she said again.

I swore impatiently under my breath. I hated the formality of this. We both knew she wanted the year. Why didn't she just ask me for the year? "April 10th, 2073."

"What is your name?" Her voice was as sterile as the room.

I opened my eyes for a second, then closed them against the pain of the light. I gave up on standing and fell to my hands and knees. *Do not lie down,* I told myself. I opened my eyes again for a moment and glanced to where I had dropped the chest. It was already gone, along with the sphere. The padding on the floor felt like a grubby old gym mat. "Adelaide Vivienne MacDuff." The vomit had been wiped away but the smell lingered and the padding had a grimy wet sheen about it that made me feel ill again.

I felt hands on me. They stood me up and supported me while another set started to remove my clothes. They always wore biohazard suits to protect against any contagious diseases I might have contracted while gone. The masks covered most of their faces so I could never tell who they were. I wondered if that was intentional.

"Mission accomplished?" The final question. The longer I worked here the more these questions made sense to me, but this one was still puzzling. What if I said no? There were definitely missions that had failed, but for reasons out of the traveler's control. No one had failed due to their own incompetence. Would they drag me out some other door along with my chest for a different kind of debriefing? It was hard not to be paranoid in this place. Most likely the question merely directs what they do with my journal and chest while I'm going through the rest of my recovery process. "Mission accomplished?"

I thought about it. There would be more discussion on this mission, I was sure. Without actually catching William in the act with another man, it was impossible to prove his orientation. It had been agreed amongst the higher ups that this would be a first step, and I would find out what I could.

"Yes."

I heard the electronic thud of a microphone being shut off as the speakers cut out. Whoever had asked the questions was satisfied and left. If I squinted I could see shapes. I didn't mind it though. The people in their white biohazard suits and helmets were unsettling. They had removed my clothes at this point and led me to an unmarked white door. No doubt they already inspected the journal I left in the chest. I had never been in this room long enough to determine where all the exits were, but I was almost certain that was by design. For a while now, there had been a dull curiosity about where the aides went when they left me. They guided me through another door and made sure I had enough strength to stand before retreating and shutting the door behind me.

I heard the hiss of the air handling system isolating the doctor and me from the rest of the world. I often wondered why she had volunteered for this, even with minimal risk. We took plenty of precautions before leaving on missions. I had been vaccinated against all known diseases of the period before I left.

It was darker in the examination room, and I was able to open my eyes more fully. I automatically struggled over to the examination table. This was my least favorite part of the return. The nausea had passed, but I was still feeling unsteady. Now I had to be subjected to unpleasant medical tests.

"How are you feeling Miss MacDuff?"

The formality in Doctor Crebbs voice betrayed only a very small amount of concern, but I knew better than to try and capitalize on it. I had asked her repeatedly to use my first name in the past. Part of me wanted to keep asking, to not give in to the formalities of the procedure, but I was especially weary this time around. "Dizzy." I took her hand to steady myself as I moved onto the examination table to lie down. I tried to take a mental survey of my body, but the vertigo made it hard to focus on anything. "Very dizzy."

"Subject MacDuff experiencing more dizziness than past missions. I note again my objection to such lengthy visits." Within the first few seconds of lying down, she had already taken blood, my temperature and blood pressure. I knew the readings were automatically logged along with all vocal notes and a video recording of this session.

In the back of my mind, I agreed with her assessment. The length had been too long. Not just for physical reasons but also psychological ones. Admittedly, it was a highly personal mission for me, but even a few weeks earlier it would've been a mentally easier decision to leave. No, not a decision, I had no choice. But that last climb upstairs to retrieve the sphere might not have been regretted as deeply.

She kept up a stream of notes, did countless more tests and gave me several injections while I tried to recall my mission. In my mind, I reviewed the past few months and especially today, mostly to keep myself distracted from the external stimulus. I didn't particularly care for doctors or being subjected to a battery of tests. We had only been time traveling for a few years, and we still weren't certain about any long-term effects on the body, so the examinations were a necessity. Everyone suffered the dizziness and nausea. They told us it was our body trying to readjust to the time shift, but they could not explain why it happened.

"Exams passed. Subject MacDuff released from quarantine, 0912." I gave a silent cheer and sighed in relief. The disorientation was passing. One thing I would say for Doctor Crebbs, she was fast. It had only been 12 minutes since my arrival. Everyone arrived at 0900. They liked to keep us awake for at least 12 hours once we returned, no matter what time it had been when we left. She helped me up from the examination table. Once out from beneath the spotlight, I found my eyes were now well adjusted. I thanked her and carefully made my way to a door opposite the one I had entered.

The next part was my favorite. One of the aides offered her arm to assist me, but I waved her off and descended the steps into the sanitation bath. The water with whatever chemicals they laced it with was nice and hot, and about two-dozen soft bristled brushes enveloped me from the sides and bottom of the tub and started scrubbing. I leaned my neck back into the arch on the tub as an aide placed the shampooing helmet on my head and started scrubbing my face. I was sure I had quite a bit of grime on me. Given William's affluence, his family bathed every month, but it was not expected that the servants would bathe more than once a year, and I hadn't wanted to make a fuss about it. There had been experimentations with automated facial cleansing shells, but many of us had complained of feelings of suffocation and claustrophobia. In the end, they were convinced that given the extreme variability of facial features they were better off scrubbing our faces manually.

There was a soft beep, and the brushes around my arms retreated. I lifted my hands out of the tub and placed them in the manicure pods on either side. The first time it was explained to me what these were I was terribly frightened of the idea of a machine being able to adjust the ends of my fingernails, but the pods proved to be experts at their jobs. Another soft beep, and the shampooing helmet was removed. My facial scrubber retreated as well. I reluctantly stood back up as the tub drained and an overhead shower rained down on me. I felt like my skin might squeak as I climbed out of the tub and into a soft robe. I smiled at the aide and walked over to another soft chair where the hairdresser, Vanessa, met me.

"Welcome back, Addy." I liked Vanessa, though I was fairly certain that she, like everyone else here, was trained to be watching me. The pleasant conversations that followed were inevitably monitored for any signs of dissent in the ranks. I had only minor training in this. Enough to keep an eye on my fellow librarians. Hairdressers were known for their ability to get people to open up.

I closed my eyes and murmured, "Thanks," as she started to brush my hair. She had quite a task ahead of her. Before I left for my mission, my hair had been roughly chopped and the ends destroyed to help me fit in with my class. "It's good to be home." I gave a hearty sigh and my shoulders, already relaxed from my bath, sank just a little further. She tugged at a particularly tangled spot the conditioner hadn't even made a dent in. "You could just cut all the ends off."

She gave a soft laugh. "Eventually, but it'd be nice if your hair lay flat while I did it." She succeeded with the rough patch and moved on to another spot on my head that had decided to misbehave. My stomach grumbled while she worked out the tangles. I realized I had been awake at least nine hours and had only had that one slice of bread to eat. Vanessa knew my nerves often prevented me from eating on the last day of a mission, and she patted my shoulder. "Don't worry, they're on the way."

She finished detangling me and was parting my hair to cut it when a door on the side of the room slid open and another aide came in. Teddy, I thought. In their white tunics and shortly cropped hair, they all blended together. He handed me a small cube, which I immediately popped into my mouth. I chewed till it was malleable and swallowed. He handed me a glass of water to wash it down. It was largely tasteless, but it would settle my stomach until I could have a proper meal. He waited silently with a placid but not unfriendly look on his face for my order.

"Argent salad, goat cheese, floogberries, bacon vinaigrette. Dry aged duck breast, medium rare, braised golf potatoes." Though I had eaten a lot of meat and potatoes in the past few months, the preparation and seasoning had been lacking. The cube I had just eaten was dual purpose. In addition to settling my stomach, it would aid with digesting foods I hadn't eaten in a few months to assist in acclimating my system back to normal. Though I no longer felt the hunger pangs, my mouth watered at the thought of my meal. "Bordeaux."

"Any particular vintage, Adelaide?" he asked.

"Surprise me."

The aide I thought was Teddy nodded, turned to go and left me to Vanessa again. She had trimmed the first section of hair and was changing my part to attack another section. "So, Shakespeare."

I could hear the smirk in her voice even if I couldn't see her face. "I know!" I knew I sounded like a star struck teenager. The truth was I had looked forward to this mission more than any of my previous ones. Growing up with a last name like MacDuff made it hard not to become engrossed in William Shakespeare.

I already knew most of the material given to me for my research. I had already read everything he was known to have written, in both modern English and the original quartos. In addition, I had read several of his biographies. Vanessa knew of my mild obsession. It had come up in previous post mission haircuts, but she was also one of the few non-librarians I got to see around the complex and actually have any lengthy conversations with. I had to assume that was also by design. I suspected that she was actually a psychologist who had been trained to cut hair. She knew more about the work than any of the other aides. We were warned not to talk with most of the staff about where we had been or what our future missions would be, but she always knew.

"I think he liked me. He would come into the kitchens often to chat. Made it easier to get him to talk about his work when no one else was around. He was not at all like what I was expecting." I paused for a minute, remembering my final conversation with him. "It was harder to leave there more than any other place I've been."

I realized a long time ago there was no point in trying to keep thoughts like that to myself. I had no idea what they made of anything I said, and second guessing motivations got me nowhere. Vanessa once told me she thought I was holding something back. I hadn't suspected her at the time, so I divulged my thoughts, which could have been considered slightly seditious. I had realized that the mission I was on at the time would have been completed more quickly and thoroughly if I had simply told the target who I really was, and I very nearly did it that way. I was still employed here though. I had to imagine certain feelings of doubt in the laboratory complex were natural, and they'd rather know my thoughts, than suspect I was keeping things from them. When I was interviewed and had to go through the lie detector test, they warned me they would rather be told about my questionable behavior than lied to.

"It's understandable. I know this mission was particularly personal to you." I heard the snip of the scissors and wondered briefly if saying the wrong thing would ever get them driven into my skull. There were stories of people disappearing from the complex, but I usually waved those off as rumors.

"Frankly, I didn't care about the outcome either way. I don't think it'll affect the way anyone thinks about his work." I paused and realized that it would still fail to be true for some people. "Or at least, it shouldn't." A bit of tension crept into me and I tried to push it away. I knew the conversations that would be surfacing amongst the higher ups and the planters about what my discovery meant. In here though, I still had some time to keep myself removed from that. *Enjoy your recovery*, I told myself. "Really it was just so amazing to be able to meet such a brilliant man. Though I admit, it takes away some of the mysticism about him as well. I half expected his normal speech to be rhyming couplets!" I laughed out loud and realized my head jerked slightly. "Oops, sorry."

"No harm." She repositioned my head firmly. "I have to admit I'm jealous. I would've loved to meet him as well."

I didn't know how to respond to this. Maybe someday you will? Not likely. The regulations put in place were rather immobilizing. It seemed a shame to have such an awesome technology and not be able to share it with the whole world, but the consequences of it getting out to the general public or other countries could be disastrous. I was told we had a hard enough time convincing the military it wasn't worth the risk for them to try and use it. "Have you ever thought about becoming a librarian?"

Vanessa had moved on to blow-drying my hair, but paused it for a moment to respond. "Nope. I've no desire to go through what you have to go through upon your return. I'm not sure the vomiting and doctor visits are worth it."

I smiled. After my first two trips, I had started to feel the same way. I was sent back into the recent past to check on the actions of some people I had never heard of. It all seemed so pointless to me at the time. I couldn't imagine who would find the discoveries I had made important, but someone must have need the information. So after two trips to see people completely unknown to me doing terribly unimpressive things, I began to think I had made a mistake transferring to this lab. I had been promised exciting and important work with the transfer. At the time I was pursued, they couldn't tell me exactly what I would be doing, but having worked on classified projects in the past I, was used to this idea and accepted it.

I knew classified projects usually turned out to be more dull than the mystery shrouding them implied, but something about this offer had intrigued me. It might've been the directions in the application to list every skill, no matter how irrelevant it seemed. They even broke it down into sections to help guide us. To this day, I have no idea how being able to play a bagpipe could be relevant to this line of work, but things like my scuba certification, community theater work and horseback riding ability now made sense. The idea that a hobby was more relevant to my new job than my engineering background was intriguing. At the time, I didn't know that was what they looked for frequently in librarian candidates. They wanted someone who showed a high level of intelligence and learned quickly but could also fool strangers into thinking they belonged in whatever time period they happened to be in.

Finally after the first two, I had earned their trust well enough to go on a simple but rather important mission. I was sent to Egypt in 2572 BC to see a few days of the construction of the Great Pyramid of Khufu. I went through hell to be made to look like someone who would fit in and not be mistaken for a slave just in case I was spotted. The skin tinting alone took three hours to accomplish and another two to get me back to my normal, pasty, Irish white when I returned. It was worth it because I spent three of the most memorable days of my life hiding in solitude in the desert with a pair of binoculars and some food and hydration packs, watching the great stones get moved into place. It was the most surreal thing I had ever experienced and definitely not something I would forget in my lifetime. To see what humans accomplished first hand with such primitive tools was awe-inspiring. After that I realized there would be missions that I would suffer almost any method of torture to be a part of. Just like this most recent one.

"All done here." Vanessa gave me a smile and a quick hug as I stood up. "Good luck."

I stepped over to the dressing area and exchanged my soft fuzzy robe for a clean purple tunic and shoes. The clothing in this place made me feel like I was in some sort of commune. I supposed that was not completely untrue. At least they weren't white like the aides wore. The starkness of the walls of the chambers gave such a sterile feel; it was nice to have a bit of color in at least one aspect of our lives.

I stepped out into the hallway and was greeted by my boss, Jim. "You've just pissed off a lot of people, Addy."

I made no attempt to hide the mischievousness behind the grin I returned.

# Chapter 3

Jim started off down the brilliant hallway. I fell into step next to him. We passed by several unmarked white doors before I finally spoke. "I don't know why everyone thought he was being so literal about it. It's not like the witches or fairies in his plays are real." It occurred to me as the words came out of my mouth, that witches and fairies might not be real, but witchcraft was definitely considered real in Shakespeare's time. Mary was a perfect example of that belief in mysticism. Perhaps my argument was not that valid after all.

Jim stopped to open a door for me, then followed me in. A small round table was set with my meal and his. Though it felt like mid-afternoon, for me it was only mid-morning. Opposite my duck and salad sat a tea pot and some small pastries. In addition to the table, a couple sets of armchairs dotted the room. I had been in this room many times. This was another part of the debriefing process: an interview given while the experience was still fresh in the librarian's mind, but after a chance to adjust to the time shift and think more clearly.

I sat at the table and eagerly dove into my salad. Jim sat across from me, watching for a moment. "Well, of course not," he said. "But while people love to ascribe meanings to things they know can't be real, they're equally enamored with reading into literature. Finding symbolism in places where none was intended."

I held a floogberry in my mouth for a moment, my tongue savoring the juiciness. Stratford was not known for its fruit. "I guess that's part of the fun. Trying to determine who's right. And we're killing that. That opportunity for speculation."

"It was a dead topic anyway." Jim poured himself a cup of tea and pushed the small plate of pastries away before settling back in his seat. "It's been decades now since homosexuality has been the least bit scandalous. Even if people take this as absolute proof, which they probably won't, the most it will amount to is an 'oh well' in the minds of the scholars who were looking for proof."

"It's not absolute proof. It merely refutes one of the most widely cited examples that supported the case that he was gay. It's not like I found him in bed with the footman." The tension crept back into my shoulders. It was easier to dismiss now that I was actually in Jim's presence. He was my advocate, and I thought of him also as my protector. I couldn't be faulted for anything. I did my job. He was right anyway; it was largely a dead topic. "So I haven't really proven anything, just taken away a bit of their argument. In the end, this isn't over."

"It might be for us. Regardless of what it does or does not prove, it's a question that has been answered. It was a fairly important point of argument in its day. Learning the meaning behind such a hotly contested sonnet will not go unnoticed. The task now is to determine if we continue along this line or let it go."

"That makes it sound like this was a pointless mission." I frowned down at my salad.

"Are you sorry you went?"

"Of course not, but that's hardly the point. You know I was thrilled about the chance to meet Shakespeare." A pang of guilt hit me. Perhaps I had pushed to go more than I should have. In the grand scheme of things, it really was no longer an issue. "But was it worth it?"

"That depends on if it was worth it for you. Look, we've all had our pet projects that we pushed extra hard to see through. It's impossible to come up with a mission that will have meaning to every single person in the country."

I tried to figure out an example to refute that. Given the general apathy of the majority of the population, I couldn't. Some people cared about politics, some people cared about literature and art. Some people cared about nothing but themselves. With all the advancements of technology over the past fifty years, life had become a piece of cake. Without the drive to better their situation, most people merely floated from day to day. What difference did it make to them how they got there?

Jim had not spoken while my mind wandered. I looked up, realizing he had been staring at me. He gazed at me over the lip of his teacup as he took another sip. "So?"

"So what?"

He put the cup down and gazed at me again before continuing. "Was it worth it for you? The weeks of preparation, months of living someone else's life, the recovery?"

A grin spread over my face as I remembered the desire to stay in Stratford. "Absolutely."

"Then I declare a success. You got a question answered and came back without regret. It's worth feeding a pet project every now and then if it keeps you a librarian." A proud smile crossed his face. "And one of our best at that."

I rolled my eyes at his compliment and relaxed again. I had heard of a few missions that were complete failures, but so far I always managed to accomplish my objective. "Do you know what the planters are leaning towards?"

"Of course not. You've been back for less than an hour. The further back in time a mission takes place, the more opportunities in time they have to plant the evidence. And you were gone for a long time. Knowing your obsessive note taking habits, they're still probably trying to read through your journal."

If nothing else, I had given them real insight into the man's everyday life. I nearly dropped my fork. It seemed so obvious all of a sudden. "They'll plant my journal."

"It's likely. I've only read a small amount of it, but it's a highly plausible scenario."

Of course it was. More and more people were learning to read and write in that time period. I had told William myself about my father wanting me to know how. The details of my visit were all there, my interactions with him. I would just have to expand the text out a bit; make it less scientific observation and more girlish whimsy. Then add the conversation that proved that the 20th sonnett was not about a man he loved, but his son. Then the planters could take it back in time, perhaps with a note to give it to someone in the household. One of the daughters, maybe. I tried to quell my excitement. They wouldn't allow further interaction with the family, I was sure. Too many years for a minor change in history to ripple outward.

Jim lifted his hand to touch the implant in his ear. It was an obsolete gesture, the speaker was internal to his brain with no outer controls. He felt it was considerate to give people around him a visual indication that he was at least momentarily going to be distracted by whatever he heard. He gave me a somewhat patronizing look and set his hand back down on the table. "Sounds like you're right. They've transcribed the journal, the file's already on your server. Embellish and expand beyond your departure point. Looks like you'll need to come up with a reason for your disappearance from Stratford after all to add to the journal. They'll find an antique book dealer's store to plant it in and provide an anonymous tip to a collector to go find it."

"Someone discovers the long-lost journal of a maid in Shakespeare's household? That'll get some attention."

"You've got a week to rework the journal."

"A week is way more than I'll need to-".

He didn't bother letting me finish my protest. "It's been five months, Addy. This is the longest anyone has been gone. It's going to be a while before you're let out again. Relax. Take your time."

I frowned and inwardly sulked. I was feeling fine. I saw no need to be overly cautious. "How long?"

"We're thinking about sending you on a two-week vacation after you finish the report."

I tried not to show that I was seething inside. "And then?"

"And then we'll reevaluate how you're doing."

I snatched my wine glass a little too violently and slumped back into my chair to pout. It would be at least three weeks before I even knew what my next assignment might be, and who knows how many weeks prepping for that. That meant at least a month before I could go on another mission. I scowled at the wine in my glass.

"Don't pout, Addy."

I glared at Jim from the rim of my glass, drained it and placed it back on the table. It was mostly for show. For the past five months, I had been drinking bad, high alcohol content wine and my tolerance had increased dramatically. I crossed my arms and continued to glare at him. He picked up the bottle and refilled my glass for me. I contemplated downing that one quickly as well.

Jim spoke again before I could try. "Think of it this way; there has to be something you've been wanting to do that you haven't had time to take care of."

It was true. I had not taken a vacation in a long time. I picked up my wine glass and thought about it again. I realized I had not taken a vacation since I started here a few years ago. When I really thought about it, aside from my missions, I had not left this place since I started. I wasn't even sure where I would be allowed to go. "Maybe." I never really thought I needed time off. I enjoyed my work learning about cultures from long ago, the dialect lessons, and the travel. What would I do with two weeks to myself? "Where am I allowed to go for vacation?" I was fairly certain they did not trust me enough to let me interact with the normal world in an uncontrolled environment.

"We have an island in the Atlantic. It's fully staffed with trustworthy people."

"You've been there?"

"I went when you were on an assignment once. Lovely spot. Learned to fence."

"Still. Two weeks?"

"You've been gone five months." He emphasized the last two words as though I wasn't aware of the passage of time. "For us only a week has passed since you left. It's important for you to spend some time in this time."

I took a hefty sip from my glass, slightly less peeved about the situation. "How about a compromise: I'll rewrite the journal during my two weeks away."

"No." His response was immediate. I knew Jim well enough to know when there was no compromise possible. I also knew he had my best interests at heart. Jim was the closest thing I had to a father since mine died when I was a young girl. Though I enjoyed the banter, we both knew I would do whatever he wanted. I didn't have much choice in the matter.

"Fine." I stood up roughly from the table and stalked towards the door like a petulant child.

"You can't start working on the journal until tomorrow," he said.

I stopped dead in my tracks. The crafty bastard knew me too well. I turned and walked back to the table. "Fine." I snatched the still half full glass and bottle and took another swallow on my way out of the room. I paused at the door, "I want a hot fudge brownie sundae for dessert."

As the door slid closed behind me, I heard Jim confirm something about Teddy and my room.

I started down the hall towards the exit. The few people I passed nodded in acknowledgement or welcomed me back. I recognized most of them but could not name them. Teddy met me shortly before the entrance to the living dome. I saw the welcoming, colorful foliage beyond the door at the end of the plain white hall. "Your sundae is on your coffee table, Miss MacDuff. Best not delay your return. The ice cream will melt."

"You're a saint, Teddy."

"My pleasure, Miss MacDuff."

I stepped through the glass door at the end of the hall and took a deep breath. Though the dome was completely enclosed, the trees and plants provided plenty of fresh air and floral scents. It was a welcome change from the five months of mild body stench and horses, followed by the stale recirculated air of the mission return chambers. I walked over to the Japanese style garden and placed my wine glass and bottle on a bench. I said to the general air, "Leave it," and continued toward my apartment. The door parted before me, and I barely glanced at the interior as I grabbed my sundae and headed back to the pond.

My wine was still on the bench. I sat down next to it and stared at the water in the fountain for a few minutes. My brain felt fuzzy. Perhaps it would be a good idea to just relax for the rest of the day, work on readjusting my internal clock to the present time. I rarely had any down time on my mission, just the few minutes before I went to sleep every night to write in my journal. Now that I was back, I hardly knew what to do with myself. My instinct had been honed to clean and tend to things whenever possible. Back here, almost everything was done for me.

Well, I thought, at least I knew what I would do for the next half hour or so. I took another sip of wine, then picked up the spoon to my sundae. I zoned out as I stared at a tree, listening to the sound of the water spraying in the fountain, and let a spoonful of ice cream and brownie melt in my mouth. The moment felt unreal, like I was in a dream. Any minute now I would wake up, and Mary would yell at me for not being down in the kitchen. Then Shakespeare would come and let me read another of plays. That was reality. This was a memory from long ago.

I shook my head, as though that would help to clear my mind.

# Chapter 4

I woke up with a bit of a hangover. I kept as still as possible for a moment. My bed felt much softer than normal. I loathed the idea of getting out of bed to begin my morning chores. Where had the smell of body odor gone? And where was the smell of fresh baked bread for breakfast? Was it still night time? What was going on? My head throbbed painfully. Of course. I was no longer in Stratford, I was home. I had drank that bottle of Bordeaux. Then I had drank that second bottle, and then that scotch. The scotch was probably a mistake.

I decided to blame the time change for affecting my ability to cope with the alcohol. There was something I needed to remember, something from yesterday. *Something about the pond.* I decided to continue lying on whatever it was I was lying on. *The pond in the Japanese garden. Japanese?* No, I had decided against learning Japanese a while ago. Even if I learned the language, the likelihood of going where I needed it meant I would also have to look Japanese. While it might have been easy to tint my pasty white skin a darker color for my Egypt trip, I doubted changing my facial structure to blend in on a more intimate mission would go well.

I rolled over and instantly regretted it. It was apparent that I was facing a window now. Though my eyes were closed, I felt the difference in illumination burning through my eyelids. My brain felt like it was still turning over as well. The pond. I thought a groan might somehow help, but the noise merely made a throbbing pain join the moving sensation of my brain. When was the last time I had a hangover? Certainly not since moving to this place. I was sure they stocked my medicine cabinet with something useful. I just had to make it to the bathroom.

Where was I anyway? I knew I was in my place. I remembered coming home. It was soft. There was a blanket. My foot was slightly pressing against something. It must be the couch. The bed was larger than this. If I was facing a window, that meant my back was to the back of the couch. That was a good start. I rolled off the couch onto my hands and knees, keeping my eyes closed. *Pond.*

I tried to get my bearings. The bathroom would be down at the end of the hall. I shuffled forward on my hands and knees to the end of the rug and pulled myself upright on the lounge chair. With my eyes still closed, I felt my way down the hall. I left the bathroom light off, opened the medicine cabinet, then opened my eyes slightly. Through the bleary slits I saw the bottle of phenederil and managed to fumble the lid off. I tossed one in my mouth and turned the tap on. I hated trying to swallow a pill without a glass of water, but I didn't want to try and make the trip back to the kitchen without some drugs in my system. I managed to get enough water from my hand into my mouth to get the pill down and plugged the sink. I watched the tap water fill the basin and thought back to the pond. I splashed some of the water on my face and gave it a good rub before looking down at the water again. Some dirt was floating on the surface of the sink water. I watched it float around for a minute before the idea finally came back to me. *Sailing!*

That was what I wanted to do with my two weeks. Learning to sail in a private tropical paradise seemed like a great way to expand my mind, yet still have fun. Besides, it might come in handy someday. I dried off my face and took a deep breath. The drugs were already doing their magic. I strutted back to my living room and said to the space, "Message to Jim, I want to learn sailing. Send." A soft beep let me know the message had been sent. I went into the kitchen to put some water on to boil. I pulled a serving of steel cut oats out of a cabinet. "Mail." A screen appeared in the air over the back of the range. The most recent message was from the planters. The one before that was from Noah, another librarian. Noah was one of my better friends in the complex. We were discouraged from mixing with people not in our field. I focused my eyes on his message and said, "Read." Noah's voice filled my kitchen.

"Hey Addy, my guess is you're either making yourself a grilled cheese sandwich with some of that horrible processed cheese substitute you seem to love, or you did the right thing and left business off till the morning, in which case you're stirring your oatmeal. Either way, when you have some free time during the next day or two, I could use a little help with my prep for next week. I need a woman's opinion on something, and you're the closest thing around. Missed ya!"

I couldn't help but laugh at his message. We frequently made up excuses to consult on each other's prep work to force ourselves to have some fun and not burn out. Not that we often had missions we weren't looking forward to. Often another perspective helped with the prep work though. It was strange. I hadn't seen Noah in over five months, but for him it had only been a few days. I heard another soft beep as I stirred my oatmeal. Jim had responded to my message. It was barely 6am, and I wondered if the man ever slept. "Read."

"Sailing sounds like a wonderful idea. I'll see if I can set that up. You should have your files from the planters by now. Remember, one week. If you finish early I'll make you translate it into another language."

I knew he was not joking, and somehow doubted he would let me pick the language. I mixed some brown sugar in with my oatmeal and poured a glass of orange juice before retiring to the couch. "Mail." The screen disappeared from the kitchen and reappeared in the air over the coffee table. My eyes rested on the message from the planters. "Open." The message opened on the screen and the attachment showed up as a smaller document on the side. I read through the first sentence and decided I did not want that sort of formality with my breakfast. I focused on the attachment of my transcribed journal. "Open." I settled down to read through the account of my time in Stratford. Most of the journal entries were fairly banal. During my first few weeks, I worked as a maid at an inn near the center of town. I gradually built up trust with Mary, and arranged a convenient absence of her other maid. Most of the entries were about me complaining of my treatment and my gradual befriending of Mary, but one in particular caught my attention.

> *Wednesday, July 8th, 1598*
> *Another interesting sighting today. Henry Wriothesley, the*
> *number one man of interest on my scout's list came to the inn*
> *today and is spending the night. He was accompanied by*
> *another man also on my list, but further down, Byron Goodfell.*
> *I tried eavesdropping on their conversations but there were so*
> *many people about today it was difficult. It mostly sounded like*
> *they were talking politics anyway. Henry, like William, largely*
> *ignored me, but Byron kept giving me queer looks. I wonder if*
> *he thought I might be of service in other ways. Something*
> *about him seemed off, it was kind of creepy. Maybe I'll try to*
> *talk to him tomorrow, see what he can tell me about Henry.*

I hadn't paid that much attention to Byron since he wasn't that high on my list of potential sonnet subjects, but I remembered the feeling he gave me the few times I did see him. It was like he knew something wasn't right with me. I had shrugged him off as being eccentric at the time. "Search Byron."

A list of four more entries popped out to the side of my journal. Each of them had a mention of Byron in them. I focused on the top one first, "Open."

> *Thursday, July 9th, 1598*
> *Well no luck today. Henry and Byron left rather early to head*
> *to William's house. I asked the innkeeper if they often come*
> *through town to visit Shakespeare, and he told me to get my*
> *head out of the clouds. He said that an Earl would have no*
> *interest in a simple maid like myself, and I should remember*
> *my place. I wanted to smack him, but demurred to his*

*intolerable wisdom. Definitely don't need to be attracting more attention to myself.*

I didn't think that entry very interesting, and focused on the next. "Open."

*Saturday, July 11th, 1598*
*I can't wait to get to the point where I can write about something other than the innkeeper's daily tortures. Today was a fun one-he found me*

*Never mind that. Byron just came back. The innkeeper brought him up to my room and told me I had to show him a good time or risk being thrown out in the streets. When the innkeeper left, I told him that I hadn't agreed to this when I was hired. Byron said something about me having nice teeth for such a lowly maid. I pleaded with him to leave me be, and he said he would enjoy my company for a few more minutes then tell the innkeeper I had been well worth it.*

*I never thought to prepare for this in my training. Perhaps I should step up the timeline. I got lucky with Byron, but who knows who else the innkeeper will bring up to my room. I wonder if this is the sort of thing that could get him in trouble with the authorities. Probably not, it would probably just bring them around more often.*

I hadn't given much thought to the few weeks I had spent at the inn before moving to work for Shakespeare. Frankly, I had wanted to forget most of it since it was largely unpleasant. This entry was the only occasion where the innkeeper had tried to sell me off as more than just a maid. I had forgotten about it almost immediately after leaving the place and wasn't very keen on reliving it now. Perhaps I would leave this part out of my rewrite. I glanced at the last entry in the search list. "Open."

*August 1st, 1598*
*Byron and Henry came by the house today. Byron gave me a funny look and mentioned how fortuitous it was that I happened to be picked up by William Shakespeare as a maid. I agreed that he was a much better employer than the innkeeper. The smile he gave me betrayed something, I'm just not sure what. I think maybe he knows that I somehow had a hand in the other maid's unfortunate incident. Perhaps he thinks Mary and I were in on it together. I didn't notice any particular treatment of Henry by William. I'll admit, he's a pretentious little fop, but*

*that's not unusual for men of his status in this time. They took him somewhere out of the house. At least now he seems to be past his highly focused phase.*

I realized that even if Byron had suspected me of orchestrating the former maid's demise, there was little to be done about it. Furthermore, it no longer mattered. Byron was long gone, and there would be no need to even mention him in my rewrite. I ignored the fourth entry involving him, knowing I would read it soon anyway.

It took me a good hour to read through my journal. I had no idea where to begin, so I looked back at the message from the planters. Their plan was to create a blank journal and rewrite my embellished journal entries with a quill pen. Then they would chemically age the journal and plant it at an auction for a well-known book collector. In the back of my mind, I wondered for a moment if they would also kill a well-known book collector to speed the discovery. I made a mental note to mention the thought to Vanessa as a joke at some point.

I took my dishes back to the kitchen and placed them in the cleaner. There was no sign of my hangover left, so I decided to go for a run. I had a fair amount of exercise in Stratford, but it was mostly heavy lifting and climbing stairs. It would feel good to get a nice long jog in and clear my head a bit. I changed clothes and stepped outside my door.

I paused just outside to gaze at my surroundings. Though I had only been gone a few months, it felt unfamiliar. A short distance to my right, I saw the entrance to the Mission Enclosure where I had arrived yesterday. It was where we did our prep work and some of our research for time travel. The faint outline of its own dome-like enclosure was barely visible on the other side of the glass. Further along the circumference of the main central living dome was the entrance to the agricultural department. Like the living dome, its enclosure was glass to allow sunlight in. It was also much larger than any of the other domes because it housed gardens and fields.

On the opposite side from the traveling chambers was another enclosed dome, larger than the one where I worked. Next to that stood the entrance to the outside world. I had no idea what went on in the other dome. I didn't even know what it was called. By way of experiment once, I ran around the circumference of the living dome. Though the doors to the agricultural dome and my own research dome slid open easily as I ran by, the other doors did not. I turned left and headed down the row of apartment doors to the gym.

The place was deserted this early in the morning so I had no trouble finding an empty running simulator. I selected my favorite trail and headed inside. It was a mostly level trail that wound through the woods, across a few small streams and past a waterfall. Within a few minutes it was painfully obvious that I was out of shape. I stopped near the halfway mark at the waterfall for a break. "Journal entry, November 18th, 1598."

The general computer voice used for text transcription sounded like Sean Connery to me. It seemed like such an odd choice for something meant to be generic. I paced back and forth in front of the waterfall trying to catch my breath as he repeated the words from my journal entry.

"Wednesday, November 18th, 1598. Today was dull. William was gone for most of it, so I had almost no interaction with him. The scout plugged tomorrow as the day he finishes his 20th sonnet. I feel I'm ready. He shows me almost everything he writes now, and frequently asks for my thoughts. Wish I had brought some sort of stronger alcohol to spike his drink, and loosen his tongue a bit. Guess I'll have to rely on my wits alone."

Even without Connery's surreal voice transcription, I knew it was going to take a fair amount of work to get the journal ready for the planters. It hadn't been hard to learn the rules of Elizabethan era grammar and verb conjugation based on my status. Even getting the accent down had been a relatively simple thing, but the speech patterns were so different it was hard to come up with sentences on the fly. It had helped that I wasn't supposed to be a terribly intelligent person or have very involved conversations. The vocabulary I had used was very limited, and the more time I spent there listening to other people, the easier it came to me. My journal, on the other hand, was very much written in my style of thought and speech patterns. The task wouldn't be as simple as changing verb forms and replacing some words. Perhaps the rewriting would actually take the whole week.

I pushed myself to finish the rest of the trail run, then walked back to my apartment eager for a long hot shower, even though I was also looking forward to seeing Noah. "Mail. Respond Noah. Hi Noah! I'm about to hop in the shower in an effort to procrastinate starting my post trip work. Care to help me in that? The procrastination, not the shower. Nothing scheduled today so let me know when you're free. Addy."

By the time I had finished my shower Noah had responded with a suggestion of lunch. Because of my early start to the day, I still had a few hours to kill, so I sat down at my desk and pulled up my journal again. I stared at the first entry for a few minutes and wondered if anyone in this place could produce a translator that would convert my text into Elizabethan English.

Once I started, creating a more thorough narrative of my time in Stratford was more fun than I thought it would be. Though I didn't write many descriptions of people in the original journal, I had strong memories of impressions and personality types. It was easy to expand upon the inn keeper's slave driving attitude and Mary's innocent mischievousness. Since everyone involved had been dead for a long time already, I didn't have to worry about accuracy of characters until I wrote about Shakespeare himself, but even he had been written about in such a variety of ways, it probably wouldn't matter how I portrayed him in the end. Though for my own conscience, I wanted to represent him as accurately as possible.

I added in a little background about myself as well. I made sure to mention my father and his desire that I became educated to explain why I could read and write in the first place. Mary was the only person I had talked to at length about my life history. No one else cared, and most people would have found it inappropriate to have a conversation of that nature with me. Naivety was also simple to impart by just narrating things at face value and focusing on relatively banal parts of my days.

The difficulty came with the actual grammar and speech I used. I found myself frequently double checking words I used to be sure someone of my stature in that time period would have written them. I tried to avoid idioms and metaphors as well.

After three hours, I had made a decent dent in the first section of my journal. It covered my arrival in Stratford to when I was picked to replace the maid who disappeared from Shakespeare's house. I felt like it sounded sufficiently uneducated. I reread through it once to check for anachronisms and decided that was enough for the morning.

I pulled on a red wrap around tunic and black drawstring pants. As much as I missed the fashion choices of the outside world, I had to admit the clothes they gave us were at least more comfortable than anything I remembered from my prior life. I asked Jim about it once, and he rambled off some excuse about remaining inconspicuous and blending in with all the other types of lab workers. As though if we all looked the same, people would just assume we all had the same jobs. It seemed unnecessary to me. It wasn't like putting on jeans was the equivalent of wearing a big "librarian" sign across my chest, and "librarian" didn't sound anything like what my job actually entailed, aside from the research aspects of it.

I looked around my kitchen for something to take to lunch with me—a well-ingrained courtesy leftover from my time before coming to the lab. It was only a halfhearted attempt. I knew Noah would have more than enough food prepared for us, so I gave up quickly and headed for the door. As it slid open and I stepped outside, I was greeted by a gloomy, ominous looking sky. My favorite kind.

# Chapter 5

Noah lived on almost the exact opposite side of the living quarters dome. I set out across the central courtyard in a nearly perpendicular path from my own door and wound my way through the copse of elm trees that marked the center of the dome. I paused in the middle of the trees and looked up for a moment. The silence was oppressive. In Stratford, there were birds flying about and insects buzzing and people and carts and horses. I had forgotten how artificial this place was while I was gone. There was a low drone in the distance that gave away the presence of some massive power generator, and the faint noise of a few voices also wandering about in the dome, but otherwise it was too quiet.

The sky was keeping most people indoors today. I didn't understand why since the rain would never touch us in here. The gloomy blue-gray color reminded me of my later days in Stratford. During my residency there almost every day had been cold and gray, once the fall season arrived. Stratford was given to frequent drizzle, and I always found the patter of raindrops on the roof of the house calming. Here the glass ceiling was so high it was impossible to hear the rain unless it really poured, and then it just became another muffled drone that added to the ambient noise level.

I knew I would get used to it again, but for a few days at least, I would feel like I had left the real world behind to come back here, to my carefully constructed, isolated home.

I continued on through the courtyard and nodded hello to the couple of people I passed. I recognized them, but again, could not have named them nor said what they did here. Librarians were probably the most gregarious people in the whole laboratory complex, but we also kept to our own kind. Partly by coincidence, but mostly by direction. We all had offices in the Mission Enclosure but did most of our research in our own apartments.

I knocked on Noah's door, and he answered it with a nonchalance that reflected his difference of opinion in the passage of time. Without a moment's hesitation, I assaulted him with a bear hug and a mocking, "It's been forever!" He laughed and stepped aside to let me in.

Noah's place mirrored my own in layout, but his decorating style always struck me as lacking. It was sparse with only a handful of personal touches. His furniture choices were very utilitarian. It gave me an impression of an extension of the White Box and the adjoining rooms of the return chambers. Almost immediately off to the right was his kitchen, which was a mess. He had obviously been cooking. I appreciated that he put in the effort and didn't just order a fully prepared meal from the lab kitchens. It also afforded me the opportunity to try things I would never think to make for myself. I gave him a curious look and asked, "What have you been up to?"

"I'm trying out a new risotto recipe. I think you'll like it." As he lifted the lid off the pan a puff of steam escaped into the air along with a delicious scent. I couldn't identify the colorful bits of food speckling the rice, but I knew based on past experiences that it would be good. Noah's experiments often were. I did remember one experiment involving a new fruit that turned out too mushy for human consumption, but he had a lot more experience with gauging the consistency of food now. "Outside?" he asked. I nodded in return. I always preferred the grass to his dining area table and chairs. I never felt comfortable in the hard plastic curves of his seating choices.

He spooned servings out into bowls and grabbed a bottle of viognier from the fridge. Though I tended to prefer reds, I trusted his judgment of what best complimented his creations. I silently grabbed my bowl and two glasses and followed him out to the courtyard. We plopped down in the grass. I held the glasses for him as he poured the wine. He took his glass and held it towards me before taking a sip, "To a successful mission."

I did not hesitate to take the compliment this time, so I clinked his glass readily and took a sip. It was perfectly drinkable, but I decided to reserve judgment until I tasted how it complemented the risotto.

"So who was the lucky man?" he asked as he started on his food.

"His son, Hamnet."

Noah tried very hard to keep the partially chewed risotto in his mouth as he barked out a laugh. His gaze drifted off to the edge of the dome. I gave him the moment I knew he needed to mentally review the sonnet. He snickered and shook his head slightly in disapproving amusement. "Oh, how you're going to piss off the literati."

"I hate to think of my poor scout and all his investigative work." My scout had spent several weeks sneaking around Stratford to figure out the exact dates of events and get a more accurate picture of Shakespeare's daily life and acquaintances for me. He was also the one who came up with the plan for the maid's disappearance. "His 'List of close or relevant men' completely led me astray while I was there. I barely paid any attention to the children."

The thought came with a pang of regret. "Had I known they were such an influence in his life, I would've made more of an effort to know them," I said. The idea was accompanied by a bit of doubt. The children, while not haughty, gave me little attention as a maid. It's likely I would have had to be a tutor or some other position more meaningful to them to gain any insight into their lives. It wouldn't have been hard to prove my qualifications as a tutor. I certainly was educated enough to teach whatever subjects they studied. Though it would've been more difficult to fake governess credentials.

Noah gave me a sympathetic look. We both knew it was pointless to think such things. Going back again would absolutely be out of the question. Scouts were the only people allowed to cross visits, and that was only because they were so good at hiding from the rest of us. For some reason, they thought that stumbling upon another version of yourself would be disastrous.

I always thought this was a rather silly rule though. If I ran into another version of myself or a colleague, I would understand what was going on. I wouldn't even think it shocking to find a stranger who appeared to be out of time. I actually found it rather hard to believe that there were not already other people traveling through time. If we had the technology, then what was keeping the European Coalition from finding it as well? If there were other travelers, I had to believe they had rules like ours. Maybe our lab just didn't want other countries to know we had the same technology. It all seemed rather sophomoric to me; the idea that everyone thought they had with this big secret, when in actuality everyone knew.

However, in the opposite extreme, if we were the only ones who had the ability to travel through time, then that was definitely something we needed to guard. We were strictly forbidden from making any changes that would seriously alter the course of history. It was hard to not fantasize about killing Hitler and saving the lives of millions of people and preventing a world wide war. I understood the reasoning behind it, but what's to say another country would agree with that assessment of non-interference?

I thought back again to my journal entries of Byron and realized that the strangeness I felt from him could actually have been a sense of misplacement. "Have you ever suspected someone in the past of actually being from the future?" I asked Noah.

He cocked his head at me and raised an eyebrow. "Where did this come from?"

"I was just thinking about some of the rules. About not going back and interfering with your previous timeline and thinking that at some point in the future, I imagine more countries will have this technology and send their own people back."

He mused about the idea for a moment. "Can't say I ever had that suspicion. Have you?"

I looked down at the wine as I swirled it. It was mostly for dramatic effect, not hesitation. There was nothing I wouldn't tell Noah. "I think maybe on this mission."

"Did you tell them?" he involuntarily smiled at the idea of me committing a potentially seditious act, even unintentionally. Although Noah enjoyed this life as a librarian, he also found these stretches of real life boring. That was why he developed his hobby of experimental cuisine, to break up the monotony of his time in normal time. Any bit of scandal was exceedingly intriguing to him.

"I'd completely forgotten about him by the time I got back," I said. "It wasn't until I reread through my journal that the memory was triggered. Guess they're finding out now." Without realizing it, I looked around as though expecting to see a microphone somewhere. Someone, no doubt, was listening. Someone was always listening in this place. That was no secret. I couldn't fault them for that. We were dealing with such an explosive technology that they were very serious about guarding our secret. It took an enormous amount of trust on their part just to let us go on a mission in the first place. I figured I might as well expand on it for their benefit. "It was an acquaintance of William's. Actually, it was someone on the list."

"Your scout's list of men of interest?"

"Yep. He came around to the house a couple of times. He seemed different somehow. I don't really have any proof that he wasn't who he said he was. It was just...a feeling. Like he knew more than he was letting on about my being there. Some things he said seemed out of place." I thought back again to my survey this morning of the entries mentioning him. Perhaps his suspicions about me were rooted in his own history.

"Maybe he was from another lab, just like ours and on a similar mission," Noah said.

"If so, he's very good at it. The two of them were quite chummy when he was around." I frowned at the idea and felt a bit jealous. Though William had liked me well enough there was a definite distance forced by my relative station. Mary had frequently warned me I was too familiar with him, and it was not just her paranoid jealousy speaking.

"You succeeded well enough. We're subject to the rules of the time. It's not like you could've joined his theatre troupe or anything. Any man would have had an advantage over you."

"Ah, wouldn't that have been sweet though," I mused. "Performing in a Shakespeare play with him at the helm!" Noah was right, of course, and I felt a little guilty that my obsession with all things Shakespeare was what got me that mission. A man surely would have had an easier time of it. Then again it was also said that if you wanted to know what was going on in a house, work in the kitchen. Mary had certainly known all the dirt on the household and was more than willing to share any gossip.

My mind kept returning to Byron. I suddenly had an overwhelming desire to return and question the man further. Again, a useless thought. I sighed in frustration. "Well, he doesn't matter. He wasn't the subject of my mission, and there's not much in my journal on him." I laughed once without humor. "We need their surveillance systems." I glanced around the grass again.

Noah caught the reference immediately. "They really need to fix that." It irritated him immensely that nothing electronic could be sent through time with us. It was not such a problem for recent trips when we could simply purchase the surveillance products we needed. Though as I had just demonstrated by my lack of memory, there were so many details we missed that could prove essential later on.

"Well, enough of that," I said, with a dismissive wave of my hand. " What are you working on?"

"Salem."

"Ooh, a witch hunt?"

He smirked. "Something like that. My scout has nailed down an event that nobody can explain by mere visual examination. A witch survives a burning."

"Really. What happens?" I asked. I was enjoying the wine much more with the risotto, and scarfed down a few more bites of my meal as Noah talked.

"She gets tied to a pole with a bunch of hay and wood piled at the bottom. When they set the hay on fire, she screams for a few minutes as the flames start to engulf her, then she simply jumps off the wood pile and runs away. The crowd is too stunned to do anything. We're pretty sure the fire burns through her binding, but the flames are up to her chest at that point. So, how would she do it?"

"Who are you supposed to be?" I leaned back into the grass on my hands to listen, full from the meal.

"A doctor," he made a quote motion with his fingers, "and sympathizer for the dark arts. I get to befriend her, then hide in the woods where she runs. Try to get to some meetings, see what sorts of rituals they do. It's more a research trip than anything else. They have a low expectation that I'll actually be able to get her to tell me how she does it."

"They'll be distrustful of a man. Why are you being sent on this one?"

He puffed his chest up and grinned. "I'm the best fake doctor we've got around here."

We were discouraged from talking about our pasts, but I knew that before Noah was recruited here, he was a medical consultant for the government. He made it about halfway through his residency before getting too bored to finish. I imagined being a medical consultant wasn't that exciting either, but the hours would've made it easier for him to pursue interests outside of work.

"Not that it'll be that hard," he said. "They had very little in the way of modern medicine in that time period. Most likely I'll just treat a few wounds that have a good chance of becoming infected and pass out a bunch of meaningless herbal remedies to people with various ailments." He smiled conspiratorially at me. "They'll probably think I'm a witch myself. Done?"

"Yes. It was delightful." I sat back up and picked a soft but fibrous yellow square out of my bowl of unfinished risotto with my fork. "What are these?"

"Monty just created them. He's calling them montbeats," he said with a small flourish of his hand. "He showed it to me when I was wandering around in the gardens the other day and asked me to give it a try. What do you think?"

Though I was plenty full, I plucked the montbeat off my fork and chewed slowly to give it a more thorough exam. I never went to the gardens. Noah found them fascinating, but I found them dull. It was probably an extension of his medical background to be curious about herbs. "A bit chewy."

"Sorry about that. I should've tried a few methods of cooking before throwing them into something."

"It's okay. I didn't notice it until I had one on its own." Now well satiated I stretched out my legs and leaned back again and sighed. The gloom had started to dissipate, and the sky, though still cloudy was getting lighter. "Well, I should probably get back to work."

He groaned slightly. "Same here. I need to get my trunk list in to the prep team today."

"What are you planning on taking other than the basics?" We were allowed one small trunk or appropriate container for the time period on each mission. Almost every librarian left with a journal, money, a toothbrush, and an adequate supply of toothpaste for the intended length of our mission. We could do without most toiletries, but we all hated not being able to brush our teeth. That reminded me; I was probably due for a cleaning.

"My scout applied to an apprenticeship with the main doctor in the town on my behalf. I'll need to look like I've traveled from afar, so they've also reproduced a fair amount of money for me to buy a real trunk and clothes and necessities. Unfortunately, this is far enough back in time that there isn't really any medical equipment I can take with me. They didn't even have stethoscopes back then." Noah had a collection of ancient medical equipment from his missions hanging on one of the walls in the dining room. It added to the unsettled feeling I experienced when in his quarters. "Well, come on then," he said as he rose from the grass.

We carried our dishes and the empty bottle back to his place. I helped him get them into the cleaner and waited as he wrapped up the leftovers. He walked me back to the door, and we hugged again. "I'm off in a few days, and I guess you're swamped with your work for the next few," he said.

"Yeah, this journal rewriting is going to be a pain. It's fun, but trying to get the grammar right is rough."

He nodded. "Well, maybe we can do a quick lunch again before I leave."

"Maybe," I said, as I turned away to walk back across the courtyard to my quarters. "Good luck with the witches!"

# Chapter 6

I finished rewriting my journal the afternoon before I was to leave for my vacation. I had forced myself to take my time going over it, checking on the style before handing the first draft off to the planters. They had only minor edits for me to make on that last day. I was excited about getting out of the laboratory complex for a while, but slept more soundly than I would have the night before a mission.

Shortly after lunch, I walked to the entrance of the complex. Jim was there waiting for me. The door in front of us slid open, and we entered the vestibule that separated us from the outside world. I heard the hiss of an air handling system as the door closed again. We waited in silence for the scan to confirm our identities. I had only been through here once before, about five years ago when I was hired. At the time, I was uncertain what I was getting myself into, and the vestibule unnerved me. Connery's voice confirmed our identities and permission to depart. The door opposite the one we had entered slid open. We stepped out to find a car waiting for us. We both got in, and it automatically set off.

We moved fast enough that most of the scenery was a blur. Jim remained silent, and I took my cue from him. About ten minutes into the ride, the view on the left side opened up to ocean, and we began to slow. The car stopped on a sandy peninsula, and the two of us got out. A small seaplane was tethered to a short dock at the end of the road where we stopped. I followed Jim down the dock towards the plane and a man I assumed was the pilot. He nodded hello and opened the door for me. I turned back to Jim. "Well, I'm off then."

"I assume you'll be a proficient sailor by the time your two weeks are over."

"How could you expect any less from me?" I smiled condescendingly at him.

"I'll be here to meet you in two weeks. The island residents will know how to get in touch with me if there's an emergency. And I *mean* emergency. If you get bored, build a raft or something, but you're not coming back for two weeks." He waited for a confirmation. I rolled my eyes and nodded, and he turned back to the car.

I boarded the tiny plane with just a small bag of some personal effects. I had been assured that there would be ample clothing, food, and other necessities available when I reached the island. Since I was the only passenger on the plane, I opted for the copilot seat for a better view. "Hey," I said into the headset.

The pilot turned his head slightly and smiled. "Welcome aboard. Hope you're not prone to being airsick."

"I've spent plenty of time in these small planes. My father was a pilot. How long's the flight?"

"About 2 hours."

I nodded and looked out the front window as we took off. For a long while, there was nothing to see but ocean. Then a dark spot appeared on the horizon. The pilot pointed to it and informed me that was where we were going. I watched as it slowly grew into a mass of land. The plane splashed down not far from a long dock that led to a beach. A large sailboat was tied up halfway down. Beyond the palm trees lining the beach, I saw the tops of a few thatched roofs.

The pilot left the engine running as I jumped out onto the dock and shut the door. He immediately turned to taxi away. I lingered at the end of the dock for a minute to watch him take off again. I had never been in a plane capable of landing on water before and enjoyed watching as the pontoons cut through the water. The plane headed out of sight, and I turned back towards the island. I took in the sailboat as I walked down the dock. It looked like it could hold a dozen people. I had been hoping to learn in something a bit smaller and more manageable, but it was a lovely boat. The hull was hard wood, and it had a sturdy yet rustic feel about it.

I saw a man standing under a palm tree on the beach. I hitched my backpack higher on my shoulder and headed to meet him. The man standing there was barefoot, in a loose pair of shorts, wide brimmed hat and sunglasses. He had the physique and coloring of someone who spent most of his thirty something years outside engrossed in physical activity. "She's a beauty, ain't she?"

I stopped short at the end of the dock. "Pardon?"

He stepped out from under the palm tree and gestured back at the sailboat. "The sailboat. Her name's 'Time Passes Slowly'."

I snorted slightly but kept the thought of appropriateness to myself. As I stepped off the dock into the sand, I took my cue from him, slipping off my shoes and picking them up with my free hand. I extended my other hand in greeting. "I'm Ad—"

He cut me off giving my hand a quick shake. "Adelaide, I know. It's not like we get a ton of visitors here. I'm Adam. I'll be your activity manager and chef during your stay."

"Call me Addy." I smiled in as flirtatious a way as I remembered.

He tipped his hat in acknowledgement. "If you'll follow me then, Addy." He turned and headed for one of the thatched roof huts. They were exactly like the pictures I had seen as a young girl, complete with coconuts dotting the ground around them. The place had a surreal paradise feel to it, which was really quite something considering the places I had been. It was also completely relaxing. The sand was cool and soft on my feet and the wind blowing through the palms sounded like rain. I was immediately glad to have agreed to this, however reluctantly I might have done it.

Adam led me to the hut closest to the edge of the beach. The door was unlocked, and he held it open for me. Rustic and a perfect gentleman, I mused. "I hope you find it comfortable while you're here." It was smaller than my usual living quarters but not by much. It had the sparseness of Noah's place, but the colors were warm and soft, so I did not find it as unsettling as his. Adam walked over to a small closet and opened it. "They told us your size, so you're stocked with pretty much everything you should need while you are here, but if you find anything lacking, please let me know, and we'll produce it as quickly as possible." There was an array of shorts and pants, lightweight tunics, bathing suits and sandals. Most were neutral in color.

"We?"

"My wife lives here with me on the island. She gardens and handles most logistics."

I felt a small pang of disappointment from a long submerged part of my consciousness. It passed quickly. "When do I get to meet her?"

"Dinner tonight, if you like, in about an hour. You can take your meals alone or with us. It's up to you. We enjoy the company, but we know people like their private time." He slightly pulled out a linen shift and gestured to it. "We're usually a little more formal at dinner," he let the shift go again and it swung back into place, "but whatever you're comfortable in will be fine."

"Dinner sounds lovely."

He gestured for me to follow him to the door, pointing out across a small pool to a somewhat larger hut. "That one is where we stay. Your kitchen is well stocked, but if you need something additional, we might have it in ours. If not, we'll get it for you as quickly as possible. We can discuss further details at dinner. I'll leave you to settle in for now then." With a quick nod he was off toward his hut.

I opened all the windows in the place and savored the breeze for a moment. Even with the amount of trees and gardens in the dome, the air never smelled as fresh as this. I started poking around the hut. He wasn't kidding, the kitchen was amply stocked. I filled a glass with cold water and carried it around with me while further investigating. The bathroom was a pleasant surprise. It had a tub large enough to drown in, and I realized I had not taken the time to have a leisurely bath in years. I made a mental note to take advantage of that.

Despite the warmth of the air, I took a long, hot shower and slipped on a plain, tan, floor-length linen shift. I stared at the sandals for a moment and decided that during my stay here I would forgo any footwear whenever possible. As I shut the door to my hut behind me, I realized I had no key. There did not seem to be any security recognition devices embedded in the door or the wall next to it like back home. With a small amount of effort, I turned my back on the unlocked door and walked toward the hut Adam had indicated earlier. There was never any crime in the domes, but I had become used to the reassurance of the security systems there. We were miles away from any other land, and though Adam had not mentioned anyone else, it was not like there was an easy method of escape if something did happen.

As I approached Adam's hut, I noticed a woman in a small garden patio in front. She was setting some food down on an ornate teak table and looked up at me and smiled as I approached. She was similar in coloring to Adam and just as well toned. My thoughts flashed to the spot on my hips I always thought was just a little too wide. She was wearing a soft white tunic, loose pants, and to my dismay, sandals. Adam had said to dress however I was comfortable, but I suddenly felt like I had pushed that too far.

She extended a long slender arm towards me. "Adelaide." It was not a question; she knew who I was. "I'm Marina." Her voice was soft and her smile inviting, but her grip on my hand belied a strong and powerful physique. Yet it was not threatening in the least, and I could not help but return the smile. Like Adam, she immediately made me feel at ease.

"Call me Addy."

"Sit, sit!" She gestured to one of three chairs at the table, and I claimed it while thinking it strange to have only three chairs at a table. Several other huts were visible from the patio. The place looked like it could hold at least a dozen people. "Adam is just finishing up the main course. Can I pour you some wine?" She picked up a bottle of Petraud and held the label out for me to see. I didn't recognize the vineyard, but the grape was one I enjoyed.

"Sounds wonderful," I said. She poured while I glanced around some more. I could see five huts in all, scattered around the area. Most were the same size as mine, though Adam and Marina's was larger. If this was their permanent residence though, that made sense. A pool surrounded by thatched umbrellas sat in the middle of the huts. A few lounge chairs were about. From where I sat, I saw out to the ocean through a clearing in the palm trees that lined the beach. The foliage grew thick very quickly on either side of the clearing. Tall flowers and plants surrounded the table, offering some privacy from the pool area without blocking the view of the beach completely. I noticed each hut had a similar area with smaller tables in between the front door and the pool area. "No one else will be joining us?"

"You're the only guest we have at the moment."

"Oh. I'm sorry to intrude-"

"Nonsense! We love the company. It's rare that we have more than one guest at a time, and I'd say at least half the year we have none. So you are a welcome addition, Addy." She handed me a glass and watched as I swirled the wine and sniffed. "It's Adam's own wine."

"Really?" I took a sip. It had a leathery undertone that seemed out of place in a tropical paradise.

"Well, he owns the vineyard land and dictates the process, though he doesn't do any of the work. It's a rather lengthy trip as you can imagine. He only makes it twice a year. He doesn't like to leave me on my own for long, though I've never minded a bit of solitude now and then." She sat down next to me. I felt silly about my prior concern of formality. Yes, she looked nice, but there was no air of pretension about her.

"She likes to get rid of me." Adam had joined us from the house carrying a platter of what looked like roast beef. He gave Marina a quick peck on the cheek before setting the platter in the middle of the table and sitting down with us. "If you'll indulge us for a just a few moments, Addy." He took Marina's hand and the two of them bowed their heads slightly. I was about to question what they were doing when Adam began to speak. "Heavenly father, we thank you for the opportunity to meet our new guest, Adelaide."

He continued, but I was too surprised to hear what else he was saying. I was glad that their heads were bowed and eyes closed so they would not see my blush and confusion. I wondered if I should bow my head too or grab their hands? My mother had spoken of growing up in a religious household, but all I knew of religion was what I had read in books. I squirmed in my chair and finally settled for placing my hands in my lap and casually looking down at them as though deep in thought. I timed it so my head raised as theirs did and smiled at them.

Adam gave me a polite smile. "Sorry, did we make you uncomfortable?"

I tried a nonchalant wave. "No, no. I just never…didn't…" I was not really sure what to say.

Adam smiled again but looked slightly concerned. "Please don't let it bother you. There's no need for you to join in if you're not comfortable with it."

"I just wasn't raised on any sort of religion." I was no stranger to it though. The topic of religious missions was frequently discussed, especially between me and Noah. Noah was raised some variant of Christian, though I could never remember exactly which branch or sect. The differences between them were always hard for me to remember, but from our discussions I was now well versed in the histories of Jesus and Joseph Smith. Noah argued that Mormonism being, in his opinion, a cult, deserved to have its origins exposed. I usually argued that since he was biased, he was missing the obvious point that all religions could be considered cults and therefore exposed. I also argued that for all he knew things went exactly as Joseph Smith said they did. He had laughed at me, but acknowledged that I could be right. Before I had met Noah, I just assumed that anyone who believed in organized religion was an idiot. I tended to think people like Noah would not be all that shattered to find out their messiah never existed, but that we were still a few generations from when most people would be readily accepting of it. "I'm not uncomfortable, I was just a bit surprised." I paused for a moment but decided to be honest. They seemed like very understanding people. "And didn't know what to do with myself."

"Not at all. So long as you don't dig in while we're praying, we won't be offended no matter what you do. Speaking of which." Adam gestured towards the plate of meat. "Roast beef in an apple nesbit jus reduction, braised beets, and asparagus."

I realized how ravenous I was, but out of politeness only took one slice of roast beef to start. The meat was delicious and had a wonderfully fresh flavor. I was doubtful that they had a ranch somewhere on the island but felt it would be a little bit rude to ask where they got their meat. "This is fabulous. Where did you learn to cook?"

"My mother taught me when I was young. She was one of the few natural farmers left in the plains. She refused to try any cross breeding of plants herself but let me plant a small garden and experiment on my own. I was never terribly good at it though."

Marina laughed. "He tried it again when we moved here. Created this rutabaga green bean thing. It was awful!"

I joined her laugh. "You have my friend Noah's sense of adventure with food. When did you start your own vineyard?"

"When we were working in Washington, DC, we met quite a few people from the Virginia wine country area. One of them mentioned he had a vineyard he was looking to sell, and though I didn't have much free time with the hotel, it was always a dream of mine. So we bought it and hired some people to take care of the day to day business, though I always had a hand in how the wine was made."

"Hotel?"

"Ah, sorry. Let me start a little earlier. We met at a small business conference where I was catering about 15 years ago—"

Marina grabbed his hand. "It was love at first sight."

"Yes. It was a bit of a whirlwind. We were married within a year, and Marina took over my catering business."

"He needed some help with the management aspects of it."

Adam smiled at her again. "I was in it for the food, not the money."

"But when you're not turning a profit that makes it hard to continue-" she countered.

"So Marina helped me grow my business, and before I knew it, we had enough money to buy an old hotel in DC that was in a bit of disrepair."

Marina smiled at the memory and continued. "The place needed to be gutted, to be honest. But I saw the potential. And with DC being such a popular place for travel, I knew one thing it would always need was more hotels."

"Between her business sense and my creative touches it became popular more quickly than I could imagine. And important people were staying there."

"Senators, visiting dignitaries. We got quite a reputation for being discreet about our guests and their activities." Marina could not hide the pride in her voice.

"And apparently word spread. The laboratory approached Marina about 8 years ago with an offer to build a resort on this island. They explained their need for people who could be trusted, given the nature of the guests. Frankly, we were excited by the idea of something a little more low key. The hotel was grand and very profitable, but the life was exhausting. And this place, is truly a paradise."

I smiled in agreement, amused by the back and forth meter of their narrative. "And what did they tell you would be the nature of your guests?"

They exchanged a nervous glance before Adam spoke. "We try not to ask questions. We know the lab has a variety of research projects and some of the researchers, yourself included, are involved in time travel, but generally people come here to escape their work, and we encourage that."

"We've also been warned that you're quite the workaholic and likely to throw yourself into the task of learning to sail." Marina smiled, and the tension immediately lifted with her tone.

"And to that end, we should probably retire for the night. I plan to wake you up bright and early to start challenging you!"

I laughed. "I have no objection to that." Adam stood, and Marina and I followed suit. "Can I help clear?"

Marina wouldn't allow it. "You have a big day ahead of you tomorrow. Get some rest."

"Good night then." They both nodded good night in return. I headed back to my hut. A silky looking nightgown in the closet felt wonderful on my skin as I brushed my teeth. I nearly jumped into the large fluffy bed and was out almost as soon as the sheets had settled over me.

# Chapter 7

The next thing I knew, Marina was knocking on my door to wake me. I mumbled something close to "come in", and she entered with a tray full of some beautiful looking scrambled eggs, bacon and potatoes. The glass of orange juice had the thickness of fresh squeezed style. I decided I could get used to this. "Good morning."

"I figured you should have a filling breakfast on your first morning with Adam. He's going to feed you a lot of information today, and you'll need to be able to focus well." She placed the tray on the table in my kitchen area and pulled out a chair for me.

"Thank you so much Marina, this looks wonderful." I sat down in the chair and smelled the food appreciatively.

"Enjoy. He'll be by around 0730 to start on your first lesson." She gave me another smile and left.

As I ate the eggs, I mused that if they didn't have cows on the island, they must at least have chickens. The eggs looked gorgeous and tasted fresh. Again, I thought I could get used to this. I finished my breakfast and took another long hot shower. I decided that for sailing, an airy long sleeved shirt and loose pants would give me good coverage from the sun, but not be too hot.

After dressing, I opened my backpack and pulled out the few things I had brought with me: a few books for some leisurely reading, and a link to my present day journal, which I was never without. I opened the journal file and had made some notes on the previous evening, including a few more observations about religion when there was a knock at the door. "Come in!"

Marina entered, followed by Adam. She took away the tray that held my empty breakfast dishes and nodded before leaving again. Adam gave me an excited smile. "Ready?"

I stood up, equally as excited. "Absolutely!"

"Right then!" He sat down at the table gesturing for me to do the same.

I sat down, a little crestfallen. "Aren't we going out to the sailboat?"

He laughed. "Eventually. But first you need to understand some basic principles about wind direction and forces!" I smiled again at his enthusiasm as he pulled a pen out from behind his ear and flipped to a clean sheet on a pad of paper he had brought in with him. *Pen and paper, how archaic.* I settled in as he started drawing diagrams of boats and sails and wind vectors.

It boggled my mind that sailors could steer a sailboat towards the wind and still make forward progress. I was assuaged by the fact that math doesn't lie, and the vector addition he showed me at least made intellectual, if not common sense. It bothered me, but Adam assured me that I was making good progress if I could at least accept the idea, even if I didn't quite feel it.

He made up a quiz for me involving a diagram of a boat and a list of parts. As I labeled the diagram with what each part was called, it felt like I was back in grade school. He explained that I needed to understand the purpose of each part before trying to use it. Though his style was simplistic, I knew I was learning a lot.

By the time Marina knocked on the door with lunch, I had a basic understanding of the principles of sailing. I was struggling to keep straight which rope hoisted or turned which sail. Adam told me it would make more sense when we were on the boat. "It helps to see the lines in action. It'll feel natural after a few hours. We'll go out late tomorrow morning."

"Not today?"

"Wind's a little strong, not too great for learning. Anyway, I'm sure you'd like some time to yourself. Relax? Maybe explore the island a little bit?"

"I have been curious to look around. Maybe go for a swim. How big is the island?"

"It's roughly circular and about 6 miles to walk around the circumference. There's a good sized stream on the other side that flows out from near the middle of the island, but it's easily crossed. There's a small mountain towards the middle. Not so steep it isn't easily climbable, and there's a 360 degree view from the top of it. There's a hydration pack and some sturdy boots in your closet if you'd like to climb it."

"Nice view?"

"You can't see much of anything but ocean from the top. Some people find it a little unnerving to be so isolated from the mainland, but given you spend most of your life in a big bubble, I can't imagine that would bother you."

Something from his tone when he said "big bubble" left me feeling that he didn't exactly approve of my work place. I kept the thought to myself, even though there were times I didn't exactly approve of it either. I justified to myself that the sacrifices of freedom I made were worth it in the end. Since he and Marina shied away from talking about it much last night, I decided to remain silent on the issue.

We finished lunch and Adam left me to myself. I found the hydration pack and loaded a couple of protein snacks and a towel into it, then tied the boots to one of the hooks on the back. I changed into shorts, found a wide brim hat in the closet and headed out to the beach barefoot.

I took a counter clockwise trek along the edge of the water. The waves were fairly calm, and the water was just cool enough to be refreshing. The place really was paradise. I walked what I gaged to be about two miles and stopped to look around. I was not able to see more than a hundred yards or so back down the beach. The trees were thick and nearly reached the edge of the water. Adam and Marina were well around the other side of the island. For the first time in a very long time, I was alone. No people. No surveillance equipment watching me or listening to me. At least I hoped not. I scanned the trees briefly and thought about it.

The lab owned the island, so it was highly possible they were watching everything here too. That could explain the look Adam and Marina exchanged at dinner last night. I realized I did not care. I shook off the suspicion and yelled at the top of my lungs, a long ecstatic "Wahoo!" The noise was swallowed almost immediately by the ocean.

I dropped the pack to the sand and started to roll up the sleeves of my shirt. I looked at my pasty white arms and thought of Marina's tanned slender arms. The only other people on the island were two miles away. Suddenly I no longer cared if anyone else was watching. The recovery crew at the lab had seen me naked often enough on my returns anyway. I stripped off my clothes and ran into the ocean.

The water was delightful and crystal clear. I could see my feet on the sand at the bottom. I had not been swimming in the ocean since I was an adolescent and it had been in New Jersey waters which were cloudy and nearly brown. For the first time, I felt comfortable in ocean water. I swam out away from the beach until I started to get tired, then turned around and headed back with a lazy backstroke. By the time I got back to the beach, I was fairly exhausted.

I took a sip from my hydration pack as I laid my towel out. I lay down on the towel and let the sun dry my skin. A breeze blew across me raising goosebumps on my arms. I suddenly started feeling uneasy. Perhaps solitude was not meant for me. Everywhere I went in my day-to-day life, I was watched. Though it was a severe invasion of privacy, it was also somewhat reassuring. Someone was always there. I had no doubt that if I ever had a heart attack or started choking on something, within seconds someone would be there to assist me. In this place with so much open air, I felt oddly exposed, uncertain if someone who had my back was watching me.

I pulled my clothes back on and untied the boots from my pack to put them on. I hitched the pack back on and opened a protein bar as I headed into the trees towards the center of the island.

A few dozen yards from the edge of the tree line the ground turned into harder dirt. The ground started to slope upwards, but the trees were still dense and tall and provided ample shade from the mid afternoon sun. There was no trail so it was slow going, picking my way through the underbrush, but the mountain was easy to see, and I kept making my way straight towards it. I hoped from the top I'd be able to see the huts, so I wouldn't have to make a complete circuit of the island to find my way back.

There were plenty of birds in the trees. Although I heard something rooting around in the bushes, I couldn't see what it was. Adam hadn't mentioned any dangerous animals on the island, but I was a little wary not knowing what made the noise.

The ground eventually became even more steep, and the trees thinned out a little. I slowly picked my way through the brush and remaining trees up the side of the mountain. The ground finally flattened out. I emerged from the last few trees onto a rocky surface about the size of a tennis court.

I was immediately able to see the ocean in front of me on the other side of the island. I walked towards the middle of the clearing and slowly turned around, taking in the view of the water from all sides. It was a first for me to be able to see only ocean all around me. I understood what Adam had said about people feeling isolated, but the unnerved feeling I had earlier was gone. Now that I was able to see all around me I felt reassured that I was alone. There was no stranger in the bushes with ill intentions watching me. It calmed me.

I noted where I had come up the mountain and started to walk around the edge of the clearing. One side of the mountain was a rather steep drop off. It looked like there was very little beach at the bottom of it. I was just able to make out the tops of the huts through the trees on another part of the clearing and decided to head back down that side of the mountain to shorten my return trip.

I sat down on a large rock towards one edge of the clearing to rest. I pulled out another protein bar and sipped some more water while taking in the view again. Aside from the immediate foliage, the view to the horizon was nearly indistinguishable from one angle to the next. The lack of visual stimulation caused me to zone out. Eventually I realized I was thinking about sailing again.

I sat for a while trying to remember everything Adam had taught me that morning. With my eyes closed, I tried to picture the wind vector diagrams he had drawn and again disbelief clouded my thoughts. I smiled and shook my head at my own stubbornness. It would make sense eventually, I reassured myself. Everything would come together when I was out on the sailboat. I tried instead to remember the diagram with the parts.

My silent contemplation of sailing was broken by another rustling noise in a bush at the edge of the clearing. I turned quickly to look. Although I still couldn't make out what had been in the bushes, I was able to tell from the flash of light off its surface that it was metal. I immediately rose to my feet. "Hello?" I called out. Silence answered me.

I stood for a moment watching the bush closely but saw nothing moving. I took a few steps towards the bush before it shook again. I ran to the edge, listening to the rustling sound traveling away from me and down through the underbrush. I caught another flash of light and saw the unmistakable form of a surveillance bot withdrawing.

I turned away and started the trek down the mountain towards the huts. The calming feeling of being alone had suddenly passed as I looked over my shoulder at least a dozen times on the way back.

# Chapter 8

My first few days on the island were wonderful. Adam and Marina were happy to leave me alone whenever I wanted, and Marina was quick to produce a drink and conversation whenever I wandered by. I had been spending my mornings out on the boat with Adam, and my afternoons indulging in mostly mindless physical activities. I did a proper trek around the edge of the island one day, and finally took a lengthy bath in the whirlpool tub when I returned. I swam frequently and worked on my tan as well.

I ate dinner with Adam and Marina every night. I enjoyed their conversation. Since they were cooking for themselves anyway, I didn't want them to make something different for me.

Now that I had confirmed I was being watched, a bit of the magic of the island had died. It was still a glorious place to be, and I took delight in all the things I did, but the metal creature had reminded me that I was still at the whim of the laboratory. I wanted to ask Adam and Marina how it felt to have their lives spied upon, but I realized, just as I felt about my job, they probably thought the good parts outweighed the intrusions.

I let them talk about themselves much more often than I talked about my past. The lab had already learned enough about me through my conversations with Noah. For some reason I felt the need to let some part of myself remain secret from them, as though on the island I was a different person, Island Adelaide.

My fourth day out sailing, I felt like I really had the hang of it. At least, getting out and back was easy. Maneuvering around the dock was still tricky, but with everything else Adam mostly sat back and let me handle things. I found it exhilarating but also very relaxing. It was so quiet and the gentle rocking of the boat in time with the waves was soothing.

I still confused some of the rope lines, but I generally knew their purpose and when to use them. So even if I was surprised when Adam told me to do something with the sheet and I was expecting him to say the halyard, I still did the correct thing.

We were just preparing to do another man overboard drill when Adam pointed into the sky and said, "Look."

I looked in the direction he was pointing. For a moment I saw nothing, but then a glint of light attracted my gaze to a spot off in the distance. It was tiny, and impossible to make out any sort of shape, but it had to be a plane. "The seaplane?"

"Nothing else would be flying this way. The seaplane is the only thing that comes here. We better head back." I detected a bit of anxiety in his voice though his demeanor remained calm. I helped him swap over the jib, and we ran an aggressive pace back to the dock. The plane grew in size as we approached and passed by us as we were navigating our way to the side of the dock. I saw Jim in the copilot seat. Panic gripped me. This could not be good. Jim wouldn't just decide to come on vacation while I was here.

The plane landed as we were coming around to the side of the dock. I noticed Marina standing ready with my backpack. Someone must have contacted her that I had to leave. The plane managed to dock right when we did. I jumped out as Adam was tying up the sailboat. I grabbed my backpack from Marina and ran along the dock to where Jim was just getting out of the copilot seat. He hopped out of the plane just long enough to open the door to the back, gesture for me to get in, and climb in after me.

"What's going on?"

"Later." He didn't talk to me the whole ride home. I assumed he didn't want the pilot to hear what he had to say. Panic started to churn through me. My first thought was something had gone very wrong with my mission, that time had taken a turn it shouldn't have and it was my fault. I argued with myself that I would have known immediately upon returning if something was wrong. Perhaps instead, something I had said to Adam and Marina made them angry at me. I tried to calm myself, but the drone of the engine fighting against the turbulence of the small fuselage and Jim's detached manner amplified my uneasiness. The flight was only two hours, but it felt like an eternity had passed when we landed.

We silently got into a car and took off for what I assumed was the lab. My stomach was in knots. I stared at Jim, hoping he would break the silence, but he stared out the window, seemingly lost in thought. A few times his hand went up to his ear as he listened to someone, but he did not volunteer any of what he heard. We finally got to the lab and quickly passed through the vestibule again. Still not speaking, Jim started stalking off towards his office, and I dutifully followed for a moment before realizing I was still in my bathing suit and shorts.

"Jim!" He stopped and turned to look at me. I merely gestured at my shorts but he got the point. He changed direction and started walking towards my quarters instead.

He stopped in front of my door and said, "Two minutes." That didn't even leave time for a shower. I put on clean clothes in a soft blue which I hoped conveyed an air of innocence. I had been hoping to take a hot shower to help calm myself but splashing some cool water on my face had to suffice. When I couldn't get a brush through my windswept tangles, I quickly gave up and pulled my hair into a bun to keep it out of my face. With a sense of dread, I went back outside.

Once again, Jim led the way to his office. It was in a separate wing in the Mission Enclosure. Though most of us worked from our quarters, Jim preferred to keep his business life separate from his home life. He sat in his desk chair and gestured at the one across from him. "Sit down, Adelaide."

My panic increased. Jim never used my full name. I thought back over my actions since I had returned. Nothing stood out as being out of the ordinary or out of acceptable behavior. I shook a little as I pulled the chair out slightly and sat. The nervousness must've been clear on my face.

Jim sighed. He glanced around the room as though looking for someone, then looked back at me and softened his gaze a bit. "You're not in trouble."

"But something's wrong."

"Yes. Yes, Addy, something is terribly wrong. I need to show you something. Subject 34, file f." A picture of a man sprang up on the desk between us. "Do you recognize him?"

I stared at the three dimensional representation of the man's face. "Turn once." The head spun once slowly in a clockwise direction. It was an older man, probably in his early hundreds. His hair was long and wiry, like he hadn't kept it up at all. It was almost entirely gray. He was scruffy, but clearly not from lack of trying to shave. His eyes were familiar, but I couldn't place him. "I'm not sure, Jim. Some of his features are familiar, but I know very few people that old, and he's definitely not one of them."

Jim sighed again. "Ok. Subject 34, file a."

I understood that this would be the first file on this man, whoever he was. I expected it was some research on a new case, so I was very surprised to see the well-lit White Box with its light gray mats now displayed on four different camera angles in front of me. I could never see the room well; the lights were always so blinding, but I saw it clearly now. The aides who collect our personal effects and the sphere were standing by ready for someone's return. I deduced I was about to see that old man arrive. He must have stolen the sphere from someone.

He suddenly appeared in the space and chaos erupted. A look of shock and confusion crossed his face for a split second before he fell over and started screaming. I could only imagine the terror of someone, suddenly arriving in a strange place, blinded and completely disoriented. It was hard enough on us, and we were trained for this. We were from this time period; we were used to it.

I watched with sympathy as the man writhed on the floor and vomited. The aides stood back, too frozen with shock to do anything. "Sound," I said. I cringed slightly as his screams filled Jim's office. I heard Jennifer over the loudspeaker asking what to do. One of the aides had wandered a little closer and grabbed the sphere away from where the man had dropped it on the floor. From one of the camera angles, I saw the old man's eyes as he looked desperately at the retreating aide. Again, something about his look was familiar to me. He closed his eyes again and continued screaming. The other aides had wandered a little closer as well. Jennifer was giving instructions, but from the record I was watching it was hard to hear her voice over the screaming man.

A new panic suddenly filled me. Noah was on his mission this week. It was Noah who should've come back to the return chamber. This man must have discovered the sphere, and not knowing what it was, accidentally activated it. And then more panic. Noah was a man who was clearly smarter and cleverer than those around him in that time period. What if he had been mistaken as a witch? What if they had burned him then gone through his belongings? "My God, what happened to Noah?"

"That's what we need to find out."

I watched for a few more seconds before another dread overtook me. Jim was responding to a different question. That's why the eyes were familiar. He hadn't been left behind. The man screaming and writhing on the floor was Noah.

I leapt out of my seat and screamed at the video. "Noah!"

"Addy, sit. Focus." His voice was commanding. "Close Subject 34, file a." Jim gave me a concerned but warning stare.

I sat back down. My head was swimming. "Subject 34, file b!" I said, before Jim said anything else.

The emotionless voice of Sean Connery greeted me; "Subject 34 files subject to clearance level two or special access channels."

"All in good time. Calm yourself."

"Jim what is going on? I need to see Noah!"

"You will, trust me, but I need you to focus." I took a few deep breaths, but my hands were still gripping the arms of the chair as though it was keeping me from falling off the Earth. "You'll have access to all the files, and we'll let you see him, but we need to go over some things first."

"Like what?" The question came out almost as a scream. My breathing had calmed a bit, but I was still overly anxious to see Noah. I was barely sitting on the edge of the chair. Jim didn't say anything, but glared at me for a moment. I took another deep breath, relaxed my death grip on the chair, and slid back into it to sit properly. I grasped my hands together in my lap and focused on slowing my breath. Noah was alive. That was something at least. I would help him. I would find a way. "Okay. What do you know so far?"

"He's been back for about ten hours. His body is of course adjusting to the time shift so he's not in the greatest state right now. He won't eat and can't seem to talk. He appears disoriented. We don't know if he knows where he is or even who he is. However, he is doing things that suggest he has some knowledge of what's going on."

I thought back to his pleading eyes looking at the retreating aide. I assumed it was a general plea for help, but perhaps it had been more specific than that.

Jim had paused to take a deep breath and said the next sentence with hesitation. "He appears to have aged about seventy-two years."

I did the math. That would put him at one hundred and twelve years old. How long did people live in the late 1600s? I had no idea, but I was sure it wasn't that long. From the images I had just seen, I guessed that he would look to be in his mid-60s to them. "But if his body adjusted to the time period, it would only have been twenty years-"

Jim cut me off. "It doesn't quite work that way, as far as we know. He has aged as he would here, more slowly than he would in the late 1600s. "

I tried to imagine being stuck in Stratford for seventy-two years. I would have gone insane. "So he was there through half of the 18th century." I rested my head in my hands and my elbows on my legs. It was hard to fathom.

"It would appear so. We're keeping him sedated. He looks at Doctor Crebbs like he knows her. We're hoping he'll respond to you in a more significant way."

"When do I get to see him?"

"I'd like you to review the rest of the files first. It's mostly clips of more significant moments since his return, but I want you to be prepared. The sedation is keeping him calm, but he had a few rather aggressive moments." Jim looked at me with concern again, trying to judge my demeanor.

The shock had passed. I lifted my head from my hands, sat back in my chair again and looked back at him. I felt a bit defeated but gave him a nod.

"Release Subject 34 records to Adelaide MacDuff, authority two charlie whiskey five, James Grovner."

It unnerved me to hear him refer to Noah as a subject number.

"Do you want me to stay?" Jim said.

"No. I'll find you when I'm done." Jim stood and left, pausing for a moment to rest a hand on my shoulder and give it a soft squeeze. As soon as the door closed behind him, I was back at the front of my chair. "Subject 34, file b."

Four images of the examination room came into view. In one of them, Doctor Crebbs was obviously out of her element. She stood back from the door, hesitating over what to do. Another camera showed that the aids from the first room held Noah's arms and tried to force him to the examination table. He freed one of his arms and ripped a hose from one of the aide's containment suit helmets. The man screamed and backed away, afraid of exposing himself to whatever disease Noah may have contracted. The remaining aides tried to regain control of Noah. While he was distracted with the struggle, Doctor Crebbs injected something in his arm. He immediately started to calm, and after a few seconds, collapsed into the arms of the aides. They kept him upright and moved him to the examination table. Doctor Crebbs secured him to the table with some straps and the aides retreated. The file closed.

Doctor Crebbs accepted the risks associated with her position. She found the contamination suits unwieldy and too intrusive on the examination process. She liked to be able to interact with her patients directly. The aides were not as trusting of the medical process, with good reason. I had heard of a librarian who came back infected with the black plague. Our vaccine had not been adequate. When she realized that she was getting sick, she abandoned her mission and returned early for fear of being quarantined. She was in bad shape when she reappeared and the aides were afraid to go near her. It was at that point that they had requested the containment suits. They also argued that we should go through our decontamination process immediately, but the scientists in charge wanted to know if we brought something back.

"Subject 34, file c." Again, four images of the examination room came into view.

"Patient DNA confirms match with Noah Kent. Patient-" Doctor Crebbs had been dictating to the recorders but was interrupted by another voice I didn't recognize.

"Pardon Doctor, repeat that please?"

"Patient is Noah Kent. Patient bone and tissue samples compared with initial indoctrination samples indicate an aging of about seventy-two years." I heard something that sounded like a swear from the other voice before the mic cut out. "Patient is suffering from severe disorientation and malnutrition. 0952, attempting to restore consciousness." She approached Noah with another injector. Noah started coming to, but before his eyes even opened he started to scream again. "Restoring sedation." I forced myself to listen to the screams. It didn't sound like screams of pain, but I couldn't be sure. The file ended again with Noah settling back down into sleep.

The next file was a reawakening of Noah, but this time he didn't start screaming. He cried. In Subject 34, file e, Doctor Crebbs was trying to talk to Noah. His face was blank. It was as if he didn't even know she was there. "Subject 34, file a."

The images of the White Box came into view again. When Noah stared out at the aide retreating with the sphere, I paused the image. He wasn't looking at the aide; he was looking at the sphere. The sphere was the only thing he had had in his hands on his return, which implied this wasn't a planned return. We weren't supposed to leave anything behind. Something about his stare gave me the feeling he knew exactly where he was. "Jim."

The door opened behind me almost immediately. Jim had not gone far. He walked to the side of his desk and looked down at me but didn't say anything. I stood to meet his gaze. The shock and fear were gone. This was business again. Though I cared immensely for Noah, I wanted nothing more than to find out what had happened. My researcher instincts had kicked in. "I want to see him." Jim nodded once and led me out of the room.

# Chapter 9

Jim led me down the hall away from his office. He motioned to a door and nodded to the guard, then walked further down the hall, leaving me with the guard. No doubt Jim was heading to a room somewhere to watch my reunion with Noah. I waited till Jim was out of sight, stalling my entry. I wasn't sure what I was going to say to Noah, but I knew there was no point in further delaying it, so I turned to the door and nodded to the guard. He opened it to let me in. Noah was sitting in an armchair when I entered in the room. His arms gripped the sides of the chair.

I paused just inside the doorway. I heard the guard close it behind me. Noah made no move to look at me or acknowledge my presence in any way. Fear gripped me in place. This man I had known for years was foreign to me. He had exhibited violent behavior. I hadn't thought to ask if he was still under sedation. I knew there were guards just outside the door. If I screamed, how long would it take them to get in here? If I was able to get a scream out, at least. Someone must be watching. If I kept my distance and Noah made any sort of threatening move towards me, they'd be on their way in before he reached me.

The room was mostly empty. A cot sat along the far edge of the wall. The chair Noah sat in was next to a table, but he was turned away from it, facing a blank wall. His shoulders and head moved up and down ever so slightly with his breath. I forced myself to walk over to the other chair at the table. I stood behind it for a moment, gripping the back for support and just looked at him for a few moments. He didn't blink. He didn't look at me. Nothing changed about his demeanor. I pulled the chair out from the table. The wooden legs made a scraping noise against the floor. I sat and again waited for a moment to watch him.

This was not my Noah. He was completely different. He looked weak and tired. Yet behind the fatigue his eyes were wild. I found it hard to believe that this was the same person I had lunch with just over a week ago. It took every ounce of courage I had to speak his name. "Noah." I didn't want him to react. I didn't want it to be true. This couldn't possibly be him.

His breathing paused for a moment. He blinked once then returned to his previous state. It was definitely a reaction, but I wasn't sure what it was a reaction to.

"Noah, it's Adelaide." Again he paused. I thought I saw activity behind his eyes as though he was processing the information, but it had no impact, and his breathing pattern reverted to its first state. My voice was a little more urgent, "It's Addy, Noah."

Once more he paused. When he began breathing again though, the breaths were more accelerated. His eyes moved around but still seemed unfocused. He was thinking. It was clear, he was thinking about something. "Addy." He didn't look at me. "Addy?" His breathing paused again. A pained look covered his face, and he slowly turned his head to look at me.

I wanted to cry, and I wasn't sure if it was due to joy or pain. "Yes, it's me, Addy." I tried to look kind and smile, but I was sure I failed.

"Addy." he said again. He looked more intently at me, like he was trying to see something in my face. "Why are you familiar?" He looked me up and down, then focused on my face again.

"Because we're friends. We've been friends for five years."

His expression changed to one of distrust. "An impossibility."

"Well, I mean, we were friends. Many years ago." From his point of view it would have been years.

He looked me over again. "You are far too young to be a friend of mine. And you certainly are not from Salem." His gaze wandered around the room. "What is this place? I wish to return to my home."

"Noah, this is your home."

He stood up from his chair and yelled, "My name is not Noah!"

I could almost hear Jim in the other room echo the gasp I tried to subdue. This was Noah. There was no doubt about that in my mind any more, but trying to convince him of that was pointless. Instead I thought I'd play along for now. "Then who are you?"

His breathing was still heavy with anger. "My name is Doctor Montgomery Welsher, and I demand that you return me to my home."

My brain tried to grasp this new information. Montgomery Welsher was the name Noah used on missions. It was the same as the gardener's. He used it because it was familiar to him and for most missions he'd been on, time period appropriate. I couldn't think of anything else to say and hoped my legs would hold out as I stood up from the chair. I wanted to stay on his good side at least. "I'll see what I can do."

Jim was waiting outside the door. "We need more information. How did he get here? What does he remember? What has he been doing these past seventy-two years? We need a general timeline of his life to get an idea of where things went wrong."

I flattened my hand against the wall for support. My head was spinning. How could Noah have forgotten who he really was? "Jim, I need a minute."

"Of course." He put his arm around my shoulders and led me to a bench a little way down the hall. He produced a glass of water from thin air and handed it to me. I tried to steady my breathing and drink the water. "You realize you're the best person for this task."

I nodded. From what I had seen, I was the only person Noah had spoken anything coherent to so far.

"We have to be better informed before we can decide what to do next," Jim said.

I nodded again.

"Find out what he remembers."

I finished my water and handed the glass back to Jim before rising and going back to the door. The guard opened it. I took a deep breath before going in again.

Noah had been rocking in his chair with his arms wrapped around him. When I entered the room, his rocking paused, but he kept his arms wrapped around himself. He looked at me warily. "Are you going to send me home?"

"It's not my decision." I sat down in the chair at the table again. He looked at me with a terribly distraught face. "Look, No-," I paused for a moment after realizing I nearly called him Noah. "Montgomery, I need you to trust me. I know you don't remember me, but I am your friend, and I want nothing more than to help you."

"Then tell me something. Demonstrate your trust in me and I will return it in kind."

I tried to proceed with caution and keep my voice as gentle as possible. "What do you want to know?"

"How did I come to be in this place?"

Of course. At least I could be partially honest about this one. "I'm not entirely sure. What's the last thing you remember?"

He sighed in frustration. "I had retired to my study. I was reading an essay by my good friend, James Otis. My granddaughter entered and asked to borrow my magnifying glass. I went to open my case and in the course of removing the glass, I knocked a little metal sphere onto the ground. It rolled under my desk. My granddaughter fetched it for me, and I traded her the magnifying glass. I went to return the sphere back to my case and suddenly found myself here."

I couldn't move or speak. Granddaughter? I tried to put that aside and focus. "Tell me about the sphere."

"It is just a metal sphere. It had been in my case since..." He frowned. "Well let me think. I acquired it at..." He trailed off again lost in thought.

"Montgomery do you remember your childhood?"

He looked down at the floor and seemed to struggle. "I...do not."

"Do you remember how you ended up in Salem?"

He was silent and squirmed in his chair. His eyes widened with fear and confusion.

I had to try and calm him down again. "Tell me about your wife."

"Oh, Marie." He relaxed a little. "She is a blessed woman. She has been such a good mother, and an excellent homemaker." He smiled for the first time since he came back, but it was quickly replaced with a frown. "I hope she is well."

"How many children do you have?"

"Two. My daughter, Juliet, and son, Thomas. Juliet has two daughters, my two grandchildren."

"I'm sure they're all doing fine." I smiled, willing him to relax.

"What is this place?"

I hesitated and glanced around the room, wondering what they wanted me to say. Technically, Noah already knew this. "The future."

He looked at me like I was crazy. "Whose future?"

"Where were you born? What are your parents' names? Surely I can't be the first person who's asked you this."

"What has happened to me?"

"I don't know." It was the truth. I had no idea why he didn't come back when he was supposed to. Perhaps he was in an accident and lost his memory. He had no idea what the sphere was for, but had felt compelled to keep it. "What is your earliest memory?"

"There was a woman. I woke up from a sleep, and there was a woman in the house with me. She thanked me. I explained to her that I did not know why she was thanking me and she said she knew. Then she departed. I wandered out of the house, and another man found me, a doctor. He seemed to be familiar with me; he told me he was my employer. I had no choice but to believe him. I went to work for him and hoped that in time things would be clear again. I never saw the woman again."

So he didn't remember what the sphere was. "You did something to the sphere, didn't you? Just before you came here?"

He lowered his head and pressed his fingers against his temples. "I honestly do not remember. I was thinking about it as I went to put it back, I remember that. Perhaps I did." He raised his head again and shook it. "Those last few minutes are difficult to remember."

I tried a smile. "You've been very helpful, Montgomery. I'm sorry I can't explain more right now, but I'll do everything I can to get you back to your family." As I stood up from my chair, I hoped I hadn't just lied to Noah.

When I got to the hall, one of the guards motioned for me to follow him. I was led to a room a few doors down. Inside were Jim and a bunch of people I didn't know, sitting around a large table wearing more formal clothes. I guessed they were Jim's bosses and heads of the lab but I couldn't pick one out that I recalled seeing in the habitat domes. In the middle of the large conference table, a video display showed that Noah had returned to his seat. He was hugging himself and slightly rocking back and forth. Jim nodded to an empty chair next to him, and as quietly as possible, I took it. Everyone's gaze followed me as I took my seat. It was unnerving. I preferred not to see the people who were keeping track of me.

A woman across the table sat up in her chair, leaned her elbows on the table and tented her fingers in front of her throat. She was dressed in a severe, stark manner, and the look she gave me matched. I didn't know if she was expecting me to speak, and I glanced at Jim with concern. His face was blank and he looked back at the woman as she started to speak. "Well Miss MacDuff. It looks like we have a problem on our hands. What do you suggest we do about Mr. Kent?"

I was surprised to be asked my opinion and positive they wouldn't like it. "We have to send him back to when he left."

"There's only one sphere. We'd lose it."

I tried to sound confident. "Send a scout back first. A few minutes before you plan to send Noah back. He'll wait for Noah then come back with the extra sphere later."

"The timelines don't work that way. We'd end up creating an alternate timeline, and he wouldn't come back here. We'd still lose the sphere."

"But you send scouts back to the same point all the time."

"Scouts are trained very thoroughly on how to perform their missions. I don't have time to explain to you the physics of multiple spheres overlapping, and the potential danger that puts them in."

A man further down the table cleared his throat and spoke up. "We have to send someone back to when he was supposed to return, to prevent this from happening to Noah at all."

"He has children!" I said. "You can't just erase that timeline, you'd kill them! And then what happens to him?"

"Those children were never supposed to exist in the first place!"

"How can you be sure? "I asked. "Maybe this is the timeline that is supposed to happen."

"Miss MacDuff." The first woman interrupted us. "That is a pointless discussion. Do you know who James Otis is?"

"Who?"

"The man whose essay Mr. Kent was reading."

I squirmed in my chair. I didn't like being uninformed. "No."

"He was one of the early voices of the revolution."

I quickly did the math. Salem witch trials I knew were late 1600s. If Noah had aged just over seventy years, that would put him right around the start of the revolution. "Oh."

She looked at me coldly. "If Noah starts interfering with the progression of the revolutionary war, I'd call that a pretty damn big ripple in time." She paused to make sure I was following the repercussions. "Someone has to go back and stop this from happening. One way or another. That is all for now."

Jim rose, and I took that as my cue to leave as well. I was more than anxious to be out of there. I turned on Jim in the hallway. "Why did they bother to ask my opinion if they already knew what they wanted to do?"

"I'm not your enemy, Adelaide."

I deflated slightly. Jim was right. I was unfairly taking my anger out on him. "I'm sorry. But really, what was the point of that other than to make me look stupid?"

"They know you know Noah the best out of anyone here. They thought you might have had a different, viable option."

"Maybe in the next few days I can come up with one."

"I'd give it hours. They don't want him here. They'll move on this quickly."

"Hours." I wanted to punch something in my frustration. "Why don't they send someone back to the lab, just before Noah was supposed to go on his mission?"

"Like she said, Addy, introducing a second sphere into a point in time is tricky business, especially for the person traveling. "

"Who was that bossy woman?"

"My boss."

"But I mean, is she head of the lab?"

"No, but she is head of this department. The head of the lab was no doubt listening in."

"Great. So now everyone above me thinks I'm a useless idiot."

"No one has called you an idiot, certainly not me. They're actually quite glad you were able to get through to him. I didn't show you the other files, but they tried several methods before you arrived."

"Like what? They didn't torture him, did they!"

Jim stared at me for a moment without saying anything. "No. But there was some rather harsh verbal abuse and threats."

I watched him glance up at the ceiling and back down at me again. I felt like I was missing something. "And they thought my idea was bad."

"Your idea is the humane thing to do. But like they said, it's not an option to send him back. He cannot return to that timeline and continue with his life. So what's the next best thing? Figure that out." He turned and started walking back down the hall, gesturing for me to follow. "Why don't you go back to your quarters and try to relax for a bit. Think things through. You might come up with something." He walked me to the entrance of the living dome and turned back there.

I walked back to my quarters trying to remember the details of the past hour. I thought about Jim's reaction to my torture question, and the last things the woman in the boardroom had said, "Someone has to go back and stop this from happening. One way or another." I didn't like the way that sounded. At this point, my only hope was that the person they sent back would be me.

# Chapter 10

I reached my quarters, too wound up to relax. I paced back and forth across my living room, thinking things through. Even if someone did go back and warn Noah about what was going to happen, there was no way they would send the Montgomery version of him back. They really didn't have a choice; they would have to kill him or keep him here indefinitely. That was only my secondary concern at the moment. More important was to either come up with an alternate plan, or convince them that if they sent anyone back to deal with this, it should be me.

The fact was, Noah was back here and no longer interfering with history. We had the sphere in our possession. For all intents and purposes, they could just get rid of him and carry on with life as usual. If I tried to look at the situation from an unbiased standpoint, it made the most sense. It was terribly cruel to Noah, but we take our missions knowing the risks. We know that we might not make it back. They could afford to leave things alone and let Noah suffer the consequences, but I couldn't accept that as an option.

Jim once told me that even the people above him were never quite sure what actually happens when we travel back in time. They were taking advantage of a technology they didn't understand; it was only natural that things might go wrong while we traveled on missions. Noah knew that as well as I did. So how could I convince them it was in our best interest for me to go back to warn Noah, to risk sending someone who wasn't a scout back and let them interfere with a mission.

For all we knew, he had already set events in motion that could have a significant impact on the progress of the Revolutionary War, but of course, we didn't know what that meant for us. Would history change for us? Wouldn't it have already happened? Or did it split off into a separate timeline that we'll never know about? And if we've pulled Noah out of that timeline, what happened to it? I doubted that the people in that room, sitting around that table, knew the answers to those questions. So perhaps it was simply a chance they wouldn't be comfortable taking, to leave things as they were.

We were not supposed to make waves in the past. That idea was drilled into us before they allowed us on our first mission. We did our job with as little interference or influence on the events unfolding around us as possible. Noah knew this when he went back in time; at what point had he forgotten it? I should have asked him when he lost his memory.

Curiosity burned in me. I needed to know more of what happened, but I knew my desire for information wouldn't qualify as justification for the lab to send me on a mission back to see Noah. Perhaps their own curiosity about what happened and fear of potential effects would be enough to satisfy their mission requirements. Perhaps I could play up their responsibility in fixing whatever mess Noah left behind as a reason to go back.

Assuming they would go that route, how would I convince them that I was the best person for the job? I was certainly not an unbiased party, but Noah knew me better than anyone else in this place. I was the person he would trust the most. I knew that for a fact. If a scout or one of the higher up, faceless people who listened behind the walls, went back to warn Noah what was going to happen, he wouldn't believe them. He'd probably think it was a trick or a test. His natural mistrust of this place would kick in. He'd wait for them to leave, then proceed with business as usual. And then what? He loses his memory again, and we start all over? I was certain that if one person went back and failed, they wouldn't allow a second person to go back and try again. He would be lost forever.

Or worse, if someone went back and failed, maybe they would send a second person back to eliminate him.

I stopped pacing. I was at a loss. Normally at a time like this I'd go see Noah. He'd open a bottle of wine or make us a snack, and he'd listen while I vented my frustrations. I wondered what Jim was doing; if they'd let me go back and talk to the Montgomery Noah again. Maybe I could get more information out of him.

I decided to take a shower and let my mind drift. Solutions to my problems presented themselves most often when I was no longer focused on them. I let the hot water wash away the salt that still clung to the hairs on my arms. I found it hard to believe that a few hours ago I was on a sailboat and oblivious. I imagined the diagram of the sailboat Adam had drawn and tried to remember the names of the ropes again. When I closed my eyes, I realized I still felt the rocking of the boat. It calmed me but induced a small amount of vertigo. I opened my eyes again and watched the water swirl down the drain, trying to steady myself.

An alert from my door startled me. I stopped the shower and pulled on a robe before heading to answer it. After the route my train of thought had led me, I half expected it to be Noah. This had all been a mistake, and he was back from his mission just fine and wanted to see me for lunch. I closed my eyes as I reached the door and made a silent wish. Then pushed it out of my mind. I knew the truth. It couldn't possibly be Noah. I nodded my head to open the door and found Jim standing there.

This surprised me. Jim never just stopped by. He always just sent word that he wanted to see me, and we met in his office. "Jim."

"They're still weighing the risks versus the gains of us going back and warning him, but it looks like it'll happen."

I didn't like his use of the word "us." I had to make Jim understand it had to be me. And not just because I wanted it to be me. "He won't trust any of them."

"They know."

"It has to be me, Jim. I'm the only one he'll believe. The only one he'll listen to. I'm the only one-"

"Addy!" He grabbed my shoulders to get my attention. "They *know*. If anyone goes back, it'll be you."

The relief immediately subdued me. It was a step towards my chance to help Noah. Somehow, I knew, I would get my chance to fix this.

*One way or another.*

I had the feeling my version of "another" was not the same as theirs. I kept that thought to myself. They had to trust that I would behave and do as they asked when they sent me back.

Jim continued, "They're not thrilled about sending you, but they know you'll have the best chance of finding out what happened. We need some more information before they make their decision though. We need you to see if you can nail down a date when this memory loss took effect. We'll let you talk to him again. Tell him whatever you need him to know, whatever he wants to know. It won't matter."

"What do you mean, it won't matter?"

"Addy, you know he can't go back to his life."

"So I'm supposed to lie to him."

Jim looked uncomfortable for a moment and glanced past me into my quarters. "Use your best judgment. If you think telling him the truth will get him to cooperate, then that's what you need to do. Once we have a better idea of the date, we can plan what should happen. It's likely they'll send a scout to find out where you need to be, but we need that information first."

"Ok. Just give me a minute." I ran back into my bedroom and dressed as quickly as possible. I ran back out to the kitchen and grabbed a bottle of red wine, a bottle opener and two glasses. "Let's go."

Jim led me back to the return chambers and the room where they kept the Montgomery Noah. He stopped outside the door for a moment and gave me a serious look.

"I've got this, Jim." I said, trying to reassure him as much as myself. I had doubts about my own ability to get Noah to talk.

He nodded after another moment and motioned to the guard to let me in. "Good luck."

Noah immediately looked up when the door opened. He sat in one of the chairs at the table, and his hands gripped the armrests. He looked a little less frantic than before and even smiled slightly, seeming a little relieved that it was me. A sudden pang of guilt washed over me, but I tried to keep my expression pleasant. I'd do my best not to lie to him, but I couldn't possibly tell him the truth about his future here. Something told me this Noah would not be allowed to live. *One way or another.*

I tried not to grimace as I set the glasses down on the table and opened the bottle of wine. Noah watched me in silence while I poured two glasses and set one in front of him. He stared at it with mistrust. "I promise, it's not poisoned," I said, as I sat down across from him. I plastered a smile on my face and took a significant sip from my glass. I'd have to be careful. It wouldn't be wise to get drunk and try to have this conversation. I held up my glass again. "See? We used to drink together often."

He took the glass and seemed grateful for it. He took a sip, then a longer swig and let out a grateful sigh. "Thank you. You say we drank wine together often?"

"Yes. Back when we were friends. Whenever I had a problem, you'd be there with a bottle of wine and let me rant about whatever I needed to."

"That hardly seems an appropriate relationship for a man and an unwed woman.

I doubt my wife would approve."

"Well, this was before you were married."

"We were acquainted prior to my marriage in Salem?"

"Well, no." I squirmed in my chair slightly. I had been hoping for more small talk before things became more serious and awkward. "You used to live in this future. I knew you here."

He barked out an angry laugh. "That is quite absurd. I have already explained to you, I have never been in this place before. I do not understand where I am, but time travel is an impossibility. It is not possible that I am in the future."

"Don't things seem out of place to you? The furniture, the rooms, the clothing and tools?"

"It has been rather a blur since I arrived. I recall a medical examination with some instruments that seemed very unfamiliar to me, even though I am a practiced physician."

"Watch this." I tried to think of something I could show him that wouldn't reveal too much. Although at that point, maybe "too much" wasn't a consideration I should have worried about. "Personnel file Adelaide MacDuff." My picture materialized above the table.

Noah jumped out of his chair and knocked it over as he backed away. "What is this, witchcraft?"

"I'm sorry, look, it's okay!" I waved my hand in the air above the table. It passed through my face, and the image flickered for a moment. That didn't seem to help since he looked even more frightened. I tried to remember when photographs were invented. I couldn't recall actual pictures from before the Revolutionary War, so probably not in his timeline. "It's like a drawing of me, but it's... a projection. Close file." My picture disappeared again. I thought perhaps that wasn't the best start. "Please, sit back down. I'm sorry I frightened you."

"A projection?" He hesitantly sat back down, took a larger sip from his wine and tried to steady his breath again.

It dawned on me; they wouldn't have had movies either. "Think of it as taking a drawing and shining a light through it. It casts a shadow of itself on the wall, right?" I struggled to continue when I realized they wouldn't have had electricity either. I should've done some research first. "Like a lantern with a cover."

"Where does the light originate?" His gaze wandered around the room. He looked under the table. The light in the room was ambient with no obvious sources. I didn't know how to possibly explain a computer to him when he didn't even know about light bulbs. It encouraged me to see him try to figure it out. The curious investigation was a very Noah thing to do. He continued to stare off at a wall as he spoke again. "I used to have these dreams..." He looked down at the table again, lost in thought. "Dreams about a place. An enormous dome, made out of glass. And grass and trees grew within. And I ate such strange foods." He looked back up at me. "Was that here?"

"Yes. I can ask, maybe they'll let me take you there." Perhaps it would jog his memory and he'd be able to tell us what happened to him. Perhaps he'd be able to have a say in what happened to him. Perhaps everything would turn out just fine. I tried desperately to cling to that idea.

"How is it possible that I could have dreams about this place?"

"Because I've been telling you the truth; you've been here before."

He shook his head slightly. "How can that be?"

I sighed. At least now I could be honest. "I don't really even understand it myself, how it all works. But you were here. That place is here. The two of us used to sit out there in the grass under that dome together. Just like this." He looked like he didn't believe me. "The grass, it's a circular area right? And there are benches and buildings lining the edges of the circle?"

He looked astonished. "You can see my dreams?"

"No. I've lived them. You've lived them. They aren't dreams." I could tell he didn't believe me.

He glanced sideways at me, calculating something. Again, it was a gesture I recognized from Noah. "I would appreciate seeing this dome for myself."

I realized this conversation wasn't getting us anywhere. I needed to get more information from him. "Montgomery, look, I want to help you. I promise I can help you, but I need to know more about what happened to you first."

He still looked a little dazed by my knowledge of what he thought of as dreams. He closed his eyes and rubbed them briefly. When he reopened his eyes, he focused on me again. "What do you need to know?"

"When you lost your memory, do you remember what day it was?"

He thought for a moment. "It was the winter. Snow covered the ground. Almost Christmas I believe."

"Anything else?"

"It was a Sunday. People were exiting the church as I wandered the square."

"Do you have any idea how close it was to Christmas? How much time passed before you celebrated the holiday?"

He closed his eyes and worried his forehead. "The wreath... The Advent wreath in the main square." He nodded to himself and opened his eyes. He had a look of smug triumph on his face. "They lit the third candle that day."

That meant nothing to me. "I don't understand. What's advent?"

He seemed surprised that I didn't know this. He straightened in his chair and pushed his glass aside, folding his hands in front of him. It felt like I was about to be lectured.

He cleared his throat and began. "There are 4 candles representing the 4 weeks of Advent that mark our watch for the birth of our Lord. Every week, another candle is lit to mark the passage of time. Supposing the third candle had been lit that week it would mean it was the second to last Sunday before Christmas." He focused on me, talking almost like he would to a child. His voice slowed towards the end of his explanation.

"Noah, that's perfect!" For the first time since I entered the room, my smile came naturally.

He looked at me intently. He didn't seem to register my slip of his name. "You were there."

"What?" My face fell with confusion. "Where?"

"You were in my dreams. You were in the glass enclosure with me. That is why you seem familiar." His voice started to break. "But that can't be," he paused. "I believe I would appreciate some solitude."

"Of course. I'll come back again later, if you like."

I sat for a moment, waiting for a reply. When he didn't say anything in response after a few more moments, I excused myself and left the room.

I found Jim waiting for me just outside the door again. I had no idea where he had been watching us from that he would meet me so quickly. "Addy, that makes no sense."

"What makes no sense?"

"His mission was supposed to end in August. The witch burning happened in August. What was he still doing there in December?"

I fought to try and understand why Jim was so rattled. "I don't know."

"The nature of this mission has changed. They no longer think this was an accident. They think Noah was intentionally trying to escape."

I had to laugh. "That's ridiculous; Noah would never do that."

"Think about it from their perspective. He's never been exactly quiet about his disapproval of the way this place is run. Now he's stayed well past the completion of a mission. No matter what the reason, they think he's making them look bad, and they won't have it." He paused and took a deep breath, "And they're rethinking sending you."

The anger flared in me immediately. "They don't trust me?"

"Can you blame them?"

I couldn't argue with Jim. My hostility wavered. I knew deep down I would be more loyal to Noah than those people in the boardroom, even if it meant losing my job. "I'm still the best person they have for finding out what's happening with him."

"I'm not sure they care about that so much as... making an example of him."

I caught the hesitation in Jim's voice. I knew him well enough to know he didn't voice out loud what he was actually thinking.

# Chapter 11

The next few days were busy ones. They had agreed to give me a chance to convince Noah he should come back, so I started studying up on the 1690s and went for my costume fitting. The scout went back and returned a day later to confirm the date of Noah's memory loss and the existence of the woman he had mentioned in his house when he woke up.

I was anxious to get my new mission underway, but Jim was adamant that I didn't rush into it. He kept quizzing me on random information about the time period that I found completely unnecessary. I tried to assure him that I would only be there long enough to find Noah and warn him what was to come. Though I knew I wasn't as stealthy as a scout, the preparation was still overkill. I knew they intended it to be that way. They were trying to assert their control over me in relation to this mission. If they were already giving in by just letting me go, then they would have me do the mission on their terms.

I could tell Jim still hid something, but since it was likely I was being watched even more closely in the days before my mission, there was no way to find out what he wanted to tell me. My mind feared the worst: making an example of Noah meant that he would be severely punished, possibly even dismissed, if I managed to get him to come back. I despaired at the idea that even if I got him back, he could be taken away again just as quickly. Getting him back was still preferable to doing nothing.

Montgomery Noah had been moved to a more comfortable living space at my repeated request. He was still guarded, but I saw him whenever I liked. He was happy to have someone to talk to but tended to retreat from me whenever I tried to discuss this place or the technologies around him. He had accepted now that he was in the future. With so much evidence to support the idea, it hadn't taken long to convince him of the truth. He believed it, but he didn't like it.

Aspects of his personality poked through from time to time which I found reassuring. He took comfort in trying to cook and made lunch for me one day when I had told him I would come by. However this didn't change the fact that an entire lifetime had been taken from him. He frequently talked about his wife, children, and grandchildren, and I could tell that he missed them terribly. It comforted me to know that he had been such a devoted husband and father. It also devastated me to think that not only had that life been torn away from him, but that if I succeeded in my mission, it was a life he'd never know.

He had asked to see his quarters and also the grassy area in the dome where we sometimes had lunch. Both requests had been denied. Although I believed that taking him places that should be familiar to him might help him recover his memory, the powers that be didn't think it was worth the risk. They weren't very clear on what they thought that risk was though. More and more I got the feeling they just didn't care. A sneaking suspicion grew inside me that while I was gone, something would likely happen to Montgomery Noah.

Every time we got together, the first thing he asked me was if he was being sent back to his home. Every time I told him no, he asked when he would be. I kept telling him I wasn't sure, which was not necessarily a lie. For all I knew they would find a way to get our Noah back and return this one to his own time. He had been subjected to all sorts of brain scans and tests. They seemed to be interested in his memory loss and were very eager to find out how it happened. I hoped, rather than believed, this was for altruistic reasons concerning him. All the scout had been able to find out was the name of the woman who was with Noah at the time of his memory loss. The general consensus was that she must be involved somehow.

My last visit with Noah before my mission started out as usual, and I tried very hard to push away the fear that this was the last time I would see him. I hadn't been allowed to tell him that I was going back.

"I know your ideal solution would be to be sent back to your family, but if that turns out to be impossible, what is the next best alternative?"

Noah sat in silent thought for a few moments. I knew he would answer, as he did all my questions, and that he just needed time to process the idea. "Death."

Though my paranoia had convinced me that he was headed for death, I couldn't yield to that. "You can't be serious."

"What do I have to live for here? Trapped in this cell of a house, not allowed to do anything useful, no family left."

"What if there was a way to integrate you into this society?"

"From what I have witnessed, I do not want to be a member."

I couldn't blame him for that, considering how he had been treated. "Okay then, the outside world. Forget about this place."

"This is all I know of your world."

That was certainly true. He wasn't allowed out, he wasn't allowed to read anything about current events or the history that brought us to this. The information I had given him about this place was sporadic at best. "It's much nicer than in here. You enjoy cooking, perhaps you could be a chef."

"You have food here I'm not even familiar with. And cooking machinery I've never used before. It would take me a long time to learn how things work in this time." He looked sad again, "Besides, I only enjoy cooking for company, and I know no one out there."

And he barely knew anyone in here. "And you think death is preferable to even trying?"

"I'm too old to be starting over."

"How old do you think you are?"

He hesitated. His aging process had slightly increased while he was gone, near as we could tell, but he was still a product of this society and had already outlived most people he would have met in Salem. When he left on his mission, he looked to be in his early twenties to the people there. "I have to be at least seventy."

"One hundred and twelve." No reason to lie about this.

He inhaled through his teeth. "But I look-"

"About sixty, I know. A lot of developments have been made in health and medicine. The average life expectancy of a person born these days is about one hundred and sixty years."

"But I had no access to these developments."

"True. There are things we can easily cure now that would've killed you back then. So you were lucky in the respect that you didn't have some horrible accident. But your advanced immune system protected you from certain common diseases, and the fact that you born and raised in this time gave you a pretty good head start. Your time in the 1700s seemed to negate some of these advancements, so it's not likely you would've lived the full one hundred and sixty years."

"How old are you?"

"Forty-two." Though I knew I looked in my early twenties to him. He didn't seem to believe me. "Personnel file, Adelaide MacDuff." My file opened again before him. He had become used to this now and did not get frightened. "Computer, date."

Connery's voice responded, "Wednesday, April 26th, 2073."

He looked at my birthdate on the file and did the math in his head. "This could have been falsified."

"Why would I lie about my age?" I smiled at the notion of vanity.

He had no answer. He looked over my profile more intently. He wasn't allowed access to many documents, so naturally he would be curious about anything he could see. Most of our conversations went this way. It was obvious he still did not trust me, and I couldn't fault him for that. I wanted to tell him the truth, but I knew there was no reason to worry him. Still I couldn't keep the fear from my face. "Why do you look so uneasy?" he asked me.

"Someone is going back tomorrow. To find out what happened to you."

"What are you worried they'll find out?"

I couldn't answer that. I was eager to find out what had happened, my worry had to do with what was to come. "I just miss my friend."

"Why don't they just send me back?"

"We need to know any potential repercussions. This is dangerous stuff we're playing with here."

"Then you shouldn't be playing with it."

I laughed at his indignant tone. Noah and I had arguments like this all the time. "Seventy years ago you didn't seem to mind that much."

He shook his head at me. "I can't imagine someone like me ever approving of what goes on here. You're interfering with people's lives, with history."

"No. There are rules that we strictly adhere to, to prevent interference with the way history would normally unfold. We're very careful."

"Not careful enough, it would seem." He gave me a condescending look.

"Noah knew what he was doing. I know him and I know that much. We're very good at our jobs." It felt strange to be referring to Noah as a separate person from this man. Although they shared a few personality traits, this was definitely not the same person. "And he is one of the best." I wasn't sure why I said that in present tense. I guessed I just wanted to reassure myself that when I went back in time tomorrow morning, I would find the same person I knew and missed. And he would not be this old man who had given up hope.

He caught the inference and his temper flared. "You see? It would be easier on you if I died. Then you could remember that other man you knew who seems like such a great man and not this old, useless one."

This is not how I wanted our last moments together to go, but I fumed at his dismissiveness of his former self. "Maybe you're right!" I sprang out of my chair and stormed out of his place.

I went back to my quarters, angry with myself for leaving things that way, and angry with him for not accepting who he really was. Once I had calmed down, I decided to write him a note. I casually pocketed a pen and took one of my books into the bathroom with me, hoping for the first time ever, that my bathroom was not under video surveillance. I turned to a page near the back of the book that had one blank side and began to write. I explained my anger at him and what my mission really entailed. It felt cowardly, I should've told him the truth to his face. I fought with the idea of telling him not to trust anyone at the lab, but it wasn't like he had any way to resist them. Not cooperating would be worse for him than merely being confused at what they wanted to do with him. I promised him I would do everything I could to get him back home to his family. I knew it was an empty promise since there was nothing I could actually do, but I didn't want to leave with him thinking I didn't care to try.

Even with a sleeping pill, I had a fitful night of tossing and turning. I woke up in the morning feeling worse about how I had left things, but knew there wouldn't be time to see him again before I left. And in a few hours, it wouldn't matter. He would likely be gone. Even if that old man never knew the truth, the real Noah, the one I was going to go help, would know my intentions were good.

I met Jim at the entrance to the departure chamber and surreptitiously handed him the note addressed to Montgomery Welsher. He gave a slight nod and slid it into his pants pocket, but I wasn't sure he'd be able to deliver it after I left. I changed into my costume and had my hair done up in a bun which I was able to hide under my bonnet. I had a picture of the aged Noah in a pocket in my skirt.

It was the only thing I had decided to take with me. My orders were strict; if I couldn't convince Noah to return or prevent his memory loss, I had to leave immediately after it happened. They decided to send me back early in the morning, so I had about 3 hours to complete my mission. The scout had found a patch of dense trees for my arrival not far from the house where Noah would be. I had memorized the map of the area. I knew by heart where I would arrive, how to get to Noah's place from there, how long it would take, the path the woman took upon leaving him, and the square he wandered into afterward. Three hours should be more than ample time.

The medical team administered a sedative and a health packet to me before I entered the departure room. The sphere sat on a small pedestal in the middle of the plain white room. Without hesitation I walked up to it, flicked opened the lid with my thumb, and pressed the glowing red button.

Arrival was always an easier transition. I found myself surrounded by trees, almost as though they had been there the whole time. I closed the lid on the sphere and shoved it down into my coat pocket before moving on. A strong breeze whistled through the trees. I cinched my coat tighter and tied my bonnet down over my brow a little more snugly. Most people in the town were supposed to be at church at this hour, so I knew I wasn't likely to run into anyone.

I left the safety of the trees, and keeping my head down against the wind, walked hurriedly through the square past a wooden platform in the middle. I glanced up long enough to see the Advent wreath Noah had mentioned hanging from a wooden beam structure. There were only two candles lit. I stopped in panic for a moment before it occurred to me that they probably lit the candle after the church service. I ducked my head back down and continued across the square to the house where Noah lived. I made it to the front door less than two minutes after arriving in 1693. *So far so good*, I thought to myself. My heart fluttered with nervousness as I knocked on the door. I kept my head down, breathing deeply to try to calm myself while I waited. The sedative helped me focus on getting here, but it wasn't doing much for my mental state now.

The door opened and before I could lift my head I heard Noah's voice say, "You're early." He stood to the side to let me in. I walked through without saying a word, eager to be out of the cold. "Do you have somewhere you need to be?" he asked.

I lifted my head and took my bonnet off. "Noah."

He looked disheveled. He was wearing proper clothes for the time, but they looked dirty and untidy. His hair was a bit of a mess, and he hadn't shaved in at least a few weeks by the look of it. His eyes blazed with some intense emotion I couldn't place. "Addy!" He rushed towards me and embraced me roughly. His grasp on me felt desperate. He let out a maniacal sort of laugh.

I was overwhelmed with relief that he recognized me as I hugged him back. I had half expected him already not to know me. I couldn't help but notice the resemblances between him in this chaotic state and the older version of him I had just left. It dawned on me that the intense fear I had seen in the older version of Noah was mirrored in his younger eyes. I wondered why he was frightened.

He released me from the hug but kept his hands grasped on my arms, as though he was worried I wasn't really here. "How did you know?"

I pulled back to give him a puzzled look. The fear was gone but there was still a desperate look about him. "Know what?"

"That I wasn't able to come back."

I was confused. After spending so much time with the future Noah I had assumed the choice to stay was intentional. "What do you mean you weren't able to come back?"

"The sphere, it's not working." He let go of my arms and vaguely gestured to some spot in the room. "How did you know?"

This news did not ease my confusion. "Noah, you did come back."

Now it was his turn to be confused. "But I'm still here," he said gesturing at himself.

"Well yes." I hesitated, since I knew this news would upset him the most. "You didn't come back for seventy-two years."

He still didn't seem to understand. "Why would I wait seventy-two years?"

"That's what I'm here to find out. You're about to lose your memory, Noah. You won't even know what the sphere is for in a few hours."

Some small amount of clarity dawned on his face. "Oh, Adelaide. Oh no. That woman, the one who survived the witch burning..."

"The one you came here to learn how she survived? What about her?"

"She's coming here shortly. She's coming to erase my memory."

# Chapter 12

I stood dumbstruck for a few moments. A witch was coming to erase Noah's memory. What did he do to make her so angry at him? How could she possibly have that power? And why would he know this was going to happen and just accept it? I wasn't sure which question to ask first. "How soon?"

"About two and a half hours."

"Then I think you better start from the beginning of your mission."

He moved to the kitchen area, grabbed a bottle of something and poured two glasses. I didn't know what it was, but I could smell the alcohol from across the room. "Sit down." He took the glasses and set them on a wooden table in the corner. As I walked over I got a glimpse of the space for the first time. It was the equivalent of a studio apartment. A fireplace filled the wall where I entered. A wood burning stove and some cupboards comprised the kitchen. A small bed was arranged in front of the fireplace. The table had a few papers scattered over the top of it, barely large enough to sit two people comfortably. I sat but left the cup untouched as Noah began his story.

"Sarah Clayes is the woman who survived the burning. It was simple enough, actually. She knew what was coming and donned a leather bodice and leggings that had been soaked with water. She also covered her exposed skin with a mixture of dirt and a chemical that seems similar to asbestos. All she had to do was wait for the ropes that bound her to catch on fire, then she was able to break free and run. Her overclothes burned well enough. No one thought she could survive let alone make it very far, and they were too afraid to pursue her right away anyway. I met her during her escape and helped her dispose of her burnt clothing and wash and find a place to lay low and recover from the wounds she did receive.

"I tended to her burns and left her with directions on how to treat the wounds. I gave her some antiseptic ointments. Then I promised to check on her in a few days and left, with every intention of not following through on that promise. I came back here, updated my journal and packed my things. Here." He pulled the journal out from under a stack of papers and handed them to me. "April 23rd. Look it up, it was supposed to have been my last entry."

I leafed through the journal to April 23rd. There was Noah's explanation of the witch burning, just as he told it to me. I turned the page and found the next one.

> *April 23rd, still.*
> *I don't know what's wrong, I activated the sphere but nothing has happened. I'm still here. The button is not glowing, it usually glows. It can't possibly be out of power, can it? They never mentioned that as a possibility. They never mentioned getting stuck as a possibility either. I'll try again tomorrow. I don't know what else I can do.*

I turned the page again.

> *April 24th.*
> *There's still no light. I think the sphere might be dead. Nothing is happening when I push the button. Dear God, I think I might be stuck here in 1693.*

I turned the page again.

> *April 25th. Still nothing.*
> *April 26th. Still nothing.*
> *April 27th. Still nothing.*

It went on like that for a week until finally:

> *May 1st.*
> *A new month. I went to see Sarah today. I didn't know what else to do. Her wounds are healing nicely. A few more weeks and she should be back to normal. Today the doctor asked me today where I've been. I told him I was sick with a fever and didn't want to run the risk of infecting anyone else. He was pleased with my dedication to the town's welfare. I left in a daze. Is this what my life is reduced to? The sphere failed to work again. I've been trying every few hours. I'm not going to give up trying. There is hope, I'm sure of it.*

I closed the journal. I was relieved to know Noah's delayed return was not intentional, that he did want to come back. I had doubted the lab's belief that he was rebelling. I knew he enjoyed his job too much to give it up, and here was my confirmation.

I turned my attention back to the sphere. I knew at the very least that the sphere hadn't run out of power since it wouldn't have worked in the future if that were the case. Perhaps some external influence rendered it useless. "Did you try taking it outside? Perhaps this place is interfering with it somehow?"

"I did, Addy. I tried outside. I tried back in the woods where I arrived. I tried on the platform where they kill the witches. I tried in the church. I've been carrying it around with me ever since the day I accomplished my mission. I don't even care about my notes or my journal anymore. I'd leave them behind in an instant if it meant I could get back."

Panic struck me. I pulled out my own sphere and inhaled sharply. I opened the lid and saw the faint glow of the red button. I exhaled with a slightly frantic laugh as I closed the lid again. I looked back up at Noah and felt a pang of guilt at his face.

"Well at least you can get back." His words had no sympathy, just pure bitterness.

"Noah, I'm not leaving until we solve this." I tried to ignore the fact that that wasn't exactly what I was supposed to do. But what would they do when I got back, fire me? I didn't care. Kill me? That seemed an extreme response even for them. I'd never be allowed to go back in time again, I was fairly certain about that. But none of that mattered. What mattered was figuring out how to fix Noah's sphere. "Can I see it?"

He pulled it out of a small pouch hanging off his belt and handed it to me. "Think you can fix it do you?" His voice sounded like a sneer.

"Noah, this is not my fault!"

His face fell. "You're right. I'm sorry, Addy. I've just been so desperate."

My attention wavered from him as I held the two spheres, one in each hand.

Noah continued, "This place is just so primitive compared to our time. The people are so foolish."

I flicked open the lid of his sphere and mine again. My light still glowed. It looked fine, still as strong as normal. On his though, absolutely nothing. A fear gripped me that whatever had happened to his sphere might happen to mine. I resisted the urge to flee immediately and tried to focus on the spheres, looking for another difference. Technically, they were both the same sphere.

"I was desperate," he said again.

The tone of his voice caught my attention again. He sounded afraid. I moved my gaze from the spheres to his face and focused on him instead. "Noah, what have you done?"

"I gave up, Addy. That woman, the one I helped, Sarah. She says she can help me forget everything. I didn't tell her why I just told her I wanted to forget my past. She said she knew a potion that could help. She's making it now. She's bringing it here today in a little while for me to drink."

"Why would you do that?"

"It's been months that I've been stuck here in this hell. This place, it gets to you. The people, their paranoia and obsessive religious practices. The complaints, all the time, and I can't do anything real for them." He stood up from the table and started to pace, his hands pressing against his temples. "Simple things, like fevers are deadly. A small scratch can lead to an infection that leads to gangrene that leads to a lost limb that leads to another infection that leads to death. I couldn't take it anymore. I figured, if had never known, if I never knew what life could be like outside of this time…" He paused and tried to calm himself. He sat back down and looked at me in earnest. "I thought maybe I'd be better off never knowing there was any other way to be. She said she owed me a favor, to thank me for helping her out." He rested his forehead on his hand on the table and took a few deep breaths. "You said seventy-two years?"

"Yes. The memory erasure works. Seventy-two years from now someone makes you aware of the sphere. My only guess is that in fiddling around with it you accidentally press the button." I didn't want to tell him who it was that drew his attention back to the sphere.

"But I've lost my memory. I don't know who you are? What I'm doing?"

"No. You come back as a completely different person." I shoved my sphere back in my coat and pulled the picture I brought with me out of my skirt pocket. "This is you, in seventy-two years."

He took the picture and looked at it with disbelief and recognition. He didn't gaze at it for long before dropping it on the table with a defeated look on his face. "Seventy-two years. That's an entire lifetime for these people."

I hesitated. Noah didn't technically need to know what happens to him in those seventy-two years, but I was too good a friend to let it go unsaid. "You have a life. A good life. You get married and have children and grandchildren. You love your wife."

He snorted. When he turned to me disdain filled his voice. "That's not me and you know it."

"It's what you're about to be."

"So that's what this place turns me into is it? An average Joe?"

"Technically an average Montgomery."

He laughed at my joke, almost pathetically. "Thanks. Not a terribly appealing option though." His body nearly crumpled in the chair under the weight of the idea.

I pulled my sphere back out and looked down at the two of them in my hands. Aside from the light glowing in the one I had brought, there was no discernable difference between the two. I was furious with the situation. I glared at the broken sphere and willed the light to turn on. My face burned at the injustice of it.

I looked back at my own sphere. I could give it to Noah. Let him go back and take his place in this world for as long as I had to. Perhaps Jim knew I would consider that as an option. Perhaps that explained why he grilled me so hard on the 1690s. It didn't have anything to do with getting me to calm down, it had to do with an unforeseen complication.

*No*, I thought, *there has to be a way*. If it will work again at some point in the future, there had to be a way to make it work now.

I had been trained as an engineer before I started working at the lab, and that innate desire to fix things kicked in. I pocketed my sphere again and focused on his. I rapped it once, hard against the table, then looked back at the button. Nothing. I closed the lid and shook it next to my ear, trying to listen for a loose connection. Nothing.

I opened it again and for the first time really looked at it. The surface was a smooth transition from the outer surface of the sphere to the inner hollow where the button started. Even the button didn't seem to have a discernible edge. I pulled on it slightly, but it had no give. I'd have to break it to get at the insides and even then I'd have no idea what was waiting for me in there or how it worked. It was Noah's only way back, at some point, so breaking it probably wasn't a good idea either. But the lure of wanting to know what was inside was strong. I realized I had never given it any thought before. "I'd kill for a hammer and a multimeter right about now."

Noah laughed. Even though the situation was dire, just being around him again made me feel better. He took the sphere from my hand and turned it in his own, as though trying to see it from an outsider's perspective. "So if in the future I don't know what this is, how do I come across it again?"

"By accident. It's in a case with some of your medical stuff and it accidentally gets pulled out when you're retrieving something else."

He sighed and shifted in his seat, staring at the sphere. "I didn't even want this assignment. Jim said it was one of the board's pet projects. And for some reason it got pushed on me. In the grand scheme of life, who is really going to care about a woman that managed to escape a witch burning?" He poked at the sphere on the table and let it roll halfway across before stopping it. "Maybe I've been set up."

"You may be opinionated but that hardly qualifies as a reason for dismissal." The idea soured my mind and sounded not altogether out of question. I took his hand to try and reassure him. "Remember, at some point it will work again. For all you know that could've been a few minutes after you lost your memory." While my hand was still there I took the sphere back and regarded it again.

I had never really considered the operation of the sphere, let alone what was inside. The actual time travel part Jim had tried to explained, but without a degree in quantum physics, it had been nearly impossible to follow, and likewise difficult for him to explain. But a button I understood. It was a button that pushed some mechanism that triggered the time travel. I couldn't imagine why the glowing aspect mattered, but my limited amount of evidence at present impressed upon me the rationalization that it did. It should merely be an indication of power. But to lose power and regain it again at a later date didn't make sense either.

I tried to remember my talks with the Montgomery Noah. He said he left the sphere in his case. It fell and rolled on the floor and was retrieved for him. I dropped the sphere and kicked it across the deerskin area rug on his floor, then retrieved it as it bounced against the far wall. Noah watched me, bemused as I reopened the lid and checked it. Nothing. Perhaps static electricity had shocked it back into operation. "Hold this a second." I handed the sphere back to him then rubbed my feet on the rug. I reached out to touch the sphere and received a small shock. I eagerly grabbed it back from him and opened it again. Nothing. "This stupid thing!" I made to throw it through the glass of the window, but Noah appeared at my side in an instant and grabbed my arm.

"Addy!" He took it back out of my hand. "One day it will work again, and I'd like to keep that option open."

I nodded at him and lowered my hand to ask for the sphere again. I stared at the red button. The stupid, worthless red button. "I'm sorry, Noah. This is so ridiculous." I collapsed back in the chair again.

"You should go back." He joined me at the table again, defeated.

"I can't."

"Yes you can, your sphere works."

"Noah, if I go back and you take that potion, they'll send someone else to kill you."

His body stiffened. "Why?"

"You'll make too many waves."

He knew what that meant. "Addy..." He struggled to think. "I'll run."

"You know they can find you."

"Give me a few hours head start," he said in a pleading tone. "They can't send someone back while you're here. I'll take the potion with me, disappear, and you go back in a few hours."

"You know they can find you." I spoke more fiercely this time around. He had to see reason. He knew the truth.

"So my choices are..." He thought about it. "I can't take the memory loss."

"If you do, I'll have to leave, and within a few minutes someone else will take my place." It pained me to see the look of despair on his face. "You know how they are, Noah. You know I'm right. They won't think twice about eliminating you. And it'll be that much easier when you no longer know they're coming."

"So I'm stuck here. With this knowledge."

"The sphere works again at some point." I thought that might be an option. Even if I couldn't get him back to our time, I could take the journal as evidence that he wasn't trying to escape them.

"But who knows when the hell that will be!"

I hesitated again. What if another decade passed before the sphere worked again? I couldn't sentence him to that. If I knew that the sphere would work in another week or even a month, I might be able to convince him to just let things progress till then. I considered what the lab would say when I returned, not knowing when he'd be able to leave. They probably wouldn't be thrilled with that idea either. They wouldn't trust that Noah wouldn't get to the same point of desperation again in a few weeks, and we'd be back where we started.

"There is one other option." I stood and walked over to him. I gestured to his hand and dropped his sphere back into it when he raised it to me. I put one hand on his shoulder and slid the other back into my jacket pocket. I tried to make it seem like a calming gesture.

"What's that?"

"This." I grabbed hold of his shoulder as hard as I could as I flipped the lid to my sphere open and put my thumb on the button. In the split second before I pressed the button and we disappeared, I saw the face of a woman peeking in through the window.

## Chapter 13

The panic stayed with me as my body exploded with the disorientation that inevitably comes from the return trip. We had been seen disappearing. That was definitely a major violation of the rules. Noah hadn't seen; his back was to the window when we left. I just had to keep quiet about it and not mention to anyone that we had been seen. We had been in the time of the Salem witch trials; a few months prior a woman had escaped a burning. To the standard observer of the time, it would just seem like another act of witchcraft. Nothing to worry about, I tried to convince myself as I panted in the grassy field. I could keep quiet. I forced myself onto my hands and knees to look around for Noah. He was sitting on a patch of dirt and staring straight ahead with a look of shock and terror on his face. I tried to follow his gaze, but all I saw in front of him were trees.

Trees. No white room. No bright lights. No mats. No one to take my sphere away and ask me what day it was. We hadn't made it back. Another wave of panic struck me as I tried to focus. We had traveled, that was certain. Then where were we? What time period was this? I crawled over and sat next to him grabbing his arm to shake him out of his daze.

He looked at me, his expression unchanged as he spoke. "What have you done?"

"I tried to take us back. I don't know what happened! Where are we?" The panic had not passed. I looked around wildly.

"The more relevant question is when are we," he said. "The where doesn't matter." He leaned over and grabbed his sphere from where it had rolled after he dropped it. He flipped the top open and gasped. "Addy!" He showed me the inside. The light glowed again.

I almost laughed with relief. The other sphere was a few feet away. I grabbed it and checked it as well, just to be sure. The light still glowed on mine.

I looked around again and shivered as a breeze came through the trees. There were patches of light snow cover. It was definitely winter. At least I determined that if nothing else. The disorientation was passing for me. I grabbed hold of a nearby tree and stood up. Noah still sat on the ground. Since he had been gone for several months, I expected it to take him longer to recover. I looked around to try and find the nearest break in the trees, but one was not readily apparent. "Noah we need to figure out what year it is." As the words came out of my mouth, I heard a clopping off to our right. I crouched in some brush near the tree I had been leaning on and looked towards the sound. I caught glimpses of a man driving a horse drawn carriage through the woods. "We must be near a road," I said to Noah under my breath. I watched the direction the driver went and turned back to Noah. "Are you okay?"

He was still sitting on the ground but nodded to me. "Yes, it's passing."

"Think you can walk?"

"Don't have much choice do I?" He grabbed a nearby tree hoisting himself up. I walked over and put an arm around his waist to help keep him steady. He threw an arm around my shoulders. "Alright, let's go." We walked over to where the carriage had passed. It was a dirt road, poorly maintained. We couldn't see a break in the woods in either direction. "What was in his carriage? Did you see?"

"No, it was closed." I looked behind us one last time before turning to follow the man. I gave Noah a bit of a shove and said, "Come on. Let's go this way." He didn't protest. We had no clues which way led to civilization faster. "We could just try the spheres again."

"I don't think that's a good idea until we know what happened." He let my shoulders go and slowly walked on his own. "For all we know we're in the right time, and that guy was just out for a nice ride through the woods."

I somehow doubted that and sensed that Noah didn't believe it either, but it did no good to argue with him on the matter. We heard another horse coming toward us and clambered into the brush again to hide. This time a man with an open cart, carrying baskets of bread passed. He had on full length pants and workman's boots that came up to his mid-calf. His coat was cinched shut so we couldn't see much of his shirt, but his it was looser than the one Noah wore. I looked down at his breeches and hose, wondering how we would get him to fit in. "Well at least we know it's the future. We're going to look out of place." We stood up now that the man had passed. "So is he delivering bread to the people in the countryside or going to town to sell it?" I asked.

"A baker would work in town. He's delivering bread to people out of town. Let's keep going," he said. We walked for another half hour before the trees started to clear out ahead of us. We moved back into the brush to approach the end of the road. We wouldn't try to wander out for a few more hours, until it got dark.

From our hiding place in the brush we saw a handful of brick and wooden buildings. We caught glimpses of a grassy area with trees in between the buildings and saw the top of a brick and wood tower that looked like an official building. Possibly a courthouse or town hall. A lot of people were walking about or riding horses. The men were in suits and hats and the women were in corseted dresses with bustles and long fitted overcoats. That meant we were both going to look out of place. "This town is small. Everyone's likely to know everyone's business. This could be difficult."

"I have an idea." Noah started to walk away. I followed him as he walked away from the town and back towards the road. "We'll wait for another solo traveler to come down the road. I'll knock him out and steal his clothes."

"You're going to beat up a local? Brilliant. What happens when he comes to and tells the local authorities that he's been attacked on the road by a man who stole his clothes?"

"You have a better idea?"

I thought for a minute. We were trained to blend in. Our clothes made that a little difficult but perhaps we could be from out of the country. "How's your French accent?" I asked him.

"Terrible. I'm not pretending to be French."

"It's not like these people will be smart enough to know."

"Why don't we just wait until tonight when everyone's asleep and break into one of those official looking buildings. They've probably got newspapers or paperwork from the day with a date on it."

I frowned at the idea of waiting around for several hours. It was winter. The sun was low in the sky, but it would be a while before people started going to bed. "I guess that's the safest bet at this point." I shivered in the wind again. "But once it's dark, I say we find someplace a little warmer. There should be stables somewhere if people are still riding horses."

Noah looked down at his clothes and realized he was even less protected from the elements than me. He wasn't wearing his coat when I had grabbed him and . activated the sphere. "Agreed."

"Gas street lamps," I noticed. "Still no electricity. By the clothes I'd guess we're still not in the 1900s." Costume construction was one of the reasons I was hired for this job, Jim had told me. While training to be a librarian, I was allowed to apprentice in the costume creation unit. A driving desire to learn everything I could and a love for the theatre had given me an abundance of knowledge about the technical aspects of stagecraft and a gift for accents. It was something I had listed on my resume merely as a lark, along with bagpiping and scuba certification. When they told me to include all my interests, no matter how irrelevant they seemed, I didn't think it was possible my theatre experience would be useful, but after working with the lab for a few years, now I easily saw how even things like scuba certification could come in handy. It was part of the reason why I wanted to learn how to sail. I loved being on or in the water, and I knew there were plenty of missions in the suggested projects list that would involve bodies of water.

"You sure?"

"There was a huge shift in fashion at the turn of the century. Full length pants, I think started in the 19th century, but I can't remember exactly when. So 19th century."

"So now we wait."

I put my arm around him to try to help keep him warm. "Now we wait."

"I'm glad it was you who showed up in 1692."

"I convinced them you wouldn't trust anyone else."

He laughed once quietly. "You're probably right. I might have beaten up anyone else and stolen their clothes."

I returned the laugh. "I'd hope you'd at least have the sense to use their sphere." My stomach growled. "I should've let you take down the bread man. I'm starving."

"Come on." He took my hand and led me through the brush at the end of the woods. It was getting darker. The sun would set soon. "Which of us do you think is less conspicuous?" he asked.

I raised my hand.

"Ok," he said. "Sneak up to the back of that house and grab us some food."

It was my turn to laugh again. "Oh yeah, that won't attract attention at all."

He sounded resigned. "Fine then, I'll do it."

Before I could stop him, he dashed out of the tree line and hid in the shadows of a house on the edge of the town. He paused for a moment, then disappeared behind a small mound near the back of the house. I couldn't see what he was doing, but no one was stirring in the house that I could tell. There were no candles lit inside. A few minutes later, he came back with a lumpy bundle in a burlap sac and a mischievous look on his face.

"Where did you go?"

"When I reached the side of the house, I saw they had a root cellar in the back. Here." He spread the blanket out on the ground.

In the fading light, I saw some sort of cured meat, a head of cabbage and some carrots. "Raw cabbage?" I poked it and watched it roll onto its opposite side.

"If I knew you were going to be picky I would've been more insistent that you go."

I sat down on the edge of the blanket with him and decided to be quietly thankful. "You're insane."

"You're welcome." We ate in silence, watching as the street lamps were lit. People started lighting candles and their own lamps in the homes and businesses. After we finished the food we wrapped the burlap sac around ourselves to keep warm for the next few hours. We decided to skirt around the edge of town towards the official looking building with the tower that we had seen on our arrival. Our hope was that we'd find something in one of the buildings on the edge of town, since going in towards the tall building would require navigating the streets and passing through a small part of the town. Then there was the matter of actually getting into the building.

We snuck back up to the side of the house with the root cellar. There were no lights on inside, but I was afraid someone might still be in there and tugged on Noah's coat to keep him moving. He acquiesced, and we moved on to the next building. It looked like some sort of merchant's shop. A light from inside cast the shadow of someone moving around, but it was too dim for us to see anything inside. We kept moving from building to building, trying to see inside without being noticed. Finally on the north end of town, there were two small brick buildings to navigate between to reach our target. Both were dark but we passed between them as surreptitiously as possible.

We emerged at the back of the official looking building. There was an entrance through double doors, and a placard told us it was indeed the city hall. The doors were locked, but not very solid. "Kick it in, count of 3?" I suggested.

"Agreed." He counted to three on his fingers, and the two of us kicked at the door knobs. With a rather loud whack, the doors split open and banged against the inside walls. We froze, listening to the sounds of the town, but only heard the distant laughter of a few night owls in the pub on the other side of the grassy circle. "Come on," he whispered.

We entered a narrow hall lined with doors. We tried the first one. It was unlocked but it was just an empty room with a table and some chairs. The one directly across the hall was the same. The next room further down was locked, which we took as a good sign. Noah grabbed the handle and slammed the left side of his body into the door. The latch splintered the wood of the door frame. A small amount of light spilled in from the street lamps through the window. It was enough to see a desk with a stack of papers. I rushed over, grabbed the sheet off the top and took it to the window to see it better. "Georgetown, Delaware, Civic Court. February the 2nd, 1882." 1882. I swore under my breath. Noah joined me by the window to see for himself.

"Drop that and place your hands on your heads."

I dropped the paper and turned, startled. In the doorway behind us a man in a black suit pointed a gun at us while another man at his side held a lantern. I placed my hands on my head and nudged Noah to do the same. "Who are you?"

I put on my best accent. "We are French visitors."

I heard Noah groan slightly. "Oui," was all he could manage.

"What are you doing here, sneaking around in this office?"

"Our papers, sir. The clerk threatened to keep them from us."

"Why would he do that?"

"He wanted favors from me, monsieur."

The man looked like he might believe it. "That sounds like something you should take up with the mayor. I'm not saying I believe your tale just yet. You'll have to come with me while I check out your story." He motioned with the gun. We followed the man with the lantern, and the man with the gun followed behind. "Staying in the town inn?"

"Oui, sir." I prayed that he would take us to jail before checking at the inn, and that Noah wouldn't try to do anything stupid like steal the gun from him. I was sure he could, but it was likely to attract even more attention.

He led us to a cell in another part of the court house. "You just sit tight while I go find the clerk and have a chat with him." He left us with a lantern.

Noah turned to me as soon as the two men were out of sight. "1882, do you know what this means?"

"What?" The date had no special meaning to me. I couldn't think of a single thing that happened in 1882 of significance.

"It's exactly between 1692 and 2073." He looked around at the cell. "We need to get out of here."

"Two foreigners disappear from a prison? That's hardly blending in."

"Just be glad we're not back in 1692. They would've burned you by now." He sighed. "We'd be forgotten. They'll shore up their defenses. This is hardly a high security prison; I could break this window open easily. They're probably counting that you'd have to steal a horse to get anywhere in short order. Then they'd have you for horse theft as well." He had pulled out his sphere as he was talking.

"Okay then, we leave." I pulled out my sphere and opened it. "But what happens now? The sphere was supposed to take us back to 2073; we only went half way. But will it still be programmed for 2073? They always just take it away. I've never thought to ask if it resets after use. What if it reset to some default point after we traveled the first time?"

"That doesn't make any sense. Why would the destination change unless they specifically make it change?"

I looked down at the glowing red light. "I don't know. They said they would readjust yours so you didn't come back at the same time as your future self. Somehow they can do that. Maybe they gave something to the scout, and he fiddled with your sphere when you weren't looking."

"So it sounds like they need to be actively involved in changing the destination time."

"Then how did we end up back here?"

"Well this may sound rather simplistic, but we're halfway there." Noah paced slowly as he tried to work it out. "The sphere is meant for one person, and it tried to take two of us. Perhaps we halved its power."

"That does sound simplistic, but also reasonable. So if we tried both of us again on my sphere that should take us home."

"I'm not so sure." He started pacing again. "From the sphere's point of view, it's trying to take us from here back to our present day. I don't think it's an absolute thing, I think it must be relative to our current timeline."

"So," I tried to follow his logic. "You think if both of us try to go back on one sphere again, we'll merely get sent halfway again?"

"1970s."

"Ugh. No thanks."

"I think we got lucky with our last trip anyway. If this is Georgetown, we probably arrived right on the spot where the return chamber will be built. Imagine what else could be built in the spot in the meantime. In the 1970s. What if we end up in the middle of a furnace?"

"But your sphere is working again. Or at least, the light is on again. We can both go back now with our own spheres."

"Yeah." He looked at it with distrust. "What if they don't want me back. What if they're sending me somewhere else? We'd both be gone, and you'd never know."

"And I thought I was paranoid." I held my hand out. "Then take my sphere. Go back. Convince them that if you don't come back within an hour, I'm taking the sphere no matter where it goes. They won't let me do that if it's not back to our time period." I heard the unmistakable sound of a door opening and footsteps heading our way.

"It's a chance I'll just have to take. Go, Addy!" He pushed the button on his sphere and was gone. I pushed mine as well.

# Chapter 14

I fell hard on my hands and knees against the white mats on the floor. I closed my eyes against the brightness of the White Box and fought off the wave of nausea, breathing hard. It didn't seem to help. The air, normally clean and odorless, had an acrid smell and felt thick with decay. I coughed up a bit of bile and waited for the voice to ask me my name while continuing to breathe heavily. I collapsed onto the floor and coughed some more, trying to open my eyes against the harsh lights. The white walls slowly came into focus. I didn't see the aides come to take my sphere away. In fact, I saw it lying there still, not far from where I had dropped it. I didn't see anyone at all.

As my eyes adjusted to the brightness, I realized the normal spot lights were not even on. It was merely the whitewashed walls illuminated by the ambient light that were so intense against my eyes after the gas lamp lit night I had just left. I picked myself back up onto my hands and knees. My time must be off, I thought to myself. I came back early, or late, and no one was expecting me. I leaned over to grab the sphere and noticed the mat had a moldy look and smell about it. They never smelled that great to begin with, but this looked like no one had been in here to clean up the sweat and sick in a few weeks. How late was I?

I forced my legs to hold my weight as I stood, pocketed the sphere again and staggered over to the exit door into the examination room. I figured from there I'd be able to call someone and get some assistance. The examination room was also unlit like the return chamber, but without the plain white walls, it was dark by comparison. Once again I had to wait for my vision to adjust. "Hello?" My voice echoed in the room. Surely someone was watching, someone was always watching. I knew from watching Noah's return video roughly where a camera would be, looked up towards that direction and asked for help. Any second now, someone would come to help me.

Or perhaps not. If it was the middle of the night, there would be no reason for someone to be monitoring this area. Still, I expected the return chambers at least to have a few alarms. I leaned over the examination table for support while I waited for my eyes to adjust to the darkness. I saw a set of clothes piled on a chair near the wall to my left. I took them over to a sink and undressed, throwing the normal clothes on and replaced the sphere in one of the pant's pockets.

I turned on the faucet. It sputtered for a moment before some cool water ran out. I splashed my face and wondered if the bathing area was working. Given the lack of lighting in here, I doubted it. In fact, I didn't see any lights on anywhere. None of the medical equipment had those soft red standby lights that glowed even when they were powered down. I had never been through here at night. Did they actually power down the whole dome? The only light seemed to be coming from the return chamber. I didn't understand how that could be though, if the lights in there had been off. I rummaged around in a cabinet and found an ambient light disc. I activated it and waited as it rose to hover just above my head. With a little more light surrounding me, I realized the place looked in a state of disarray. Dr. Crebbs seemed a bit anal-retentive, so this took me by surprise.

I moved on to the next room and looked longingly at the tub, but as I moved closer I noticed the water that pooled at the bottom was dirty and had a green algae-like tint to it. Something in the recesses of my brain told me this was not good. Algae must take several months at least to form in an environment like this. I moved more quickly now through the rooms and reached the hall at nearly a run.

Like everything else, it was dark. I turned to my right, intent on heading back to the living area dome, but hesitated, remembering the room I sat in just a few days ago while the important looking people debated what to do about Noah. I turned to the left and walked down the hall past where the older version of Noah had been briefly held. When I reached the door that I thought was the boardroom, I tried the handle. The door was locked. Feeling a bit silly, I knocked on it. I was not surprised by the lack of response. I didn't want to try kicking it in while wearing the soft shoes I had put on in the examination room. My 17th century boots were still back there, but I didn't think it would give so easily as the wooden doors did. I looked around the hall for something to smash against the door, but there were only a few toppled chairs.

I looked at the door with yearning. I suspected the answers to so many of the secrets they had kept from us lived in that room. I looked further down the hall and realized I had never been past this door. I walked further down the hall, past a few more doors and turned a corner. Though the hall was exactly the same, it looked darker. I began to feel uneasy and glanced up at the ceiling, looking for some sign of surveillance equipment. I glanced behind me a few times, certain I was being watched as I walked toward the door at the end of the hall. I expected it to be locked, like the other door, but the handle turned easily and my sense of foreboding froze me.

I stood there for a moment, clutching the handle, motionless, and waited for something to happen. Nothing moved. I heard nothing but the sound of my breath. I pushed the door open a crack and tried to peek through but saw nothing. I took a deep breath and flung the door wide open, trying to convey a sense of confidence that I lacked.

It was an office. A large, ornate wooden desk that looked out of place in a facility like this sat directly across from the doorway. A door stood in the middle of each wall. As I stepped into the room, a soft light came on, and I heard Connery say, "Good morning, Dr. Lancing." I stopped immediately and surveyed the room, but I was alone. I realized it must have been an automated system. It seemed there was at least some power left.

I grabbed the light disc, turned it off and pocketed it, then walked around to the desk and sat down. A display sprang to life above the desk. The main part of the display showed a paper someone was editing. There were lines of equations and some constants I didn't recognize. In the upper right corner of the display was a chart that looked like someone's vital signs. The name said "E. Phillips," and to my surprise, the chart was updating. E. Phillips was alive and being monitored nearby.

I was about to jump up and try the doors when the lower right corner of the display caught my attention. Two folders sat there, one labeled "A. MacDuff" and one labeled "N. Kent." My eyes bored into the icon representing Noah's folder, and after a few seconds, it opened.

The folder contained a list of files; the date of the most recent one was June 3rd, 2073. It was a memo titled "Neutralization Order." Below that was a video dated June 2nd, 2073. It was titled "Interrogation Session 4." A few more videos followed of prior interrogation sessions and Noah's return. Lastly there was a long list of files of various missions and status reports. I looked back up at the first file. "Open."

Connery's voice greeted me again. "N. Kent files subject to clearance level 1 or special access channels."

The folder closed as well as the unfinished paper. I swore to the room. The remaining display was a split screen of video monitors. One showed the White Box. The other three were places I didn't recognize. One looked like a dorm room, one like a hospital room, and the last a large laboratory. I couldn't see the bed well in the hospital room, but my instinct told me that was where I would find E. Phillips.

I stood up from the desk and walked to the door on my left. It was locked. The door next to it opened into a dormitory style room. A dozen beds lined the walls. Small desks next to each bed contained papers and personal effects. All the beds were neatly made except for one. The third bed on the left was disheveled, and a mark that looked like dried blood stained the left side of the pillow. I picked up a framed photo on the desk that showed an adolescent girl grinning with a ball poised a few inches above her open hand. The picture must have been taken shortly after she tossed it in the air. She was standing next to a man grinning down at her, but most of his face was obscured by long hair. I could only guess that it was Doctor Lancing.

I decided this must have been some sort of medical research wing though I wondered why the head of medical research had files on Noah and me. I ran my finger along the top edge of the desk, but no dust had collected on it. I opened the single desk drawer. It had a few file links inside and the ball from the picture with some writing on it. I pulled it out to read it. Eliza Phillips had signed it with a date: November 24, 2068. 5 years before I started working here. I had no idea this place existed the whole time I had been employed.

Why did this place look pristine while the return chambers were in shambles? I put the ball away and walked around to the next desk. The picture on this desk was another child. He held up a card with a heart on it. His smile was elated. He was standing in front of someone wearing a lab coat who had their hands on his shoulders, but he was cut off from the chest up. "Doctor Lancing again, I presume?" When I opened the drawer, the desk was completely empty.

I sighed and continued to the end of the room. The door at the end was also unlocked, and I recognized the laboratory from the video feed in the other room. In person though, it didn't look like a laboratory at all. A single lab table and it was pushed into a corner as though it had been in the way. A single petri dish filled with some gooey substance sat in the middle of it. There was no other lab equipment visible, which I found odd.

The floor was softly carpeted, a definite change from the rest of the facility, and large pillows were strewn about. A neatly stacked pile of blocks, taller than me, stood precariously off to the side of the room. Two empty chairs sat facing each other in another corner. The lab table seemed out of place in such a comfortable setting. Spotting no other exits I went back through the dormitory to the office again.

The door on the opposite side of the office also opened easily. Before I even had it open, I heard the soft beep of a heart monitor and knew I had found Eliza. She lay in the hospital bed, eyes closed. Electrodes connected her to various machines. I didn't understand how she could be here; since no one else was around. Perhaps if I waited someone would show up to take care of her.

Perhaps Doctor Lancing was still working here. Or perhaps she had been sitting here on life support for weeks.

She didn't look ill in the slightest, and her IV drip was nearly full. Someone had definitely been here recently. She wasn't even on a ventilator; she must have been breathing on her own. I took her hand and squeezed it. "Eliza?" She did not stir. Nothing about her changed.

I glanced around the room. Next to the head of her bed was a chair with a strange looking helmet on it. A cable came out of the top and snaked somewhere behind Eliza. I walked around the other side of the bed to see where it went and immediately regretted it. Eliza's skull had been cut away. The other side of the cable looked like a claw that had been dug into her brain.

I turned away and ran from the room, trying to control the nausea that had surfaced. From the office, I still heard the soft beep of the monitor. She's alive, I kept telling myself. Someone here had done that to her, and I didn't want to stick around to find out who when they finally returned. I began to leave the place but was stopped by the mental picture of the helmet on the chair. It was linked to her brain. Perhaps it was a way to communicate with her. If I found out what was going on, maybe I could help her.

I looked around nervously. I was fairly convinced that someone would return through here at some point. I didn't want that to happen while I was in the room with Eliza. What choice did I have though? I had to find out what was going on here. I went back into the room and looked around again. There was a closet off to the left that housed medical supplies. I figured, if I heard someone come into the office, I could hide there.

I sat down, took a deep breath and put the helmet on my head. I closed my eyes and tried to listen, but nothing happened. I opened my eyes again and glanced over at her. "Eliza," I whispered.

Immediately images started filling my head. I gripped the arms of the chair; the intensity of it was painful. It felt like someone had taken over my mind and would not allow any of my own thoughts to surface. I struggled to get a handle on myself; the images flashed past so quickly I couldn't understand any of them. I forced myself to relax, clear my mind and focus on what I saw.

I recognized one image showing over and over again. It was the picture of Eliza and Doctor Lancing with the ball in the air over her hand. I was seeing it through the eyes of Eliza. The image stretched out into a few seconds during which I could feel Doctor Lancing pat Eliza on the shoulder. She stared at the ball. I felt her face as she broke from an intense look of focus into a smile. The ball didn't move during this time.

There were more flashes of Doctor Lancing, though his face was never in focus. He was frequently in the laboratory room I had seen with other children. I caught a glance of a sphere. One of the children held it. While the rest of them watched intently, the young boy disappeared then reappeared a few seconds later. I caught a glimpse of Noah, but the image vanished too quickly. Somehow my mind knew I could get it back, and I focused on bringing the image back to the forefront.

Noah was hunched on the floor in a plain room. I saw what I assumed was Doctor Lancing's white lab coat in my peripheral vision. I watched passively as Noah clutched his abdomen and screamed. Some part of my mind found it odd that I didn't care as I watched. I merely continued to focus on his mid-section as a man's voice asked, "Where is she?" Noah screamed that he didn't know.

My vision flickered to the other side of the room. There was a ghastly pale, gaunt looking boy strapped into a wheelchair with a different helmet on his head. He stared with wild fright at me. I saw the corner of Doctor Lancing's lab coat swing slightly as he turned to the boy in the wheelchair. "Where did you take her?" The boy didn't take his eyes off me as he whimpered, "I don't know," just before breaking into a heart wrenching wail of pain.

I leapt out of the chair and tore the helmet off my head. I barely had time to register that several objects fell to the floor as I ran out of the room through the office and into the hall. They had been looking for me, and they might still be looking. That little girl, Eliza, could use her mind to move things and to hurt people.

I sprinted down the hall, pulling out my light disc as the light from Doctor Lancing's office faded behind me. I turned the corner, half expecting to run into him, and slowed my pace to get around the chairs I had noticed earlier. Someone had built that helmet and burrowed into her brain as a way to interact with her. That made no sense; she could hear and react to people, why not just talk to her? It must be something more than that, a way to link to her mind and her ability to manipulate objects from a distance. A few objects in the room had started to levitate as I was linked with her; that's what fell. I hadn't realized it while I had the helmet on. Had I done that? Or had she?

I rounded another corner and saw the light from the living dome spilling in through the glass doors at the end of the hall. I kept sprinting towards the exit and refused to look back to see if I was being followed.

# Chapter 15

I burst through the doors into the living dome and only then allowed myself to turn and look behind me. Through the glass doors, the hall was still and empty. It looked as though I had never even been in there. I switched off the light disc and pocketed it again, then turned back towards the main courtyard of the living dome.

It was barely recognizable. The gardens were wild and overgrown. The buildings looked like they were in good shape, though the grass had also overgrown and vines were covering much of the central facades. I guessed Doctor Lancing didn't have much need for a tidy living space.

I walked slowly over to my living quarters, trying to ignore the fact that the most alarming part of the facility neglect was a giant hole in the roof of the dome. Something had shattered a large section of the glass and bent the frame in. Eliza, perhaps?

When I reached my door, it did not open automatically for me, but it was easy enough to force open. It was dark inside here as well, but I didn't have to go in to see from the light in the doorway that someone had destroyed the space. Either through searching or looting, I wasn't sure. I lit my disc again and cautiously wandered in.

The kitchen cabinets were open and the contents disheveled. It looked like they had been searched. I couldn't imagine why someone would want to search my kitchen cabinets. I wandered through the space, my bed had also been stripped and clothes pulled from the closet. I had so few personal effects, I had no idea what someone would have been looking for. I was simultaneously puzzled by the motive and angry at the invasion of privacy. What little I had left in this place.

I left and walked across the open space to Noah's quarters. I knew immediately upon entering that it wasn't right. The decor was off. The furniture was too fancy. Aside from a thick film of dust, it didn't look disturbed. I wandered through just to be sure, but nothing looked out of place, except that being Noah's quarters, everything in there looked out of place. I walked back outside and double checked the door. It was definitely the right room. I tried the next door over. Like Noah's place, it seemed to be undisturbed. I went back outside. My gaze was drawn back up to the hole in the roof of the dome. I tried to push my fear away. Whatever had done that must be long gone. This place was empty. I walked over to the area of grass below the hole. Through the weeds, I saw shards of glass on the ground but nothing else. Whatever came through didn't seem to do much damage where it landed. I stared up at the hole again for a minute. I felt unsettled, like I was wrong that whatever had come through had left a long time ago. I forced myself to turn my back to it.

I hadn't counted on this. I had no idea what to do with myself. I had no idea what year it was. I had been detached from the real world for so long, I was nervous about the idea of leaving the complex. I needed to know what happened. The fact that algae had been growing in the bath meant it had to have been at least a few months since anyone had been in there. But what caused the place to be abandoned? Almost certainly it had something to do with the hole in the dome. So when did that happen? Was this a split in the timeline, or was I in the future?

I certainly couldn't remain where I was. I walked over to the main entrance Jim and I had used when I left for my vacation. My stomach knotted. I hadn't been outside since my trip to the island, which hardly counted as the real world. Perhaps I could find a way to get back there. I could live with Marina and Adam and find some way to be useful to them. When I got to the doorway, it didn't open, but I was expecting that at this point. Unlike my own doorway though, there were no ridges in the door. There was nothing I could see to grab hold of and force it open. I tried sliding it using just the friction of my hands against the door, but it wouldn't budge.

Panic gripped me for a moment. What if I was stuck in here? How would I survive? I walked back to the nearest quarters and forced that door open. There was a photograph in the entryway of someone I didn't know. "Adelaide MacDuff mail." I waited for a moment, but there was no response. My sigh arose more out of frustration than disappointment. I hoped maybe a back-up power system would kick in to respond to me, but I hadn't actually expected that to work.

There must be another way in. I had rarely seen the main door used, but I knew we must get deliveries somehow. The farm made the most logical sense to me. If they had to take delivery of certain foods and supplies that would be the closest place to store things. I turned back towards the farming dome.

I had only been this way once before with Noah. He wanted to show me a new plant he created by suggesting a cross breeding of two other plants. I didn't remember the name of the original plants or what the creation was. In the end it tasted horrible, and he gave up on it. The farmer had destroyed the small section of crop to Noah's dismay. I laughed lightly at the memory of his indignation and the emptiness swallowed the sound. The glass door leading to the farming area had been propped open. A large house that I assumed was where Montgomery, the farmer whose name Noah used on missions, had lived and worked was to my left. Several fields stretched in front of me. I had forgotten the size of this section of the complex. An orchard with various trees grew to my right.

"Okay," I said to myself. "If I were an alternate entrance, where would I be?" I thought about the root cellar Noah had found just a few hours ago. It seemed like years ago to me now. I sensed I was being watched and glanced back through the doors to the living dome. Nothing moved. Not even a breeze rustled the tall grass. "Root cellar it is." Talking to myself was a habit from when I was young and my parents left me alone in my room for hours at a time. Someone had told them it would help my creative side to be left alone like that. I guess it did though I never actually created anyone in my mind who listened. It was a comforting thought to pretend someone was there and to speak to the silence.

I walked around the back of the house. From what I could see, like everywhere else, it was dark inside. I smiled when I got to the back to find an actual cellar. It was still latched shut but wasn't locked. I lifted the latch and wrenched one of the doors open. It was dark inside there as well so I relit my disc and headed down the shallow concrete steps to the cellar below the house. The room was much bigger than I expected. That made sense since at least a thousand people had lived in this complex. Though not all our food came from here a vast amount of our fruits and vegetables had. I knew that one of the fields was planted with soybar, which was made into many more types of food with the produce conversion system.

There were vast shelves full of containers. I pulled one off the shelf closest to me and read the label: carrots. "Now all I need is salted beef and cabbage." My shoulders fell as I put the container back on the shelf. Even if I managed to find a way out of this place, I had no idea what to do after that. For all I knew, Noah hadn't been taken to this time period. Perhaps he had made it back to normal time as he was supposed to. Would he try to find me? Were they tracking me right now? "First things first." I walked down the aisle a little further and pulled another container off the shelf just out of curiosity. "Juniper." I put it back and continued down the aisle. About halfway to the back, I pulled another container down and wiped the dust away to see the label. "Orange slices." I put the container back and wiped the dust away from my hand with the other, then looked at my hand for a moment. There hadn't been dust on the first containers. "Wait a minute." I turned and quickly walked back along the aisle. About halfway back, the containers were not covered with dust anymore. I grabbed

Michelle McBeth - 105

another container and stared at it in disbelief. Someone had put these here recently.

That someone was suddenly pointing a disintegrator pistol at me. "Put that back please, and place your hands on your head."

I did as he asked, my swift movements betraying my sudden fear. "I'm not here to rob you." He was old, but his hands were steady with the gun. I didn't like my chances if I tried to rush him.

"How did you get in here?" he demanded. The gun moved an inch closer to my torso.

"The doors were unlocked. I was looking for... something."

"No, I mean the dome, how did you get in this dome?"

My eyes followed the tip of the gun as it moved just slightly away from me when he gestured with it.

I realized what he meant. He thought I was from the outside world. A reasonable assumption given the state of this place. "Please lower the pistol! I'm not here to steal from you or anything. I need help," I pleaded.

He lowered the gun slightly but kept a firm grip on it. "No funny stuff now."

"No funny stuff," I agreed. I lowered my hands from my head but kept them held out in front of me as a sign of trust. "I need help."

"So you said. What kind of help?"

"I need to find a way out of this place."

He grunted in amusement. "Just head back out the way you came in."

"That's easier said than done. Do you know what year it is?"

He laughed at me. "What nonsense is that? I haven't kept track of the date in years." He gave me a look that said he thought I was either crazy or up to something. I noticed his finger twitch towards the trigger on the pistol. "What are you doing in my root cellar?"

"Your root cellar? You live here? You work here?"

"Live here, yes. Work here, used to. Nobody's been here to work for years."

I had only met the farmer a few times, but I certainly knew his name. "Are you Montgomery Welsher?"

He gave me a dark, mistrusting look. "Now how would you know that?" He raised the pistol again and pointed it at my head this time.

My pulse sped again, desperate to get him to trust me. "I'm a librarian. My name is Adelaide MacDuff, I'm a good friend of Noah Kent."

"Adelaide MacDuff?" His look turned from confusion to surprise and a small laugh escaped his lips. It built as he lowered his gun and clutched his stomach, bent over with laughter.

"What!" I yelled at him to get his attention.

"Oh, Adelaide." He stopped laughing and gave me a wry smile. "You've pissed off quite a few people, you know. Come with me."

I followed him outside and up into the house. He turned on a light in his kitchen. "You have power too," I noticed.

"Too? Yes, I have a small generator. It's enough to keep this place going. Have a seat." He gestured to the kitchen table and pulled out a bottle of some pale yellow liquid. He placed it on the table and retrieved two glasses, leaving the pistol on the counter. At least I knew I had his trust now. He poured two glasses of the liquid and pushed one over to me. "Drink, you're going to need it." He took a sip and stared at me as he put the glass down. "Adelaide MacDuff," he said again, almost breathlessly, as he looked me over.

"What happened here?"

"So you don't know what year it is?"

"No idea at all. I just got back and everything was wrong. It looks like no one's been working here for years."

He gestured to the drink again, and I took a small sip. It was harsh on the back of my throat, and I made a face.

"That they haven't. It's been just me for a long while now. The year is 2168." He watched my reaction.

I couldn't speak. 2168. How could I have ended up here? I took another sip from my glass. And if I ended up here, what became of... "Noah?"

"Oh he came back in 2073, as was expected. But boy, oh boy when you failed to show up an hour later like they had programmed?" He laughed again. "Being out here I never got to hear about much of the goings on, but Noah came to visit me a few days after his return and told me all about it. They were furious with you. They thought you'd found a way to outsmart them and go somewhere else. They grilled Noah for days trying to figure out where you had got to. And come to find out it was their own fault, a screw up with the programming." He chuckled again. He clearly didn't have much faith in the people who ran this place.

My face fell as he explained. Noah came back on time and was gone now.

Montgomery seemed a little giddy with excitement. "He gave me a note for you. Knew you'd make it back at some point."

I looked back up at him with a pleading interest. "Noah did?"

"Yep." He groaned a little as he got out of his chair and walked over to a desk. "Had to do it rather sneaky too. Came over asking about some plant I had mentioned a few weeks before, wanted to go out into the fields and see it. Talked about them the whole time while he slipped two notes into my pockets. Slid them into a book when I got inside and took it back out into the orchard a little later on." He was rummaging through a drawer of some papers. "Read the one addressed to me like it was part of the book, just in case. Always knew they were watching but could never find the damn things." He pulled an old leather bound book out of a drawer and set it on the top of the desk then kept looking. "Told me about the other letter, which was addressed to you. Told me he believed at some point you'd return, that he thought he had worked out what happened. And if I was still around when you did, I was to give you this." He produced a folded piece of paper which was sealed shut at the edge. "I'll be off to the facilities for a little while. Give you a bit of privacy."

I sat down at the table and took a deep breath. The letter opened easily enough and I recognized Noah's writing.

> Adelaide,
> If you're reading this, it means I was right and you were
> sent into the future. I have a guess about how far into
> the future, but I won't bore you with my stunning
> intellect by explaining it here. Things are bad here.
> They're furious. They think it was part of some plan on

*our parts. I'm pretty sure I'll be let go. I've heard rumors of what happens to people from here who disappear, and none of them are good. If they don't just kill me, it's likely they'll find some way to neutralize me. I think I'd prefer death, I've seen what happens to people who lose their memory. Addy, I'm sorry for that. Jim let me watch some of the videos of your meetings with him. Well...me. That must have been so hard. So before that happens, I'm going to kill myself. I don't want to lose the first half of my life to these people. I want to remember it all. So I'm sorry again. Though if it's the year I think it is I'd probably be dead by now anyway. I don't know what to suggest you do at this point. I guess return to society, live the best life you can. Don't give up like I did. You're free now, you can go wherever you like. Enjoy it. -Noah*

The stress of the past week and losing Noah for good hit me all at once. I lowered my head onto my arm and cried. I hadn't cried in such a long time. Life had been great here. I loved learning about the past and getting to travel. I hadn't minded giving up the freedom; to me, it was worth it. Now I had no friends, no job, no place to go. I thought about the sphere in my pocket. I wondered where it would take me if I tried it again. By the time I raised my head, Montgomery had returned to the chair. I sniffed and took another sip from the glass. "So what happened to this place?"

"Witches."

I barked out a laugh. "Witches don't exist. Noah proved that himself."

"Well no, not real witches per say. But you've heard of The Gard?"

"Not really."

"A religion of sorts. Worship mother earth and nature and crap like that, but with a nasty violent streak. That woman that Noah saw escape the fire, she was a Gardian."

I froze in my chair. I felt like an idiot for not realizing it before. That woman who saw us disappear in 1692, that's who she was. "She saw us. I didn't notice her in the window, I was just desperate to find a way back for both of us."

"Exactly. She saw you up and vanish in front of her eyes, then went inside to see what happened. She found this." He reached over to the desk, grabbed the old leather bound book from the top and handed it to me.

I opened the cover and immediately recognized the same handwriting from the letter I had just read. "This is Noah's journal. We left it in my haste. We left everything." I flipped through a few of the pages.

"Noah was a wordy one. And having had those months there without a way back, he wrote all about it in there. She kept it, passed it down through generations and generations. As you know, most people have lost their religion over the years, but there were some fierce believers. And the one thing they hated most in the world were the fierce believers in Jesus Christ. The people who had persecuted them so endlessly through the years. So they bided their time, working on their plans. They broke into this place—"

"The hole in the glass dome of the living quarters?"

"That very one. Didn't see it happen but heard it. Sounded awful. People said it was some witchcraft, but I think they were just freaked out by it all. So a handful of them came down with some powerful weapons. Knew exactly where to go, took out any guards that got in their way and demanded an audience with the powers that be. Said they were taking over the lab. They wanted to send someone back to disprove the existence of Jesus Christ and any miracles he might've done."

I smiled slightly in amusement. Noah and I had talked about this very sort of mission but from the different side of things, wanting to prove that it all happened. I wondered how The Gard would have felt if going back proved everything to be true instead.

"Well as you can imagine, the leaders of this place weren't too keen on being bossed around. They gave in all too quickly and set about getting a librarian ready to go on a mission to meet Jesus Christ. They decided the first trip would be to see his birth. Angels singing to the sheep and all that."

I had no idea what he was talking about but nodded for him to continue.

"I mean, these people had guns and were threatening the lives of their very important employees, of course they were going to cooperate. But the Gardians, they weren't having it quite so tidy. They wanted to send one of their own folks back in time. There were arguments about our people knowing the process, knowing how to not interfere and all that, but the Gardians didn't believe they'd be honest about it all. They thought the librarians would lie to them. Don't blame them myself.

"So they got one of their own people trained up a bit and sent back in time. Only thing is, they didn't get sent back to the birth of Jesus; they got sent back much further than that. To a time when the earth was just plates of hot magma swirling about. Surely they died instantly, and the sphere was lost."

I thought about the sphere in my pocket. Though I trusted Montgomery, and he must have known how I arrived there, I didn't want to broadcast there was still a sphere. "They stuck with their principles," I said. "They always said they'd rather destroy the technology than hand it over to anyone else."

"They told the Gardians immediately once their guy had gone, what they'd done. The Gardians got a bit upset as you might imagine, broke into some boardroom and killed the whole lot of them. Their leader was killed in the scuffle though. The followers weren't sure what to do then. Probably would've killed a whole lot more of us too if some people hadn't talked them down. Told them we were practically slaves there and had nothing to do with the management's decisions. They let us go and left. A bunch of people hung around for a while, tried to find things to do, but without the sphere and all the management gone, there wasn't much for us. Things started falling into disrepair, and more and more people left. I told them about the tunnel Noah had taken to get out."

"Noah who?"

"Noah. Our Noah. He left right when those Gardians came and stirred things up. Snuck out in the middle of the chaos."

My heart nearly exploded. "Noah's alive!"

"Well of course he is. Er, well, he was when he left. But that was what...ninety something years ago? Could be though. I'm getting up there myself."

My heart fell again. Of course. Even if he were still alive, he'd be an old man by now. Even still, a very old friend would be better than nothing. There was only one other place I knew to start. "Do you know of the island the lab owns?"

He nodded. "That I do."

"Can I get in contact with them from here?"

He shook his head. "The link in here's been down for years."

I groaned in frustration. Even if I could find a working link outside of this place, I had no idea how to connect to the island to talk to anyone. I'd have to travel there myself. "I don't know where anything is outside of this place."

"Hang on, this might help." He grunted again as he got up from the table and moved over to the desk. He reached behind it and pulled out a large rolled up paper. "I found it while wandering around the departure chambers one day." He laid the roll down on a table and opened it.

It was a large printout of the complex. The domes were labeled and rooms were numbered. A key at one side detailed the purpose for each numbered room. I double checked the listing for my room and Noah's. Mine was the same, but his listed someone else's name. I scanned the list to see if I could pinpoint a different room but couldn't find his name anywhere on the list. So this was a fairly recent map. And there it was to the right of the complex, past where the land ended. The island. The map wasn't drawn to scale but there were coordinates that would lead me to it. "Can I keep this?"

"Sure, not much use for it here anymore."

It had been a two hour flight from the shoreline. I had no idea what that would work out to in sailing speed. Come to think of it, I wasn't even sure Marina and Adam would still be alive either. "I'm going to need some food and provisions."

"I may be able to help with that as well. In here." I followed him into another room. Random pieces of equipment lined the walls. "I collected things I thought might be of value. Intended on maybe selling some of them to the outside world, but never got up the courage to leave."

"Why did you stay after all this time?"

"At first for Noah. He was so sure you'd come back, he wanted someone to be here. He couldn't hang around, even after things fell apart. Then as the years went on, I forgot about you. This place had just been my home for so long, I couldn't imagine being anywhere else. Ah, this one here," he patted a dusty looking box, "is the one they used to make money for you guys on your missions." He smiled broadly as though he enjoyed the idea of ripping off the leaders of the lab yet again, even though they were long gone.

"You are magnificent!"

He plugged it in and punched in a few numbers. "How much you think you'll need?"

"Let's say $5,000,000."

He whistled through his teeth and typed in the total. He hit a button and large bills started pouring out of the bottom of the box. "That's an awful lot of money for a young lady. What are you going to do with it?"

"First off, I'm going to find myself a sailboat."

## Chapter 16

Montgomery insisted on fixing us a meal and having me spend the night in his second bedroom. I was anxious to get on my way, but appreciated that I was the only person he had seen in at least seventy years, and obliged him. I also hadn't slept in at least a day, and with a long road ahead of me, probably needed the rest.

He loaded me up with some food, supplies and my new money in a backpack he had handy, and he found a sturdy pair of shoes. I had the map of the facility folded up in one of my pockets and the sphere in another. It wasn't clear which way the tunnel from the root cellar led out. It ended in a field surrounded by roads. It was supposed to be inconspicuous. The coast was about twenty miles east of the complex, and Montgomery suspected I'd be able to find sailboats in Rehoboth Bay. Supposedly I would be able to see the tops of the trees of a state forest not far away to the South, which should give me enough orientation when I exited the tunnel to get to a major road.

Montgomery offered me a disintegrator pistol after giving me a hug in the root cellar. I took it and shoved it into the back of my pants, hoping I wouldn't actually need it for any reason. I walked to the back of the root cellar and opened a fairly plain looking wood door. A long, dark hallway stretched out before me. I pulled out the light disc Montgomery had provided in my backpack and headed down the hallway. After about twenty minutes of walking, the floor started to slope up slightly. It went up for another ten minutes before the hallway ended with a large hatch, like one might find in a submarine. I struggled to get the wheel turning, pulling with all my weight on one side before it started to budge. I pushed open the door and had to close my eyes against the light that poured in.

I stepped out into the field and shut the hatch again. It was concealed inside a mound of hay, the handle barely visible on it. I stood up and looked around, feeling rather out of place and unprotected. On all my missions, I had been prepared for the real world, but it never really felt like the real world. In some ways, it wasn't real. I was a fake person in a time long past, and all I had to do to get back to reality was push a button. But now here I was out in the real world, in the future no less. I didn't have weeks of research under my belt to help me deal with the culture and any surprises that might come up. I stood there for a moment, wondering if this was the best course of action. I could just push the button again, and see where I ended up. "No," I said, steeling myself against the fear of the unknown. I had decided to make some attempt to fix things. Somewhere, someone must know how this sphere works. I would start at the island and see where that took me. I saw the trees that Montgomery had talked about straight ahead. I loosened the straps on my backpack slightly and set off, keeping the forest trees to my right.

I reached the edge of the field and took a right on the road. I was definitely in a rural area. I walked along the road until I reached an intersection. Neither road was marked, so I took a left again, heading further to the East. It was still early in the morning, which I assumed accounted for the lack of travelers on the roads. Since the proliferation of self-driving vehicles, the need for road sign upkeep had dropped significantly. Ninety years into the future, I imagined they were fairly non-existent. A person walking down a country road was probably unheard of. Had a vehicle driven up behind me, I'm not sure the passengers would even know how to stop and pick me up.

I wanted to avoid strangers as much as possible anyway, so my plan was to stick to as many back roads as possible. It came to an end about half a mile later, and I made a right. After a short way, I finally came to a highway. The road I was on passed under it, and I stayed on that, but from the distance and direction I had traveled, I was fairly certain this was the highway that went Northeast to the coastline. I pulled out my map and checked again. Just below the highway were the remains of a railroad, and I could follow that until it crossed the highway again. I had decided to head a few more miles on the road from that point and then stop for the evening. I would be well over half way, and I wanted to regroup and plan my next day from there.

"Hello there!" called a pleasant sounding voice.

I stopped walking and looked around, trying to find the source of the call.

"Nice day for a walk."

My mind went to the small of my back where I felt the pistol pressing against my skin. My breathing accelerated with nervousness, wondering why I couldn't see the man. "Yes, it is." I tried to relax; I was being paranoid. "Where are you?"

"Right here."

I heard rustling in the field to my left and backed off slightly. A young man emerged in overalls with a stalk of wheat hanging out of his mouth. I could tell it was for show, nothing about him suggested years of working in fields, even with technology making it a relatively simple job these days. In fact, he seemed one big cliché of a farmer. Something I expected to see in the 20th century. "You startled me. I didn't expect to run into anyone on my journey."

"Where is it that you're journeying to?"

Even his accent sounded fake. Though he seemed harmless, I wasn't about to trust anyone. "Just heading to a relative's house a bit south of here."

"Why don't you come on up to the house, and I'll give you a ride."

I tried to play to his character. "I don't think a tractor would make for a comfy ride."

He laughed, but it was overblown and clearly for effect. "Well if you don't like the tractor I've got a real car too. Not one of them fancy modern ones, but smooth enough."

"That's kind of you, but it's really not far and I'm enjoying the walk."

"Come in for a rest then. I'll have the missus make us up some coffee."

"No thank you, I'd really rather get back to it." I gestured down the road past him, trying to indicate that I would like him to move aside. Over the course of our conversation he had moved into my path.

"Well... if you're sure."

"Yes, my aunt is expecting me soon. I don't want to be late and make her worry."

"Nope, certainly don't want to worry that Aunt." He gave me a shallow smile but still stood in my way. I didn't want to walk past him, but it seemed rude to take a wide arc around him. "Say, if she's not far from here, could be I know her. What's her name?"

I couldn't think how to get out of this conversation. Perhaps rudeness was needed after all. I said the first name that came to mind, my old hair dresser. "Vanessa Parker."

His features froze, and his voice took on a brief air of malignance. "Why yes, I know Vanessa Parker."

Either he was lying or that was a very strange coincidence. Vanessa was old enough ninety years ago that she should be long dead, even if she did settle in this area. "Well it really is a small world!"

"Why don't you come in. I'll give her a call and let her know you're stopping for a rest. She'll be thrilled to know you gave an old farmer friend of hers some company for a few hours."

"You don't look terribly old." He looked about my age, perhaps a little younger. Definitely no older than forty-five. I had no idea what the age expectancy was these days.

"I meant we're longtime, old friends."

"Funny, she's never mentioned a farmer friend from the area."

"When is the last time you talked to her?"

He had shifted even closer, and I realized his farmer drawl had turned into a faster metropolitan form of speech. He looked healthy, as though he would put up a good fight. I didn't need authorities coming after me, so trying to knock him out and leave him out in the field didn't sound like a smart option. I had gone beyond politeness, I would just have to plow on ahead. "This morning, and she has plans for us that can't be changed, so I really must be moving on. Good day." I tensed myself as I brushed past him, ready to fight back if he grabbed me.

"You have a safe journey then, miss."

I waved back but kept my gaze forward and determined. I walked as quietly as possible, listening for him following me, but heard nothing.

I continued along the road and found the railroad tracks. I turned to the left to follow them and glanced to my left to reassure myself he wasn't standing right there. The encounter left me nervous. I knew he was lying, I just wasn't sure why. Everything about him had seemed off. I tried to push it out of my head, telling myself he was just an oddity as I continued down the tracks.

Trains had become obsolete in my time, but it had been decided that it wasn't worth the effort and expense to tear up the infrastructure. The tracks had been left to become overgrown with weeds, quite dense in a few parts. It slowed my progress down, but I was fairly assured I wouldn't run into anyone else this way, and it was a very easy map symbol to follow. I stopped a little way onto the tracks to rest and have some lunch. With the farmer a few miles behind me,

I felt more relaxed. I hadn't heard or seen any indication that he followed me.

I just barely heard vehicles on the highway zooming past a few hundred yards away, but it was otherwise peaceful. The tall grass hid me quite well from anyone who might walk along nearby roads. I had taken a few containers of the vegetables from the root cellar, and Montgomery gave me some preserved meat he had made. His livestock had long since died, but he sometimes went out into the woods just north of the tunnel to hunt wild game. I ate some jerked venison he had made to keep my protein levels up for the remainder of the walk today.

I didn't linger after finishing my meal; I was anxious to settle in for the night and plan my arrival at the bay. I figured with enough money, I could dissuade anyone from asking too many questions. Most of the planks between the rails had decomposed long ago, but there were a few sections where I could methodically place one foot on each plank. It slowed down my pace a little, but I found it mentally soothing. I figured it was about five miles from where I had stopped for lunch to the next highway crossing. Even taking about half an hour to make it a mile along the track, I would have plenty of time to get back to the road, walk a few more miles, then find a secluded spot to set up the shallow shelter in my pack.

I thought about Adam and Marina as I walked along. They were definitely fit, but also well-seasoned in the hospitality business. I never asked, but my guess was they were in their fifties, which would put them at one hundred forty now. Definitely old, but not an unheard of age. The fact that they led such a healthy lifestyle might have helped. Or perhaps I was wrong, and they had been younger when I met them. Regardless, it was the only lead I had to go on for now. A fair number of people had been sent there to unwind. My only hope was that a few of them considered it a good place to retire. Specifically, Jim.

I came to the highway crossing and left the railroad tracks on a road that headed south. This shortly joined another road that took me further east. In an hour, I knew I would start to approach civilization again, so I decided to call it a day. I wandered off into another field and pulled out the shelter. I unlatched the cover and threw it a few feet from me. It popped open into a low tent that was not visible above the tall stalks of wheat. I threw my pack inside and crawled in after it. The floor was cushioned enough to sleep on comfortably, and I would throw some of the extra clothes I packed over top of me if I felt too cold at night. I pulled out the map again and checked my progress. From here I could head mostly Southeast through the fields, then skirt along the North side of the bay to a marina just off the main area of Dewey Beach. I was hoping to find a boat for sale somewhere at that marina.

I put the map away and pulled off my shoes to let my feet air out a little. I flexed and rotated them and gave them a good squeeze. It felt good to get the shoes off and put my feet up for a while. I dug around in my pack for some dinner. I had some carrots, more of the jerked venison, and took a hydration cube. I was exhausted and wanted another early start, so I stretched out on the floor of the tent and was asleep instantly.

I woke up once, when I heard some rustling in the field near me. As quietly as possible, I grabbed the pistol from my pack and brought it up under my pillow, listening to my surroundings. My other hand almost instinctively checked for the sphere. A grunt broke through the rustling noise, and I relaxed a bit as I listened to the animal wander off again. I kept my hand on the gun under my pillow as I went back to sleep. In my dream I found the farmer beyond the door at the end of a dark hall.

The following morning I just had some fruit for breakfast, then packed my bag and collapsed the shelter. I continued on through the field. The sun was still rather low in the sky, so once again I didn't encounter anyone on the roads. The new day made my encounter with the farmer seem like an overreaction of my paranoia, and I easily put it behind me.

I got to the North end of the bay after an hour and a half, and started following that to the East. I was walking through a residential area and finally started seeing some people milling around their houses or getting into their cars to head out for the day. They gave me some strange looks, but no one stopped me. They seemed nervous and glad I was merely passing through. I kept the edge of the bay in sight as I wandered through the neighborhoods. After another half hour, I was finally able to see the masts of sailboats in the distance across an industrial yard. The yard was fenced off, so I had to head back to the North a little to get around it, but reached the marina a short while later.

I walked along the docks, looking at the sailboats. A few of them had for sale signs on them, but only one of them looked basic enough for me to handle. I took note of the seller and boat name and headed back to the marina's main office. An older looking man was behind the counter placing charter information on a board. I coughed to get his attention. He turned and gave me a bemused smile after looking over me. "Looking for a charter somewhere, miss?"

I hated being called miss. I let it go in the interest of making this as simple as possible. "I noticed a sailboat out on the docks for sale that I'm interested in purchasing."

"Where did you come from, miss?"

"Georgetown. Can you contact the seller for me? Tell him I'm ready to buy today."

He looked at me like something was out of place. "Which boat?"

"The Lost Traveler." I smiled at the appropriateness.

"Think you can handle that much boat?"

I fixed my smile and tried to make it as polite as possible. "My father taught me well."

"Okay, just a sec." He went into the back room, and I could barely hear the murmurs of a conversation. He came back in and seemed a little less wary. "Alrighty then, Tom, the seller, will be here shortly. Anything else I can help you with?"

"Can you point me in the direction of a store? I need to pick up some provisions for my trip."

He brought up a map of the local area and pointed out a small local store not far from there. "I can help you carry some goods back here if you need?"

"No thank you. I'll be back shortly and wait out by the boat. Please let him know." I turned and left as quickly as possible without looking like I was trying to. I hated being treated like a little girl, but I thought the father comment would get him off my back.

I found the store easily enough. I had another two days' worth of food in my pack, but figured I'd be on the water for at least three. Then if the island had been deserted, it would take another three days to get back to the mainland. I purchased a week's worth of food and headed back to the marina. I wandered back along the dock to the boat and waited for a few minutes. I saw a man approaching from the end of the dock a short while later.

"You're the woman interested in the boat?"

"Yes, sir." I walked towards him with my hand extended and gave him a firm shake.

"My father's sir. Call me Tom."

"Thanks for coming out so quickly, Tom."

"So what sort of experience you have with these things?"

"My father taught me when I was a young girl. I've spent many weekends on sailboats in the season. It's been awhile since I've been out on one though. She's a beauty." I smiled back at him. Adam had loved it when I complimented his boat. I hoped that trait was common amongst sailors.

"She is." He smiled down at the boat like a proud father.

"Why are you selling?"

"Just don't have the time to devote to her these days."

"Well, that won't be a problem for me. I've recently retired."

He cocked his head at me. "At so young an age? How will you support yourself?"

"It was a very lucrative job. Speaking of which, 1.8 million yes?" I paused as he nodded. "I can pay cash if it helps move things along more quickly."

"Lucrative sounds like an understatement." He looked me over again. I could tell he was a little nervous, but didn't want to get involved, which was how I wanted it.

"I'm hoping to spend most of my time on the boat, so I'm happy to spend as much as I would on a house for this. And I'm anxious to get the rest of my life started."

He nodded again. "You said cash right?"

"I'd prefer to do business indoors if we can?"

"Sure." He jerked his head towards the marina office, and I followed him back. "Ben, we'll just be borrowing your office for a few moments."

We walked past the counter and into Ben's office. Tom sat down at the desk. I dropped my pack on the floor and sat in a chair on the opposite side of the desk. I dug down into the bag and counted out 18 $100,000 bills as discretely as possible, then laid them on the desk in front of Tom.

He quickly counted it. "That looks about right." He opened a drawer in the desk, pulled out a thick envelope and stuck the bills inside. Then he reached into a drawer further down and pulled out a folder. He tossed it over to me.

"The paperwork, including the access card you'll need to get out of the bay. The scanners should pick it up from anywhere on the boat as you pass through the inlet. Come on, I'll walk you back down and help you off." We left the office.

I kept my head down as we passed Ben to avoid conversation. I jumped into the boat and dropped my pack down in the cabin area. Tom untied the lines and tossed them into the boat for me. "I'll push you off."

"Thanks." I grabbed the rudder and pulled hard to steer away from the dock. I was a little nervous navigating the crowded, narrow dock area, especially with someone watching me. I knew he'd watch until I was out of sight, so I tried to remain calm and remember everything Adam had taught me. "I'll take good care of her!" I called out as I pulled past the end of the dock and waved quickly before adjusting the rudder again. He gave me one last wave, and I turned the boat to head out to the channel and onwards to the island.

## Chapter 17

I found it strange to think that just over a week ago I had learned how to do this. It didn't feel as fresh in my mind as it should, but a lot had happened in that week. It felt like months had passed since I first traveled to the island. The wind was light but steady. Navigating to the southern end of the bay to the Indian River Inlet was rough. Most of my training had been in the open sea where I had plenty of room for each tack. The bay was narrow enough that each leg of my path only lasted a few minutes. As I passed through the inlet into the Atlantic, I saw no signs of security, but I was glad to have the card on board regardless.

Getting into the open ocean was a huge relief. I had felt pinned in by the bay and half expected someone from the lab to show up and drag me back to one of the secure rooms. I kept a hold on the main sail line and reached over for my pack. I dug in the front pocket and pulled out my sphere, flipping open the top for the first time since I arrived in this time. The glow of the red light was just barely visible in the daylight. From my limited experience with both spheres, that implied that if I pushed the button, it would take me somewhere. If I just found some way to reset the destination, perhaps I could use it to go back. I didn't know enough about the technology. I needed to find someone who might still be alive with knowledge of the operation of the sphere. The only lead I had to go on though was the island. Montgomery hadn't talked to anyone from the complex once they left. No one had come back to see him or told him of their plans before their departure. I only had the hope that perhaps some of them had gone to the island. I knew Jim loved it there, so I hoped at the very least he still had contact with them.

The sailboat had a fairly sophisticated navigational system on board. Once I entered the coordinates of the island into the system, I was able to pull up an image of my course. Even with a good wind, it was going to take a little over three days to reach the island. As I left the mainland behind, I started to relax even more. It was highly unlikely that I would run into anyone in the middle of the ocean.

I cleated the main sail line and explored the boat a little more. I took my pack down into the cabin area and pulled out the rest of the food to sit it with the groceries I picked up earlier. I put the rest of my clothes in a small chest of drawers on one side of the cabin. There was a safe above it; I realized I had no idea what the combination was. I grabbed the folder of paperwork and flipped through. There was all kinds of technical information on the boat and in the back a small slip of paper with nothing but a few numbers written down. I tried them on the safe combination, and it opened easily. Inside the safe was a small box. Tom must have forgotten about it. I made a mental note to go back to the harbor and return it to him at some point. I pushed it to the side, and shoved the disintegrator pistol and sphere into the safe next to it. I went back up on deck to check my progress and make sure I hadn't veered off course.

The next few days were peaceful and uneventful. It was the first time I felt really relaxed since I first sailed with Adam. Sleeping on the boat was also very calming. I pulled out one of the cushions from the cabin and placed it on the deck. The wind died at night, so I would anchor the boat and sleep on the deck, staring at the stars until I was lulled to sleep by the gentle rocking of the hull against the water. On my third night at sea, I noticed light on the horizon in the direction I was heading. There were no other islands in the area, so I was fairly certain it was the one I was headed for, and the fact that lights were on was a promising sign. I slept poorly that night, looking forward to my arrival at the island the next day and thinking of all the questions I wanted to ask when I got there. It felt like hours before my mind settled down well enough to sleep.

Despite the restless night, I awoke with the sun and pulled the anchor, eager to get on my way. I saw a dark spot in the distance and left the navigation system off for the rest of the journey. I'd be able to work my way in on sight now. I hoisted my mainsail and jib and set off for the island. I cleated the sails off again and went below deck to prepare my things. I repacked my bag with my clothes but left the food out. I opened the safe and noticed again the box that Tom had left as I put the sphere into a pocket and secured the gun in the back of my pants. I grabbed the box and shoved it into my backpack, then went back up on deck. It took another two hours before the island loomed into view. My approach so far seemed to be unnoticed. I couldn't see any lights on now, so I knew someone had to be on the island.

Leaving the dock hadn't been hard, but now I had to navigate my way back to one. I released the mainsail to slow my approach and used the rudder to steer myself alongside the dock. I was so focused on not hitting the wooden decking as I approached that I failed to notice the man standing there, pointing a rifle at me. I put my hands up and let the boat drift forward toward him. He gestured at my mooring line. I tossed it around a post and proceeded to tie the boat up, my hands shaking. I wondered how quickly I would be able to pull out my gun and take aim, but I didn't want to make enemies if it was possible someone on the island could help me. When I finished tying the line, I stepped out onto the dock and put my hands up. He looked just like Adam, but I knew it couldn't possibly be him. Though I had been here just a week ago, Adam would now be 90 years older. This man had not aged a day. "Adam?"

He tightened his hold on the gun. "Who are you?"

"Adelaide MacDuff."

"That name means nothing to me."

I couldn't help but feel annoyed. My hands dropped slightly. It was the second time inside a few days that someone had threatened me with a gun, and I found the idea that I could be considered a threat ridiculous. "Where is Adam?" I didn't try to hide the impatience in my voice.

He didn't say anything else but stared at me for a moment. "This way." He jerked his head behind him and moved to the side to let me pass. "Keep your hands up!" he said as he swung the rifle around to meet me again.

I huffed in frustration but obeyed and walked past him down the dock. I kept my focus forward but I could hear his bare feet on the wooden planks behind me. As I approached the beach, an older woman walked slowly out of the trees towards the shoreline and stopped a few yards from me. "Who are you?"

The man with the gun spoke up behind me. "She said her name's Adelaide MacDuff."

Her eyes widened with recognition, and a flicker of a smile crossed her face before being replaced again with distrust. In that instant of a smile I knew who she was. "My God. Adelaide? No, it cannot be."

"You know that's not true, Marina."

She nodded and smiled again, visibly relaxing. "Noah said you might show up one day. You're well out of your time here. It's ok Carlo, we can trust her."

"Noah was here?"

"Many years ago. He and Jim came shortly after the lab fell to ruin. We managed to hide them here when the island was invaded. People had come looking for them. Jim said he knew more than he had let on."

My head swam slightly. They had both been here and the island was invaded? I was right to come here. "I need to know everything you know."

"Of course. Come." She beckoned me back towards her hut. "You must be hungry. Carlo, get us a bottle of wine and some lunch."

"Thank you, Marina. I'm relieved to see you," I said.

"It is a pleasure to have you here again. Adam would have enjoyed it as well I'm sure. He would've been proud. It looks like you can handle that sailboat all on your own." She motioned to a chair and I sat down. "He was killed in the raid on our island. Thankfully they spared me and Carlo. He was just a baby then."

"Your son?"

"Yes. He's been my savior since I lost Adam. Jim and Noah helped me bury him on top of the mountain." She looked up in the general direction of the mountain as Carlo came out with an open bottle of wine and glasses. "Thank you, dear." She poured me a glass and Carlo went back into the hut. "So where should I start? How much do you know about what happened to the lab?"

"I know about The Gardians breaking in and one of them being sent back in time to destroy the sphere. I saw Montgomery, the farmer. He was still living there. He helped me get the sailboat and gave me a letter Noah had written for me. Noah said he was in trouble, that they thought we had planned for things to get screwed up and escape with the sphere."

"Jim helped Noah escape once things got chaotic with the Gardians. They chartered a flight here, which was unfortunately easily traceable. A few months after the lab closed for good, some people who had survived The Gardian attack came here looking for them. Adam told them they had taken a boat and left. When they didn't believe his story, he tried to force them to leave, but they wouldn't until they had thoroughly searched the island. Thankfully they did not find the secret bunker we had built years ago. Once they were satisfied that the two of them were not here anymore, they left, the damage done.

"Jim and Noah spent a few months here. They would talk frequently about what happened. They were trying to work out where you ended up, and why you hadn't arrived at the same time as Noah. Noah thinks he figured it out. He explained it to me, but unfortunately I can't really explain it back to you." She smiled wryly. "I never was one for technology. But they had a plan. They knew somehow you'd make it back here, and they prepared for it. Assuming you still have the other sphere...?"

I hesitated, but Marina was certain to know there would be no point in my tracking down Noah if I didn't have the sphere. I nodded. "Still looks like it's working as well. Did they figure out how to reprogram the destination?"

"They had theories, and they knew someone who they thought could help them, who had facilities that could accomplish the task."

"Who?"

She smiled at me. "You haven't changed at all. A bit more serious perhaps, I wouldn't have believed that possible, but you look exactly the same."

"It's been less than two weeks since I last saw you, but it feels so much longer."

"No more business now," she said as Carlo brought out a tray of food. "You will stay through the night at least, and we have plenty of time to get you up to speed. For now, let's catch up. It may only have been two weeks, but it sounds like they were pretty busy ones. So tell me, did you come straight back to this time or was there another stop on the way? Noah filled me in about your getting arrested." She laughed at the memory as Carlo left the food and went back inside. "Only you two."

I smiled. She was right, business could wait. I realized how happy I was to see Marina again. She might have looked much older, but she was still the kind hearted, welcoming person I had met just a few weeks ago. "I blame Noah. I arrived at this point in time at the same time he made it back to when we were supposed to. I thought about trying the sphere again once I saw where I had ended up, but then I found Montgomery and found out what date it was and got Noah's note. At that point, I thought I'd try to find someone. I have no idea what will happen if I push the button again, and I wanted to at least get some more information before making that kind of decision. I'm glad I did. It's very good to see at least some of the people I know are still around." Noah wasn't here, but he might still be alive. That thought alone was enough to keep me going until I found out what happened to him. "Tell me about Carlo."

"Ah, he's just like his father. Loves being outside. But who could blame him in this place." She waved her hand in a generic motion taking in the island. "He and Jim really took to each other while he was still here."

I could see that. Jim was almost like a father to me as well. "Jim was a great man. He took good care of me. I'm not surprised he got Noah out of there before they hurt him."

"It was good to have him around. He came back after a few years. He left Noah to finish the work they had started and returned here to live out the rest of his years."

"You make it sound like there weren't that many left."

"There weren't. Jim had started showing signs of Sunithe's disease while he and Noah were working on a solution to the sphere operation. When Jim was sure Noah would be able to finish things there on his own, he came back here. He survived another five or so years before succumbing to the disease. Carlo made a small raft with a time delayed fire and sent him out to drift at sea. It was Jim's request. We could see the smoke from here." She glanced back to where Carlo had gone and sighed. "I think he would've been happy to see you make it here."

We ate in silence for a little while. I was getting the impression Jim had shielded me from quite a few things going on at the lab. If they were cruel enough to kill people in their search for Noah, what would they have done to me? Given how Jim acted before I left on my last mission, I had the feeling he was more worried about me than he let on. And then there were the images of Noah being tortured that I had seen in Eliza's mind. I began to think I was lucky the lab was defunct upon my return.

Marina pulled me out of my contemplation. "You were on the boat for a few days I take it?"

"About three and a half."

"Why don't you go freshen up then and relax. We can get to more important matters over dinner."

I headed back to the boat to grab my bag and took it over to the hut where I had stayed just over a week ago. I looked longingly at the enormous bathtub for a moment before turning and heading back out. I ran into Carlo on my way to their hut. He smiled at me, just as Adam would have. "Carlo, I'd like to pay my respects to your father, if I may."

"Of course, miss. Follow me." He led me behind their hut to the start of a path. He gestured along the path, which seemed to wind towards the center of the island. "This path will take you right up the side of the mountain to his grave. It shouldn't take more than half an hour to get there. The return trip will be much easier."

"Thank you." I left him behind and climbed the steep path up to the top of the mountain. There was a clearing on top that I had remembered from my first trip. There in the middle was a small grave marker adorned with fresh flowers. I walked over and sat in the grass next to it. "I'm sorry," I said to the ground next to me. The epitaph on the marker read,

"He loved his life until he lost it to defend ours."

A sudden fury rose in me. "Damnit Adam, you didn't have to die." For so many years I had just accepted the decisions of the omnipresent people in charge. I figured they knew what they were doing and that I wasn't to ask questions for my own good, but this was just plain vicious. There was no need for them to come so aggressively after Noah and kill the people in their path. It filled me with rage that he had been killed so senselessly, and I vowed I would find a way to make them pay. I would find Noah or whoever he instructed on how to get me back, and I would find a way to avenge Adam's death.

I turned to head back down the mountain again when a flash of light caught my eye. I walked over to it and found a small metal robot, about the size of a rabbit lying in the grass. It hadn't moved as I approached. I kicked it lightly with my foot, and it rolled slightly, still not moving on its own. It was six sided and had six legs. On each side was the unmistakable circle of a lens. Below each lens was a mesh cavity that I could only assume was some sort of mic. "So you're what was following me around last time," I said to the metal creature.

My engineering instincts kicked in. I turned it around in my hands. The bottom was etched with a company logo, Lancing Electronics. The name was not familiar to me. I couldn't see any access panels for batteries, and none of the surfaces looked like energy transducers, so I couldn't determine how it received power, let alone transmit a signal back to the lab. I tried to pull off one of the legs, partly to try and open the thing and partly because of an irrational desire to make it suffer. I knew it wasn't alive and was long past its usefulness, but it was likely that this reported Jim and Noah's whereabouts back to the lab and brought the attackers here in pursuit.

I hurled the robot into a group of trees towards the edge of the clearing. It hit the trunk of one of the larger trees and fell to the ground. A clinking sound made me think I had managed to damage it slightly, but that wasn't enough. I glowered at it on the ground for a moment, fighting the urge to go over and do further damage. It was a pointless pursuit. My rage now had an edge of irritation to it as well as I turned back to the path and stalked back down the mountain.

# Chapter 18

I took a long bath after I returned from Adam's grave. I tried to relax and let the rage pass, but it wouldn't. I feared it would only get worse the more I learned on my journey. I stayed in the bathtub until my skin started to prune and the rage submerged to a dull pain in the back of my mind. I had decided to remember that moment on the top of the mountain, but I wouldn't let it overtake me. If the time came for revenge, I would remember, and I would exact it without remorse.

I went to Marina's again for dinner. Carlo joined us this time. Talk over dinner was again left to more trivial matters. Carlo cleared the table after dessert, and when he was gone, I nodded after him. "What's going to happen to him when you're gone?"

"Carlo?" She laughed. "Oh you don't have to worry about him. He has so many girlfriends he'll never be lonely. I'm hoping he'll pick one of them to join him here before I pass on." She paused. "Though I've given up hope for a grandchild." She looked thoughtful for a moment. "He might not stay here. I've told him, it was Adam and my decision to come here, not his. So maybe he'll go back to the mainland and this place will fall to ruin." She didn't seem as sad about this as I thought she would. "But it was always our dream, not his. And we saw it through very well, I think.

"And now, the story. I only delayed so you wouldn't be able to leave this afternoon, you know. Carlo is a good son, but he's so dull." She smirked after him. "But enough delay, you're right." She poured another glass of wine for herself and pushed her half eaten dessert to the side. "As I said, Jim and Noah arrived a few days after the lab had been assaulted. The four of us would eat together almost every night, and they would update me and Adam with what they had worked out that day, what their new plan was. It changed almost daily, you see. There were risks associated with what they wanted to do, and they felt that careful planning was worth the delay in getting back to the mainland. What do you know about how the sphere works?"

"Not much, admittedly. I push the button and it takes me to wherever they've programmed it to go."

"Have you ever met one of the programmers?" she asked.

"No. They keep us pretty well isolated. We're not encouraged to associate with people outside our, well, class for lack of a better description. Librarians stick with librarians, scouts with scouts, planters with planters and so forth."

"For programmers it was even worse. They weren't allowed outside of their living areas at all. They were segregated from everyone. Their only contact with the outside world was the messages they got to tell them about the next mission and who was going where. They had files on all the travelers. They had to know who they were sending, to keep a mental idea of that person in their mind while they were being sent back and forth in time. You see, during the operation of a sphere, part of what makes you able to travel back and forth is the fact that operator knows who you are and is specifically sending you through time."

"You make it sound like the programmer is controlling the sphere itself."

"The programmer is."

"But I thought," my mind stuttered a bit. "A computer does it. A programmer programs the computer to specify the destination of the sphere."

"No, Addy. It's a person who controls it. One person, to be exact. He is able to see paths through time and send people back and forth along them. The sphere is largely just a tool for them to keep track of the path, where it ends, and when to bring you back. It's a constant in time. Anything that touches the sphere when the button is pushed is forced into the mind of the programmer, and he can then send that along with the sphere to wherever he chooses. And by extension, anything that person touches as well, though my understanding is that it gets harder the more removed an object is from the sphere. Which is part of why you were never allowed more than a few important objects to complete your missions."

"What kind of person could do that?" I was in awe to find out that there were people who could see the course of time. It seemed an incredible power; I wasn't surprised the lab would want to have that on hand and even less surprised that they'd keep it a secret.

"There were at least two people who were able to do it during the years the lab was open. The first one went mad. They expected the second would at some point as well. They saw the warning signs with the first one. People ending up not quite where they were supposed to. But they're also tied to the sphere. If the button is pushed, they have to act on it. Their default response is to bring someone to their timeline, so people were still coming back.

"So when things started going wrong with their first programmer, they started looking for another candidate. Jim was there when it happened. They didn't tell him much about what was going on, but missions were halted for a few weeks. Then all of a sudden, they were up and running again, and this new person was suddenly living in the dome, unable to remember most of his life. Being the kind hearted person he was, Jim befriended him and tried to help him adjust to his new job as a gardener. Jim assumed it was one of the librarians who disobeyed an order or made a mistake on a mission and had been neutralized. The guy had nightmares about time unraveling around him.

"And then one day it started to come back to him. Like I mentioned, they can see paths in time. So he started seeing his own path. He was able to travel in his own mind to his past and feel his brain working out moving people around in time. He started to interfere with the current missions. He could feel the new programmer making paths for people and would push them just a little off course. He told Jim about it. Of course, someone overheard. The next day, the gardener was gone." She paused to let me take all of it in.

"Yes, I think that would make me a little mad too." She didn't have to explain what it meant that he was gone. "How do they find these people?"

"They have people watching for indicators. Hints that there are gifted children out there. Incredibly smart children, who dream about time travel as though it's really happening to them. They're usually terrified by it and get sent to psychiatrists who find them to be fascinating and post their cases in journals. Jim started researching the list of children in the lab with those listed in these journals. Some were on record as being admitted to a hospital. Some merely disappeared."

"They kidnapped children?" The rage flared inside me. Had I known what was going on I never would have condoned it. I would never have participated in the time travel. It was smart of them to keep us in the dark. I was almost afraid to ask. "What did they do with them?"

"Jim was never sure. He never saw any children in the complex, so he had to assume they were being kept somewhere else. He didn't believe they were killed."

A vision filled my head; a dorm room full of empty beds and pictures of children with a faceless doctor. Eliza Phillips, barely a teenager, strapped into a hospital bed. I felt ill and wondered if Jim had known about that section of the lab. "How did he figure all this out?"

"Most of it he pieced together based on things he had heard and seen in his time there. No one was explicit in explaining how things worked; he was only given a general idea. But also he had the conversations with the first programmer, the one who had gone mad. He gave Jim a great deal of information through his rambled memories. Jim didn't understand that it was all real until after the programmer had disappeared."

Jim must not have known that they were being kept there. I couldn't believe that he would have condoned such a thing. Maybe he didn't have a choice. Sadly, I couldn't ask him. I had ventured too far into the future, and he was gone. "So why did I come back when I did?"

"Like I said, they spent a few months here, puzzling it all out. Jim had kept extensive journals and uploaded them here. He had managed to work out a secure link to a database outside the lab and would post his notes and thoughts about his experiences there, where they couldn't monitor them. He and Noah poured over all of it, then set about trying to fill in some of the gaps. In the end though, they decided they needed to try and find one of these children. They found a little girl in Philadelphia who showed signs of insomnia. Because of her time travel dreams, she was terrified that she was affecting the course of history. So they went to Philadelphia to track her down and try to get her to understand her power." She laughed, "They pretended to be experts on insomnia and convinced the parents they could help. They were given an hour to do what they could and then told to leave. That night was the first time the child slept soundly in several months. The parents contacted them again the next day. Jim and Noah convinced them their child needed more work or the nightmares and insomnia would return.

"So the parents let them stay. They spent several days at the little girl's house, helping her understand what was going on and trying to get her to focus her power. They ran into some trouble though. One day when they went back to her house, people from the lab were there. They stayed hidden until the laboratory men had left then went back to the house. The parents had thankfully been distrustful of the men who arrived at their door and said nothing, even when they had been shown a picture of Noah and recognized him. At that point, Noah had to explain more of what was going on to the parents. He didn't tell them the truth, but explained that their daughter had a gift and that dangerous people might come back for her one day soon. They convinced the parents to let her go away with them for a few days. They took her to a place where Jim had lived as a boy, a farm that had been abandoned, and spent the next few days helping her focus more clearly on each of their timelines.

"Finally, one day she was able to see Noah in the past, and she followed his path back to the present time. She was able to follow him on a few of his missions; she could easily see the paths through time and his presence while he traveled. His last two journeys though, she said were complicated. The first one was the one where the two of you both traveled on your sphere. She said the existence of the second presence made it hard for the path to complete, which is why you only made it halfway. And then the second trip, Noah had the wrong sphere."

"What do you mean, the wrong sphere?" I tried to remember leaving from the jail cell.

"You both dropped your spheres when you arrived in...where was it, Georgetown?"

"Yes. We both collapsed, it's hard to keep a grip on anything when you arrive."

She laughed, "I believe it. Well you both dropped your spheres, and picked up the wrong ones. As I said, the sphere carries an association with whoever touches it, but the programmer also has a person in mind already. When Noah pushed the button on your sphere, he suddenly showed up in a path where he wasn't supposed to be. The programmer managed to get him back anyway, but in the amount of time it took him to sort Noah out and then switch over to you, too much time had passed. The paths are not reversible once you're on them. He brought you back as quickly as he could, but it was already well past the time you should have returned. The girl felt that. She felt that Noah was on the wrong path, and she could sense the change when it happened. Of course, she had no idea who you were, but given you're the only other person with a sphere, she worked it out."

"So, if I find this girl she may be able to send me back?"

"If that is what you want to do. She needs to meet you and talk to you about what you want. She's been able to sense your sphere. She's known all along and been waiting for you to get to this point. She even had a path in mind for you if you just happened to push the button randomly."

I stood up without realizing it. "Tell me where she is."

Marina smiled and took my hand softly. "Sit down, Addy. Calm yourself."

She was right. I wasn't about to head out tonight. "You're right. I'm sorry, Marina. I just didn't think I would get to this point. I'll wait till tomorrow morning to leave. I just want to know what's in store for me and how to find her."

"She went back to Philadelphia, supposedly cured. Noah wrote a bogus journal article with some medical mumbo jumbo about how she had been cured of her ailment, and she understood that if people ever came looking for her again, she should deny any dreams she might have had. But you need not trouble yourself in leaving, Addy. Carlo will bring her here."

"That's not necessary. I can sail back on my own just fine. I just need the address."

"You're better off working out things here where it's safer. Carlo can get her for you."

I did the mental calculation: three days back to the mainland, probably another day up to Philadelphia then another four days back. I could hardly stand to wait that long. "Marina really, I'm perfectly capable—"

"You mistake me, Addy. Carlo will insist upon it. She's one of his girlfriends." Marina grinned, and I couldn't help but return it with excitement.

# Chapter 19

I was relieved to find out that Carlo knew how to fly, and a seaplane was docked in a hidden alcove on the other side of the island. The next afternoon I would meet someone who could potentially erase the last 90 years of everyone's lives. Adam would live. I'd see Jim and Noah again. Everything would go back to normal. And I'd find a way to exact my revenge against a company that I grew to loathe more and more with each new story I heard about it.

Carlo left early in the morning. I was so nervous I could barely eat, but Marina insisted I at least go through the motions. I managed to get some fruit down but mostly pushed the food around on my plate. "Marina, one thing you didn't tell me about last night; Noah, is he still alive?"

"That I'm not sure of. When Jim returned here, Noah struck out on his own. He told Jim he would find him a cure, but Jim never held much stock in that idea. He hasn't been in touch with any of us, so who knows?"

I had kept only a vague hope that Noah was still alive. I knew from my dealings with his prior older self that his personality still had glimmers of my friend, probably more so given he knew who he was. Even that would be better than nothing.

Marina interrupted my thoughts. "Have you decided where you are going?"

"You mean in time?"

"Yes."

"Well I figured I'd go back where I belong. Ninety years ago when I was supposed to have arrived."

"Just a few days before the Gardian attack?"

I paused. I knew where her line of questioning led. "Yes. I don't think I have another choice."

"You know this place. You know the sorts of things they're capable of. Do you really want to go back there?"

"It's the only life I know, and as much as I hate those people right now, I need to get back there. Hope that I can just escape with Jim and Noah." My thirst for revenge was diminished by the idea of escaping with them.

"There will be two spheres," she said.

"Yes? So?"

"So they'll send one sphere back to be destroyed. And then what? Hide the existence of the other sphere?"

"Probably."

"And then the Gardians leave, and what do you think they'll do then?"

"They won't let things go on as they have." I realized the truth. Even if they took the sphere and started over somewhere else, I wouldn't be going with them. I would face the same choice that had led Noah to a desire for self-destruction. "They certainly won't let *me* go on as I have."

"What is it that you really want, Adelaide?"

"I want to go back to when I didn't know any of this. Back to when I did my job and accepted the rules because I figured they just knew better than me."

"Going back in time will never erase what you know. That's not an option. What else do you really want?"

I thought about it. I wasn't really sure. I wanted to be happy again. The more I thought about it, I didn't think I could be happy with that place going on as it did, given what I knew. The rage surfaced again as I thought of the children that had been abducted and the people who had died or had their lives otherwise taken from them. "I want them to suffer."

"Vengeance doesn't solve any problems."

I nearly snarled at her, "No, but it will make me feel better!"

She was not phased by my outburst. "For some time maybe."

I wondered if years on a tropical island gave a person such a mellow, practical demeanor, and if I could benefit from that. "I should let the Gardians take over anyway."

"Innocent people died in that attack."

I didn't want to listen to her anymore. She was making too much sense. It all went back to my first mistake; letting that woman see us disappear and take Noah's journal. But crossing back into my own timeline like that could be fraught with peril. It's why we were never allowed to go back again on the same mission if we made a mistake. For all I knew that was more of the lies we had been fed to keep us in line. That disobedience had resulted in two spheres though.

If the programmer sent me somewhere close by, I could find that Gardian woman and distract her until Noah and I disappeared and then collect his things and return. I could correct my first mistake. And then what? Perhaps go back to when I should have returned and force them to erase my memory? Would they do that? Then let me continue to be a librarian alongside Noah? I doubted that. If nothing else though, I would fix my first mistake. I would go back and keep that Gardian woman from learning too much. The rest I could figure out later.

We heard the engine from the seaplane approaching and walked out to the end of the dock to meet them. A woman jumped out of the copilot seat, and Carlo climbed down after her. She was in her early nineties by the look of her and terribly frail. I could hardly imagine her being able to move people with her mind; it seemed like it would take a much stronger person. She stuck out a slender hand towards me. "Hello Adelaide, I'm Erica."

From the stories I had heard I was still expecting her to be a young girl and was having trouble rewiring that expectation in my mind to this older woman. I took her hand, suddenly feeling very young in the present company. "Hello, Erica, it's a pleasure to meet you."

"The pleasure's all mine. I've been looking forward to this immensely. Since you arrived a few days ago, I've been keeping an extra good tab on you, though from my point of view, I've been aware of you for years."

It felt strange to be greeted as though she's known me for longer than I've been alive. Like someone who's watched me grow up from afar, even though it'd been just over a week for me. I didn't know what to say.

Marina saved us from the awkwardness. "Let's have some tea, shall we?" She caught my eye and nodded back towards the beach. I'd been anxious for this meeting all night. Now that it was here I felt strangely inadequate, like I wasn't worthy of the privilege that this sphere bestowed on me. The four of us sat around the table, Carlo and Erica holding hands. "Adelaide seems a bit lost as to what she should do," Marina said to Erica.

"That's understandable. It's a big decision. I think you need more information before making it. Surely, you have questions about what happens to us if I send you back?"

My brain started to kick into gear. I hadn't really considered what would happen to the rest of the timeline. I felt guilty for not considering those around me. "Well, yes. What does happen if I go back and fix things so the lab never gets attacked?"

"This timeline is already in effect; it cannot be deleted. We will go on, just as we have, living our lives as they have been up to this point. We're already an abnormality. As you already know, the Gardian woman Sarah was never supposed to see you or find Noah's belongings. Likewise, Noah was never supposed to get stuck there nor find his way back to his original timeline. Each of those events created separate timelines. Once established, they cannot be undone. I can sense them, though not as well as this one. There is another version of me, another Erica, who knows nothing of you or of the laboratory you came from. She grew up, eventually learned to control her nightmares though she never learned the truth of what has happened to her. Most of your missions were small enough that the splinters they made in time were able to self-correct. The people who ran your lab were right to keep you out of important events. These short splinters are able to work themselves back into their original timelines. It's like time wants to heal itself, like it knows how things are meant to be."

"And this timeline was never meant to be?"

"No. But there is nothing you can do about that now. Like I said, I can sense the other versions of myself. Even though I know it is me, it is still not this version of me."

"How many timelines are there?" I asked.

"Three major timeline splits have arisen from the events surrounding Noah's initial problems with the sphere. There was a split from his being there; he was starting to push events in different directions. Then there was another split when his older self arrived back in your original timeline. Then there was another split that started with the discovery of his journal though it remained very close to the original timeline and did not become very divergent until the attack on the laboratory. That's actually the one you're in now. So three major splits from the first timeline."

"Which one do I actually belong in?"

"You belong in different splits at different times. It's hard to say. There is one other version of you as well."

I almost laughed at her, the idea sounded so ridiculous. I tried to wrap my head around it, tried to sense the other version of myself like Erica said she could feel hers. I figured it was futile, but I needed to focus my train of thought. My head fell into my hands, and I rubbed my temples, trying to straighten out my mind. "Only one? But you said there are 4 timelines. Have I died in the other timelines?"

"Eventually both of you will die. When you travel with the sphere, your existence travels within your current timeline. But if you cause a split, you travel into that new timeline. Everyone else who existed in that one is recreated in the split. So there are four versions of the rest of us.

I smiled at the thought of that. "So I'm recreating the universe around me?" It seemed like an awful lot of fuss for one person.

"Well you're not doing it, but you're causing it to happen."

"So even if I go back and fix things so that Noah's journal is never found, this timeline will still go on."

"Yes."

"Then what's the point?"

"It will at least get you back to where you belong. That timeline is still going along."

"What happens if I never go back to my own time?"

"Neither you nor Noah will make it back to where you started. The lab will close without a sphere. It will be similar to this timeline, but the attack on the lab will not be the impetus for its closing."

"Then I should just stay here. Let things end the way they have."

"That is certainly a possibility. And the choice is yours, though you don't belong here I can feel that it's wrong."

I didn't belong here. The words hurt. She was right, I was out of place here. And I couldn't imagine staying and leaving things alone.

I had forgotten anyone but Erica was still here, and it surprised me when Marina broke in at that point.

"Surveillance is not what it used to be, and the lab has long since closed, but there are still people watching, Adelaide. From Noah's description of events and from what little they obtained from the programmer who brought you here before they killed him, they know you were sent somewhere in the future."

I turned to look at her as she spoke. "Then why didn't they keep the lab open to wait for me?"

"There were many activities going on at the lab, lots of research. But the most lucrative was the time travel. People who knew, and there weren't many of them, paid well to have their questions answered. When they realized it would potentially be many years before they'd be able to get their sphere back, they couldn't afford to keep everything else going."

I shuddered at the thought of what other activities they could be doing, given how they treated us. "What other kinds of research?"

"I know you think they're evil, Adelaide, but they were making real strides in vaccines and technological breakthroughs. They were doing good work, but it wasn't enough. The sphere was their prize."

A question that burned in the back of my mind for years resurfaced suddenly. "Where did they get the sphere?"

Erica was the one who responded, "It was an accidental creation. A man working on a teleportation device created the sphere. He figured out the need for a fixed point that the user must keep with them. He had the gift of the programmers, but thought it was space, not time, that he was seeing. Shortly after he realized what he had done, he refused to make another. He thought the technology was too dangerous for anyone to use. The lab obviously disagreed, but couldn't force him to participate. He was neutralized, and his partner took over the project."

"And what happened to the older version of Noah? The one I met before I went back?"

"In all timelines except the one where he stays in his proper time, he is killed shortly after Noah returns."

I wondered if he ever got my note before he was killed. If Jim had found a way to sneak it in. My train of thought was interrupted by a low droning noise. Another plane was heading towards the island. Marina stood up from her chair and said something in another language that sounded like a swear. I bolted out of mine as well, knocking it over. Carlo grabbed Erica's hand and tugged her towards one of the huts on the opposite side of the pool. "Erica, Adelaide, come on. We have to hide you!"

Erica placed her hand over Carlo's and held her ground. "Relax Carlo, it's okay." She turned to me and gave me her quiet, calming smile. "It's just Noah."

# Chapter 20

My breath stopped. Noah. One hundred and forty something year old Noah was on that plane and would be here in mere moments. I struggled to breathe and remain standing. I walked out towards the dock alone while the plane taxied to the opposite side of the first seaplane. I avoided looking into the cockpit at first. A rope coiled along the side of the fuselage. I grabbed it and tied the plane to a post on the dock as the door opened. Out of the corner of my eye, I saw someone come down out of the pilot seat.

I stood up and kept my eyes on the fuselage. I had seen so many different versions of Noah in the past week. I really didn't want to be introduced to yet another one. I knew he would be older and different but still the same person. I worried that I would decide that that was enough, and I'd chose to stay in this timeline and live out my life twiddling my thumbs on this island. It was beautiful and I loved sailing but somehow I knew it wouldn't be enough. I realized he was staring at me as I stood there staring at nothing. I snapped out of my daze and turned to face him.

I only had a moment to look at him before he swept me up in a giant bear hug and laughed. "I knew I could count on you to find your way back!" He set me back down and held me at arm's length. "You look so young."

"You look so old," I countered.

He laughed again and let me go. It was only then that I noticed the small girl standing behind him. He noticed me trying to look around him and stepped aside. "Addy, this is Daphne."

"Your daughter?"

He bellowed again. "Daughter? Do you really think I'd ever have settled down?"

I remembered the older version of Noah that had children. Though I always knew Noah would end up an old bachelor, there was a part of me that was disappointed he never found someone to spend his life with and want to have children. Though it certainly looked like he wasn't friendless. He was perfectly happy with the way his life had gone. I smiled. "You're right, I should know better than that. Too busy living life in the fast lane?"

"You have no idea." He hadn't stopped grinning since I turned to look at him. "Daphne is like Erica," he paused and the corners of his mouth fell for a moment. "You have met Erica, haven't you?"

"Yes. Just about an hour ago."

"Ah good, good. I wasn't sure when I got her note how far along she was. Come on, I'm starving." He grabbed my hand and Daphne's and dragged us back down the dock. Carlo must have known Noah would be hungry. There was already food on the table. Now that I thought about it, I was fairly starving myself. It had been an hour since Erica's arrival, and my brain was finally getting enough of a break to realize I hadn't eaten much of anything all day. Noah immediately gathered Erica into another hug. "Erica, so good to see you again!"

She stopped him just short of picking her up as well. "I'm not as young as I used to be, Noah."

Marina crossed over to him and embraced him as well. "It's good to see you again, Noah."

"You haven't aged a day, my dear." Carlo emerged from the hut with two more chairs and was assaulted before he could put them down. "Carlo! There's a good boy, always know when to feed your Uncle Noah." He released Carlo and took one of the chairs from his hands, placed it at the table and sat in it. Daphne sat next to him still saying nothing, though she was smiling.

The whole atmosphere had changed with Noah's arrival. Though I knew I still had a serious decision to make, it felt like whatever happened from here on out, everything would somehow work out. The stress of my situation and the weight of what was coming seemed greatly diminished.

Noah rubbed his hands together in anticipation before turning to me. "Well now, Addy, have you decided what to do with yourself?"

"Not just yet. I'm still trying to get a handle on this multiple timeline thing."

"Waste of time, really. They exist, nothing you can do about that."

"Then what have you been doing these past years, Noah?"

"Running about, not getting caught. Going on a few adventures. Learning.

Fighting. The usual."

"Fighting?"

"A natural aide to not getting caught."

I laughed. Of course Noah found all of that exciting. He probably loved being in jail back in the 1800s. He had been addicted to the thrill of time travel and the clandestine operations. It was like being in a joke that the whole world is the butt of. I missed it just as I knew he did. I wanted it back; his presence made me realize that. I was right that living out this life would not be enough. I turned back to Erica. "Can you send me back to just after Noah and I disappeared in 1692? So I can remove the journal and go back to where I should have been before this whole mess began?"

"No, I cannot get you to a timeline that I don't exist in. At least, not this version of myself. I can only send you to sometime before you disappear, before the timeline splits. You'll just have to be careful to not let yourself be seen by your other self."

Noah cut in. "You need to keep Sarah from seeing us as well, remember, Addy."

It was so strange to see him sitting there. He looked just like the older version of himself that I met only a few days ago though his hair was cut in a modern style instead of the 1700s cut he had before. And he knew who I was. He was exactly the same person I had left, merely older. It was a relief after dealing with the first older version I had met.

"If you've never done this before, how can you be so certain you're able to do it now? With the precision to get me where I belong?"

"Because I've already tried it."

My brain felt sluggish. I wondered if this was one of those strange paradoxes where something happened in my future but her past? "I don't understand."

"We have another sphere."

This was definitely a surprise. I half smiled. "Let me guess; I'm supposed to go back to steal a sphere and bring it back to you at some point in the recent past?"

She caught the snark in my voice and smirked back at me. "Don't be silly. We had a new sphere made years ago."

"How?" I was having trouble following all of this.

"What do you think I've been doing all these years?" Noah looked at me mischievously. "I found out everything I could about the lab. I found out about the researcher who invented the sphere, and I tracked him down.

"But Erica said he had been neutralized."

"He had. It took quite some time and effort, but he was able to once again sort out the logic that led him to the creation of the sphere. Without the resources of the lab, it's not quite as fancy. It's more like a box, actually. A small wooden box that would fit in say, a small safe should I need to hide it from lab people at some point." His grin was somewhere between petulant and wicked.

I suddenly thought of the little wooden box in my backpack. "How did you know?"

"I would've made a good scout, I think. About ten years ago the lab was getting a little too close for comfort. I needed to hide the box somewhere that it would find its way back to me later in a way the lab would not expect. Erica helped me track down your return. I saw you on the dock at the marina the day you purchased the boat. I returned a few months earlier to plant the box in the safe, then get them off my tail. Got to skip past ten years. I hear they were rather dull. Nothing of note happened."

"So why haven't you gone back to fix things?" The question came out more harshly than I meant it to. But I was angry. Here was Noah mucking about in the future when he could have done the responsible thing and gotten back to where he belonged.

He turned quiet for once. "Addy, we only got the sphere a few years ago. Well, I guess about 15 years ago from today, right?" He looked at Erica, who nodded. "It took some experimenting before Erica got a handle on moving me around in time, then some more experimenting with Daphne involved. And look at me. Imagine me turning up from the conclusion of my mission this age. With a wooden box. There would be questions. Even if you came back shortly after me, they would know I hadn't come straight away. There would be more questions asked and it's likely I'd end up in the same position I was before I came here." He paused, perhaps feeling a bit of the guilt I had intended to inflict on him. "Besides, I didn't see the point. I've had a good life here. I have another sphere. I'm able to stay one step ahead of the lab. I have no desire to go back to them and I strongly suggest you stay away from them as well."

I was still mad at him. He sounded more like he was trying to be my father, telling me what to do, than a friend offering a suggestion. Marina told me the lab did good work as well. If they were also saving lives with vaccines and advancing the human race through technology, why should that be denied to mankind?

Erica interrupted my train of thought. "There was another complication with that. Once you're back before the timelines split, the other programmer will be able to see you and control your sphere as well. Daphne and I have experimented with this a little bit in this timeline. One programmer can override the intentions of another, but if you manage to continue past the split into a timeline that this version of myself does not exist in, my ability to keep control over you will diminish greatly. Within a few minutes, I doubt I'd be able to do anything at all when you tried to use the sphere. Daphne's much better at this than I am, but we're not sure she'd be able to send you forward in a different timeline. We haven't tried to do that. Had I sent Noah back and he continued along the original timeline, he could have been stuck there. So if you go back and fix things, you'll be stuck in that timeline."

Noah interjected again, "If that's what you want, that is. There are other options, you know."

"Like what?"

"I know you miss it. The missions, the travel. All of it. Erica and Daphne are able to send you wherever you want in time and are fairly certain if you went back to a time before the timelines split, they'd still have control over you. So long as you don't go back to a time where another programmer is expecting someone to be, they're not likely to notice you. You could keep doing what you've been doing. Solving mysteries and finding ways to let society know the truth about them, and you could do it without having to subscribe to the lab's stupid rules."

"Their rules make sense given what we've done to the timelines, Noah!" I practically hissed the words at him.

"I'm not saying you should go tell Lincoln not to buy those theater tickets, I'm saying you can be careful without having to be as tied down as we had been. The small splits heal themselves."

I thought about it. It would be nice to be able to do my job without having to follow all their restrictions and formalities. I understood their concern and why they were in place, but I always thought some of them were a little overkill. And that awful white room with the moldy mats, I would not be sorry to avoid it every time I came back. But there were diseases to fear, and the readjustment period. "It was nice having the facilities available to us though. What if I go back and catch the black death like that other librarian did?"

Noah's face was blank. "We'll kill you before you can pass it on."

"What?"

He laughed at me. "Just kidding. But come on Addy, the black death, and all diseases of the past are curable in this day and age. You know that."

"It's not like I can run down to the corner store and get the cure for it. And the return trip recovery is always so rough. Especially after a long trip."

"Not necessary. It was a side effect of the programmers from the lab."

"What do you mean?"

He sighed. "We don't know exactly, but I haven't had the side effects on the trips I've done with Erica and Daphne. We think, given the restrictions the lab puts on their programmers, they were not able to operate as efficiently as possible. That gets carried over into our journeys. We shouldn't be getting sick on these trips, just a little dizzy from the sudden time change. But it's not like we're physically being transported..." He trailed off and turned to Erica. "She explained this better, and I still didn't quite get it."

Erica jumped in again. "Think of it as though your physical existence is not going anywhere. It's not like we're putting you in a plane and flying you somewhere very fast. It's more of a shift in the state of your existence. You're merely moving from one point in time to another, not one place to another."

"But we end up in different places as well, not just different times."

"Again, your physical existence is irrelevant. Your state is merely changing, not moving."

I was having trouble separating those two things in my mind. Actually I was having trouble keeping any of what I was told straight in my mind. "But you described it as a path through time. You kept seeing my path."

"Yes, you can think of it as a path. But I see everything at once, so a spot further back is equally as accessible as any other closer time. It's like your memories, you don't have to think backwards through time to remember something from your childhood. It's just accessible to you. And the same with locations. I'm sure you can remember the lab without having to think back through how you got here from there."

"So we can travel without any of the side effects." My mind felt so slow. Everyone else had already figured all this out for themselves. I felt like a child.

"There is still a little bit of dizziness, like Noah said. I'm not perfect at it." She smiled apologetically.

Her humility amused me, as though she was anything other than extraordinary. "Sounds like you're much better than our previous programmers."

She didn't take the compliment. "They were kept under very strict control. If someone distracted me while I was trying to get you back it probably wouldn't go well for you either."

"Are you not happy about having this power?"

"I don't see it as a power so much as a burden. Before Noah and Jim came along, it was terrifying. And even after finding out what was really going on, to know that people would kill to keep me out of the hands of other people... Very few people know I can do this, and I intend to keep it that way. In fact, I've largely been guiding Daphne at this point and letting her take care of Noah."

I glanced at Daphne again. She looked so small and harmless. "So you could send me back somewhere if I wanted?"

She didn't answer me, but looked nervously at Erica, who answered for her. "Yes, Daphne can send you wherever you decide."

"And whenever," Noah chimed in. He seemed a bit giddy. I knew he wanted me to be as excited about the idea of traveling again as he was.

So it turned out that I could do it, I could travel through time with no restrictions. Go wherever I wanted. See whatever I wanted. And not suffer the side effects I always hated. It was very tempting, but I still had a nagging feeling of guilt for starting all of this in the first place. I knew I wouldn't really fix things, that this timeline would still occur, but I didn't belong here, really.

There were so many things to consider, and I was still trying to sort through this new information. There was one thing I knew for certain, I wouldn't be able to focus with everyone hovering around me and waiting for me to make my decision. I stood up from the table with everyone still watching me. "I need some time to think," I said. I stalked off towards the beach, certain that their eyes followed me but refusing to look back to see.

## Chapter 21

I started walking down the beach on my own. I knew from my last visit it would take about two hours for me to circumnavigate the island. I hoped that would be long enough to sort out my thoughts. I felt like someone had been smacking me in the back of the head for the past few hours, and I had had enough. My brain was jelly, I needed a mental break. I needed to refocus and get my thoughts organized. I spent the first mile just focusing on the sand beneath my feet, trying not to think about anything important and letting my mind wander.

The sand was cool and hard where the tide had retreated. It stuck to the bottom and lower sides of my feet. It was pleasant in the shade from the palm trees but a little too warm without it. I stood at a break in the trees and let the sun warm me for a few moments until I was sweating. The water occasionally running over my feet helped cool me back down. I thought it strange that it should make such a difference.

I watched the bubbles push themselves up through the sand next to my foot whenever I took a step and watched the pockets of air sucking their way open when the waves retreated. I stopped for a moment and focused on the waves coming into land, letting my feet get sucked further down into the sand with each new volley of water. The repeated pattern helped me empty my mind as I drifted into a bit of a trance.

After a few moments, I pulled my buried feet out of the sand and moved onward further around the island. I tried to start thinking about what I wanted. I wanted to continue my work. That was a definite. With or without the lab supporting me, I wanted to keep finding the answers to life's mysteries. There were so many left that I had wanted to solve. The Loch Ness monster, the disappearance of flight 370, and the Roswell Incident were still on the top of my list. I wasn't sure I wanted the lab on my back though. Noah's love of staying one step ahead of his enemies and constantly dodging capture did not sound appealing to me.

I turned into the trees and grabbed a dead branch from the ground, then walked out to the packed sand. I used the stick to carve my options into the ground.

*1-Stay here and travel.*

*2-Fix things and go back to my time.*

*3-Drop both spheres in the ocean.*

*4-Meet up with Jim and Noah and travel with them.*

*5-*

I couldn't think of a fifth option. So option 1 where I merely continue along in this timeline meant I could travel as I liked, but with the ever present threat of the lab hunting for me. Noah is older here, he won't live too much longer. Marina as well. After a while it would just be Daphne and me, and I didn't even know her yet. What if she didn't want the rest of her life to be tied to moving me in time?

Option 2 would put me back where I was meant to be. I could fix things so the Gardians never find out about the lab, then return with Noah where we were supposed to go originally. I'd have to pretend I didn't know anything that I had learned in the past few days. I'd have to ignore the things about the lab I didn't approve of, like what they did to people who got in their way, and Eliza lying there with her head splayed open. I thought of that poor older married father version of Noah being killed. Is the reward of traveling through time worth the guilt, knowing who I really work for? Could I do that and live with myself? After all, it keeps their other, more noble projects funded so some good comes out of the situation.

Option 3 meant we would all be stuck here. It might be harder for Noah and me once they realize I'm here, to keep ahead of the lab once our ability to travel in time is gone. And if they found us... I didn't think our options would be pleasant. Besides, if we made another sphere, they could make yet another once they figured out how Noah and Jim did.

Option 4 would put me in this timeline, but the lab would still be destroyed. I could help them find Erica much more quickly, and the three of us could continue our work. On the con side, Jim would still die rather young, and the lab would still be on our trail.

I crossed off option 3. I wasn't going to let myself get stuck here. Did I care about Noah's age? Did I want to be back at a time when we were closer? It didn't seem to matter too much for our interaction, but I would lose him much sooner than I had anticipated. Although for all I knew, if I went back in time close to where I was meant to be, Noah could die rather quickly from something entirely unexpected. Jim would still die rather young. I wanted to find a cure for Jim. The only place I knew that could potentially cure a disease like that would still be the lab.

I finally thought of an option 5. I took the stick and wrote in the sand:

*No5-Take over the lab.*

Noah would love that. I stared at the words. My mind had trouble gaining any ground on this idea, but the words burned into my brain as though there was nothing to think about. This was the answer. It got the lab off my back, left me the convenience of a place to live and thrive, the other research areas could continue, the programmers could have a life. I just didn't know how to possibly accomplish that.

How had the Gardians done it? They broke in—that wouldn't be a problem for me given I lived there. They had weapons. But surely we had weapons. Were we taken by surprise? Was that it? I couldn't imagine them breaking in through the dome would give them much in the way of a stealthy attack plan. Maybe I should just let that bit of time carry on and take over the lab after they'd killed most of the important people. I tried to think back to what Montgomery had told me. They knew exactly where to take out the guards. They must've had inside help. If they'd been planning for years, it probably wouldn't have been that hard to get someone in the lab and work them up to a position of importance. They killed the people in the boardroom. If that was so, who has been chasing Noah? Who else survived?

I kicked at the sand in frustration. The option 5 written in the sand was destroyed along with part of 4. I left the others to be swallowed by the tide in a few hours and continued around the island. Even if I did let the Gardians take over the lab, what was to stop them from finding out I had restarted the time travel and coming back to kill me? I supposed if I found out the answers they wanted, then they might leave me be.

I needed help, my thoughts were getting me nowhere. I was having enough trouble keeping the different timelines straight in my head. There was no way I would be able to figure out what to do without talking to someone first and working through it all. I wondered if Daphne was so quiet because she had no opinions or for some other reason. Perhaps she was the perfect person to talk to. She would be largely unbiased, having never dealt with the people from the lab. I wondered if she would be willing to leave this timeline and travel back in time with me. Perhaps if she went back to before the timeline splits, she'd be able to see each of them more clearly and send me into a specific one. New possibilities opened up with that idea.

I turned toward the mountain, and my walk turned to a jog as I climbed to the top and found Adam's grave again. There were fresh flowers on top of the marker. I guessed Marina or Carlo must come up here every day to replace them and pay their respects. I had forgotten about Adam, but I couldn't change what happened to him here. This timeline would continue even if I fixed things. "I'm sorry," I said to Adam for the second time.

I stood in front of his grave for a moment. My gaze fell to the base of the tree at which I had thrown the surveillance robot. I wanted to see if I had damaged it at all in my previous encounter and possibly throw it down the side of the mountain. When I approached the tree, I couldn't find the robot anywhere, but there was a small metal structure. I picked it up and upon observation decided that it must be the lower segment of one of the legs. I had done some damage to it after all. Whoever was up here must have seen it and disposed of it, not realizing this piece was left behind.

I shoved it into my pocket intending to throw it out and turned to follow the path down to the hut. When I arrived back at Marina's hut I found just Erica and Daphne sitting at the table. Daphne had been speaking but quieted when she saw me. At least I knew she wasn't mute. I sat down at the table with them. "Can I talk to you two?"

Erica responded, "Of course."

I turned to Daphne and asked, "Do you speak?"

Her cheeks blushed and she seemed to shrink into her chair. "Yes. I'm sorry."

"Are you afraid of me?"

"No!" She seemed frightened by the sound of her own voice though. She coughed slightly and sat up straight again. "No. I'm just, distrustful of people I don't know. I've been told my gift might make some people want to hurt me."

She didn't trust me, and here I was about to ask her to travel through time with me and help start a rebellion. "Noah and Marina's opinion of me isn't good enough for you?"

"Noah does not show the greatest judgment sometimes. And I've only just met Marina."

"That's fair," I allowed. I paused for a minute as my mind shifted gears. "I want to find a way to take over the lab."

Silence filled the open space. Erica looked dubious, but an amused smile crossed Daphne's face. Neither spoke so I continued.

"My plan is sort of based on an assumption on my part though. I take it neither of you have tried to travel yourself?"

Erica shook her head no, and Daphne looked curious about the idea.

"You mentioned you can't really see into other timelines, but I'm wondering if you were to go back in time before a split, would you be able to see both options that lie before you? Is it simply because you're in this timeline that the others are inaccessible to you?"

"An intriguing thought," Erica said. "And if it turns out to be true?"

"The short version of the plan is: Daphne and I take the sphere and the box back to 1692 and alter Noah's journal to inform the Gardians that there are two spheres. My theory is that once you've traveled back before time splits, you should be able to see any timelines emanating from that point and travel into them. We then go to 1882, give Noah my sphere and tell him he needs to come up with a story about me dying in 1882 when he gets back to the present day. That way they have possession of every sphere that they know about. The Gardians take over the lab with the knowledge that there are two spheres and insist on using both of them. The lab is destroyed, along with both spheres. Daphne and I use the box to travel to when Noah and Jim escaped and tell them what is going on. After the lab is destroyed, and the board members are killed, we waltz in and take over the place. We free the programmer, or at least ease his work. We keep doing missions that will keep our funding going without the interference of the lab. We push for a cure for Sunithe's disease. We all live happily ever after." I paused. "At least in that timeline."

I knew it was a lot to take in. If Daphne came back with me, she'd never be able to make it back to this timeline. She seemed to be working it out in her head. "I've never tried to travel myself. With the box."

"Are you willing to try?" I asked. "A short trip into the past and back?"

She thought for a minute. She didn't look like she wanted to do it, though behind the fear in her face excitement danced in her eyes.

"I can keep track of you, Daphne," said Erica. "If you have trouble navigating yourself, I can get you back here. Then we'll at least know."

She nodded.

I took the sphere out of my pocket and handed it to her. She flipped open the lid and closed her eyes with her thumb on the button. Nothing happened for a moment except her head twitching slightly to the side. Then she was gone. I turned excitedly to Erica but she held up a finger to silence me. She was focusing very hard on something when suddenly Daphne reappeared in her chair. Even expecting it, I was startled. I looked back and forth between the two of them. Daphne smiled at me, and Erica seemed to relax finally. Before I could speak, Daphne held up a finger to silence me and disappeared again. I looked to Erica who merely shrugged and then focused again.

This time when Daphne reappeared she was laughing. "You are right, Adelaide," she said. "I can see into all the timelines, not just this one. Scared the heck out of a horse when I arrived in 1690." She giggled again.

I smiled. "So you can do it! You can get us back into my original timeline?"

Her laugh faded, and she went into deep thought again. "I can, yes. But I don't know that I want to." She turned to Erica.

"No one is going to force you. It's your choice, Daphne." Erica smiled, "But why stay here with us old folks. You could have so many adventures."

In the back of my mind a wretched thought flickered. She could take herself anywhere she wanted and never come back, and there was nothing we'd be able to do about it. Maybe that was part of the reason the lab kept the programmers so restricted. Their rules, while harsh, made sense. Would I be any better at being head of the lab? I shuddered at the thought. I would never force someone into this. I would never kill innocent people. But if I let the Gardian rebellion happen to my advantage, isn't that what I would be doing?

I had no choice but to trust her if I wanted this to work. And just like her a few minutes ago, I had no basis on which to lay that trust.

Daphne finally came out of her introspection. "That is true, but there is one more thing we need to test." Before I could ask what, she grabbed my hand. I found myself falling onto my butt in a field with a startled horse while Daphne shrieked with glee. "Perfect!" She grabbed my hand again and yanked me up, and we were back at the table with Erica. "Ok, so one part of the plan works."

I felt a little dizzy from the time change, though it seemed so effortless for her. Perhaps an adolescent wasn't the best choice for this sort of power.

"What plan?" Noah and Marina emerged from the trees and joined us at the table.

I explained my elaborate plan to get control of the lab and continue on with the work to Noah.

"So you're going to take my box and your sphere and Daphne and leave me here to rot?"

"Noah, you'd have Erica and the means to create another sphere. You could keep traveling as long as you like."

He looked hurt. I wondered if he felt like I was abandoning him for a younger version of himself. I wouldn't necessarily call it abandoning, but I was more likely to succeed in my plans with a younger Noah.

"Aw Addy, I can't keep this up forever. Maybe it's time I just start taking it easy." He looked sad, but there was a slight tilt to his mouth that made me think he had no intention of settling down with his life. "So what do you need from me?"

"Do you know if the Gardians had someone on the inside?"

"Not a clue. But I would assume so, given the ease with which they took over."

"It's a chance we'll have to take," I said. "If we should need to, how do we find the man who created the sphere?"

"I'm not sure where he'd be when you got back. The lab should have files on him. Once you've taken over, it shouldn't be hard for Jim to find him."

"Do you know who is following you?"

Noah's face darkened. "Doctor Lancing."

"Doctor Lancing," I repeated. It was his office I had been in. He was the one who had connected that helmet to Eliza's brain. He was still alive and working from the lab. I must have just missed him when I was wandering around.

Noah nodded. "He was above the board, the head of the entire lab. Bit of a recluse, didn't like to be seen but had his hands in everything. The board did all his dirty work for him. But now that they're all dead, I guess this is personal for him. He's young. Way too young. I think some of the research going on in that place must have been aging related. You'll have to deal with him as well, the

Gardians never got to him."

That could complicate things. Granted, he was only one man, but I wasn't about to kill him just to get him out of the way. Even if I could. With Eliza on his side, I had no real idea of what I was up against. I felt the remnant of the robot leg in my pocket, pressing against my thigh. "Lancing Electronics," I said to myself.

Noah nodded. "An offshoot of the company. Apparently the security person there was a real wizard at electronic surveillance."

I pulled the leg segment out of my pocket. "Marina, do you and Carlo go up to Adam's grave every day?"

She gave me a somewhat apologetic look. "I go every day. Carlo hasn't been in years. It's too painful for him."

"And did you find a robot up there recently?"

"A robot? No, but I don't often look around. I'm usually focused on Adam's grave."

Somewhere on the island a small robot was hobbling around watching us again. "Lancing knows I'm here," I said, holding up the leg. "We better hurry."

# Chapter 22

Daphne and I found some floor length linen skirts that would pass for appropriate costumes. The jackets available were incredibly modern compared to where we were going, but we didn't have much choice, and it wasn't like my backpack was period appropriate anyway. I told her we would just have to do our best not to be seen and get through the first two parts of the plan quickly. I described the towns of Salem and Georgetown as well as I could. She had never been there, but we were counting on her ability to sense the other versions of myself and Noah to get us as close as possible to our targets.

We said our hasty goodbyes. I promised Marina that I would come to visit her and Adam more often once things were settled with the lab, and that I would not mention anything about Carlo until after he was born. Daphne spent a while saying goodbye to Noah, and though she seemed excited to be leaving, he seemed saddened by it. His mood had turned a bit foul by the time I said goodbye. I knew he was unhappy to be cut off from the sphere, and now I was taking away Daphne, one of the few people he had left in the world. As much as he claimed to never want to settle down, there was a definite father-daughter relationship about them. I kept the observation to myself, though I thought it was telling that both this version of Noah and the version that was trapped in Salem had found their own versions of family. It gave me hope that when I got back to the Noah in the timeline I was supposed to be in, he would one day find that kind of fulfillment in his life as well.

We put the sphere box in my pack with the money I hadn't spent, some extra clothes and the necessities for our journey. We didn't intend to spend much time in the past but weren't sure what would happen when we made it back to where I belonged. I was counting on Jim's help to figure out the rest of the plan. I held Daphne's hand and waved goodbye to the people gathered on Marina's patio. My hand was still raised when we arrived behind the house Noah had stayed in while in Salem. "When are we?"

"1692, a few days before you arrive." Daphne raised her hand to silence me. Her face screwed up in concentration. I knew she was trying to see into the different timelines. A split was created when Noah had his memory erased, and she'd need to see into this for her to find a way to get Montgomery home. "Amazing," she whispered. "Okay, go."

I pushed the button again. There was a subtle shift in the trees. Leaves that had been there before were suddenly gone. The sky became a little darker and the temperature a little colder. Otherwise, I detected no difference.

I let Daphne's hand go and told her to stay put for a moment while I went to peek around the side of the house where I knew I'd find Sarah. She was looking into the window and using her hands to block the light for a better view. She backed away looking startled and ran off into the woods, so we must have arrived just before Noah and I disappeared from Salem. I had no idea how long it would be before Sarah came back, so I called to Daphne. We wasted no time in going inside to do what we had to do.

I had gotten Noah to write another journal entry detailing the existence of the second sphere which I quickly copied into the journal we had left behind. Noah had also written a note for Sarah, which I tucked neatly into the back of the journal. "Done!" I grabbed Daphne's hand and we suddenly arrived in a pitch black room. "Where have you taken us?" I hissed at her.

"The root cellar."

It took me a moment to put two and two together. This was where Noah came to steal some food while we had been waiting for our chance to sneak into town. "Ah, brilliant. How soon before-" I was cut off by a door opening. The faint lights from outside illuminated us softly as a figure descended the few stairs down into the cellar and stopped short when he saw us.

"Oh excuse me, I was just-"

"Noah." I would've loved to delay my greeting and hear what excuse he had come up with on the spot, but we were in a hurry.

He had turned to leave but stopped abruptly and turned back. "Adelaide?" He glanced behind him at the open door. "How the hell-"

"Noah I don't have a lot of time. Here." I grabbed the burlap blanket he had found and started collecting food from the shelves. "You're going to take this food back to me in the woods as you planned. You absolutely cannot mention this to me. You need to take this sphere and take it back with you, and you cannot tell me that you have it either. Don't second guess anything you're about to do, just take this sphere." I handed him the blanket with the food and then handed him my sphere. "And when you get back to the lab, you need to tell them I'm dead, that I died here, and you brought back my sphere. Do you understand?"

He hesitated, but it was clear he trusted me. "No, but I'll do it anyway." He turned to leave and grinned at me from halfway up the stairwell. "See you soon, Addy." He walked back upstairs and closed the doors to the root cellar.

"I hope that worked," I said as I pulled the wooden sphere box out of my pack and gave it to Daphne.

"One way to find out!" Even in the dark I saw the brightness from Daphne's teeth, exposed as her expression widened with excitement. She grabbed my hand again.

I squinted against the sudden brightness. For a few moments, I felt like I was back in the return chamber, but the air was fresh, I heard birds, and I didn't feel like I was about to vomit. I gave my eyes another moment to adjust. It was a little disorienting, but nothing in comparison to my last return.

"We're in the field you told me about. Look!" Daphne walked a few steps past me. I turned around to see where she was pointing. "Here's the hatch to the tunnel! Do we go inside or wait to surprise them out here?"

Admittedly, this was the least certain part of the plan. "Well, I suppose it's safer to wait out here. Perhaps we should hide in case the first people who come out aren't Jim and-" I was cut off by the sound of an explosion. From the direction of the lab, we saw a plume of smoke rising above the glass dome. "The Gardians. Come on." I tugged on her sleeve. We walked over towards a bale of hay that was rolled up in the field. I wondered if they paid someone to plant these in the field and remove them every year. I didn't imagine this field was part of an actual working farm.

"How long do you think?"

"Supposedly Jim and Noah escaped in the chaos of the attack. It can't be too long, I should think. If Jim was already planning to help Noah get out, he'd be prepared and ready to go. So a few minutes to realize what is going on, a few more minutes to find Noah, then maybe half an hour for them to get out?" I tried to remember the details of the story I had been told. I didn't remember if they had stopped by Montgomery's on the way out. I didn't think so, since Noah gave him the letter before the attack happened. It had taken me at least half an hour to get to the hatch after leaving Montgomery's place. "At least half an hour, maybe an hour."

"We could pop forward a few minutes."

I smiled at her enthusiasm. Again, the need to keep her under control seeped into my thoughts. "Impatient are we? We can wait. I don't want to miss them if they come out running."

"Fine!" It was a whine, but she gave me the box.

I stuffed it into my backpack. Her enthusiasm was contagious. "So we've got a few days with Noah and Jim before things calm back down. Where do you think we should bunker down and plan our takeover?"

"How about Paris?"

"What?" The word came out as a laugh.

"Well, we've got that sphere. I can take us anywhere. Why not somewhere fun?"

I couldn't think of a reason to object. "Let's see what Jim and Noah think when they come out." Why not Paris, I thought to myself. I'd never been there. Noah would love breaking out the French accent again, to be sure.

"Why give them the chance? Let's grab them the instant they come out and leave!"

"People don't like being whisked away unannounced unless they're being saved from imminent peril." She sulked so I decided to throw her a bone. "Paris sounds good though. Noah will hate it." She grinned again. It was odd, I felt like I had inherited a daughter. Noah's adoptive daughter. What a strange little family the four of us would make for the next few days. I wondered how much to tell Noah about his relationship to Daphne in the future. We sat in the field and leaned against the hay bale for a while. She was thankfully quiet for a few minutes, no doubt thinking about Paris. "Think you'll have any trouble traveling with two more people?"

"Nope. Easy peasy."

It occurred to me that we never traveled into the future on missions, with the exception of my accidental arrival eighty years from this point. I always assumed it was an impossibility. Yet Daphne had just suggested going a few minutes into the future here to pass the time. "How far into the future could you take us?"

She grimaced at me. "I'm not completely sure. Not far beyond what year it was when we left the island, I think. Technically, we're still in my past. But I couldn't see anything beyond the present while we were on the island or when I was working with Noah on honing my skills."

"What do you think would happen if you had tried to send someone ahead in time?"

"Noah asked us to. Me and Erica. She said no, and I was too nervous to contradict her. I can't see anything. I'd have no reference for where to put someone." She looked disappointed and a little frightened by the idea.

"But Noah said he skipped 10 years into the future to plant the box in the safe."

"Erica merely waited 10 years to bring him back. For him, it was instantaneous. She basically just had to ignore him for all that time. I don't think she could've sent him forward though."

"It was an idle curiosity. Probably better to leave the future unknown anyway. Which reminds me, you probably shouldn't talk much about the other version of Noah that you know."

"Why not?"

I sighed. As much as I resented the lab, their rules made it easy for their employees to just obey without question. "Noah didn't react that well to finding out that there was another version of him. Especially one who didn't adhere to his version of a life. I think it might be better for him to not know how he turns out in another timeline."

"Was he very different?"

"No," I said. "But had he been given the option to continue along in his current state, I think he would've turned out slightly different. But he's stubborn enough that if he knew what he was like in another life, he would want to be different. Almost like he would need to prove it wasn't him."

She giggled a little. "Yes, I could see that about Noah." We sat in silence for a moment. "How is he different here?"

"It's hard to say. I don't think he'll seem that different to you. Younger, but you're meeting him at a rather pivotal moment in his life. While we were in the lab together, his personality was much the same, but the traveling through time was really the driving force in his life. As much as he might complain about the lab, he needed it. Without the lab, he seemed like a much more relaxed person though he still seemed to be driven by the same needs."

We heard a hollow, metallic thud as the handle on the hatch moved and were instantly alert. We jumped up and watched over the top of the hay bale as the door opened. Jim's head peered out. He glanced around quickly and came out, turning his back to us. I moved around the front of the hay bale and motioned for Daphne to be silent. I leaned against it as casually as possible and waited. Noah was emerging from the door while Jim looked around to get his bearings. His eyes skimmed over me and the bale of hay before snapping back to stare at me. He was too far away for me to hear, but I saw the word "Adelaide" form on his mouth.

Noah had emerged from the tunnel. As he was closing the door he turned to see where Jim was looking. His mouth broke into an enormous grin. He ran over to greet me with a crushing bear hug and a hearty chuckle. I joined in his laughter.

"Adelaide, at some point you'll have to explain that bit in the root cellar!" He put me down and noticed Daphne. "You were there too, weren't you?" She looked at him curiously. He held out his hand. "I'm Noah."

"I know." She looked a little wary of him and didn't take his hand, but focused on his face. I could only assume she was trying to see the resemblance between this Noah and the one she knew in the future.

"We've met?" He looked amused.

"I'll explain later," I broke in. "We need to find someplace a little less exposed."

Jim had joined us at that point. "I know of a little house not far from here. I'm friends with the family. I was going to take Noah there to sort out what to do next."

"That sounds lovely. But Paris sounds even lovelier." I gave them a devilish smirk.

Noah grinned in response and adopted a patronizing tone. "Ok, Miss Adelaide. How do you propose we get to Paris?"

"With this." I pulled the wooden box out of my backpack.

"You captured Paris in a box?"

I grabbed his hand. "Hold Jim's hand, Noah."

Jim gave me a curious look. Noah reluctantly took his hand. I handed the box to

Daphne and took her hand. She flipped it open. Noah peeked inside and gasped slightly when he saw the glowing red button. We arrived on a deserted bank of the Seine. Jim and Noah were a bit stunned.

"Welcome to 2053!" Daphne said.

"Twenty years prior? Why did you take us back in time? We could've just stayed in the present."

"This is a great year in Paris' history," Daphne said. She dropped my hand and gestured across the river. "Jean DuFreulle's unveiling of 'The Slathering of Snarlak', the opening of Susan MacInnes's groundbreaking play 'Trained Monkeys'! We'll have some time for sightseeing won't we?"

Those events seemed harmless enough. "Well, we do have a time machine, and I suppose it helps that at this point the lab doesn't even know we exist. But first let's find ourselves a place to stay for the next few days and settle in. Agreed?" I held my hand out for the box.

She practically bounced with delight and seemed sated. "Alright." She gave me the box without hesitation. I shoved it in my pack again.

Noah watched me. "What is that, Addy?"

"It's a sphere, obviously."

"Doesn't look very sphere like."

"Don't be so closed minded, Noah."

"I think you have a lot of explaining to do."

"Yep, but it would be much better over room service, don't you think?" I nodded down the river toward the city.

Daphne started off along the riverbank toward the Eiffel Tower. We followed, Jim looking wary, Noah amused, and me exhausted. She led us to a hotel right off the Eiffel Tower. I knew it would be expensive, but we still had plenty of cash from my visit with Montgomery. We rented four rooms, and with a stern lecture about remaining inconspicuous, I left Daphne to wander while I filled Jim and Noah in on the events of my past few days. " I need help now to figure out how to take over the lab. From what I've been told, the board will be killed, but Doctor Lancing survives. I have a plan to get rid of him, but I'm not sure where to find him. I saw a laboratory area that seemed to be his office, only he wasn't there."

Jim had been able to fill in some of the gaps of my knowledge as I explained what was going on, however, his knowledge of Doctor Lancing was even more scarce than mine. "I've seen blueprints of the complex. He lives in a dome isolated from everyone else, but it should be connected to that office you found. Do you know when he leaves it to come after Noah?"

"Montgomery didn't mention it to me, no."

"He probably won't leave his quarters for at least a few days. He'll need time to make sure it's safe for him to emerge and plan what he's going to do next. It won't be easy to get inside; it's heavily secured and airlocked. Shame the Gardians didn't break into that one for us, but you might be able to lure him out if you can get to his lab area. You especially, Adelaide. If he sees you, he'll put two and two together and come after your sphere."

The locked doors I hadn't been able to explore from Doctor Lancing's office hadn't looked that secure to me. "That's fine then, I can handle it."

Jim gave me a concerned look. "What are you going to do to him Adelaide?"

I tried to ease Jim's concern with a nonchalant look. "Nothing. I simply plan to deliver the doctor to some people who will want to see him and leave him there."

He didn't seem convinced, but changed the subject anyway. "I'm not looking forward to going back. I've seen what you guys go through on the return trip."

"That won't happen, Jim. I've traveled a few times with Daphne now and no sickness."

Noah perked up at this news. "I'm not going to vomit all over myself when we get back? That's good news. Why?"

"You met the original programmer, right?"

"I did," Jim said. "A very troubled young man."

"Well the restrictions they put on the programmers to keep them in line inhibit their ability to perform their tasks and move us through time. Once Erica learned how to control the sphere and the person holding it and got the hang of moving them through time, it became effortless for both her and the traveller. She explained it as we're not physically moving, just time is shifting around us." I had to smile at his confused look as I remember Erica trying to explain it to me. "I don't pretend to understand it either." I thought back to my nervousness about Daphne's incredible abilities. "Let's hope he's still there though, it would be good to have a second programmer around. Jim, we'll need you to take over once we get back there. You know more about how that place runs than either of us. You're more likely to be able to talk people into staying and find ways to get in touch with the people who were funding us. We'll need to regain their trust quickly and assure them that everything is fine."

Jim's face fell as he looked at me. "I don't think I can do that, Adelaide."

"What?"

"Look, I'll put you in touch with the people you'll need to talk to, but I can't go back there."

I couldn't speak. My plan was suddenly falling apart all around me. "But Jim, we need you."

He shook his head. "I can't. That place has too many bad memories. I did too many things I didn't agree with."

"But it will be different if you're in charge!"

Jim gave me a piteous look. "Adelaide, you have no idea what that place did to me. No idea how I tried to fight back. In some ways, I succeeded, but in most I didn't. It'll be different, I'm sure, with you and Noah in charge, but I can't have anything to do with that place anymore."

I thought about telling him about Sunithe's disease and how he didn't have that much longer to live. That he needed the lab to find a cure. I kept silent because it felt like blackmail, and I couldn't do that to Jim. He had confidence in us being able to pull it off. I had to believe in that. I looked to Noah for help, but he just shrugged at me.

# Chapter 23

We spent three days in Paris. Though I was eager to finalize things, I knew I needed a break. Daphne was beside herself with glee, and I wanted to spend a few final days with Jim. The time finally came for us to put our plan into action. Daphne dropped Jim off at the island, then came back for us. The three of us grabbed hands again and found ourselves delivered into the center of the living dome's central courtyard. Noah laughed at our arrival. I found myself overwhelmed with relief to be back, even though I knew we had a lot of work ahead of us. It was like coming home to a house that had been ransacked by a tornado. Some people milling about turned to stare at us. We had appeared out of nowhere. I registered shock and distrust on their faces.

One man who looked mildly familiar came up to us. "Where did you come from?" He looked like he was ready to run from us at the slightest provocation.

"We're not with the Gardians if that's what you're worried about. We've come to get the lab back up and running."

"We were told yesterday that the lab was closing."

"Who told you that?" I asked, but had a feeling I knew it was Doctor Lancing.

"I don't know, some voice came over the loudspeaker system. I didn't even know we had a loudspeaker system in here. It was like a voice booming down from the sky." The man eyed me suspiciously.

Noah glanced at me, but I waved him off. "Well the voice was wrong."

"Who are you, if you're not with the Gardians?" His voice sounded accusatory.

"We work here too. We had to leave when the lab was attacked, but we came back as soon as we could. We're here to fix things and get the lab back up and running. Spread the word!" I said as cheerily as possible. I grabbed Noah and Daphne by the arms and dragged them off to the time travel laboratory entrance before he could ask me more questions I wasn't entirely prepared to answer.

The door slid open easily, and we started down the hallway. There were a few guards, dead on the floor. Daphne gasped beside me. I tried not to breathe too deeply. The guards looked gaunt under the harsh lights of the hallway.

We peeked into the doors as we continued. Most rooms were fine but perhaps a little disheveled. The place was deserted, though. After passing a few more dead guards I didn't blame people for wanting to stay away. "Noah, what are we going to do with them?" I asked.

"I guess we'll bury them, Adelaide." He pressed onward. I recognized the room where Jim and I had last eaten a meal together after my return from my Shakespeare mission. I knew that the return chamber was ahead. We entered the room where I had my hair cut. I wondered if Vanessa was still around, and if I could now voice my suspicions to her without fear of repercussions.

It felt strange going backwards through the rooms. The cleaning tub looked fine. There was no algae or dirt in it. I remembered the disorder from my last time through the examination room, so I was a little surprised to find Doctor Crebbs when we opened the door. She froze in place, organizing some paperwork in a drawer. Her usually stern demeanor melted in relief and surprise when she recognized us. "Noah." She put the papers down and came over to hug him. "Someone said you escaped."

"Jim got me out. He didn't think I had much of a future here."

"I'm glad, I wasn't looking forward to helping her erase your mind."

I could feel Noah tense beside me as I wondered who Doctor Crebbs had meant by "her." Before I could ask, Noah stepped forward slightly to confront her. "You mean you are the one who does it?" His temper flared.

She held a hand up and spoke quickly to stop him. "Noah, I didn't come up with the idea, and I certainly didn't approve of its use. But I know to do what I'm told or I'll end up the one with the scrambled brain."

He seemed unconvinced.

"I've saved your life more times than you can possibly know, and it killed me to know that I was basically about to undo all that." She didn't seem to be able to continue and her head fell.

I turned back to her and glanced at the box of files beside her. "Are you leaving?"

She didn't raise her head. She kept looking sadly at the floor. "There's nothing for me here. I was just trying to organize some of my research to take with me and then, yes. I was going to try and find another medical lab to take me in."

"We're going to rebuild this place. Noah and I will be in charge. You can stay, you'll never have to destroy another person's mind again, I can promise you that."

When she looked up, her face was clearly marked with pain. "I can't stay here. Now that I'm free to go, there are just too many memories here that I'd prefer to leave behind. I'm not proud of a lot of what I've done." She looked apologetically at us. "I'm sorry. There are other doctors here who can take my place. I'll leave copies of all my work, but I have to get out of here."

I thought about how Jim had the same reaction, the unwillingness to continue at this place now that they were able to leave with no repercussions. I nodded slightly. "I understand."

Doctor Crebbs's eyes welled up before she turned away from us. I led Daphne and Noah to the other side of the room and through the door. The lights of the White Box were blinding. "Well at least we'll never have to use this room again." I turned to Daphne and gave her an apologetic look.

"This is where you made people come back?" She seemed appalled.

"Well the padding protected people when they collapsed, and the mats were easy to clean up if someone vomited. Plus the lights made it easy to see if you brought back anything you shouldn't have and—"

"Enough!" She held up a hand to stop him. "Let's rip this out and put in some plants or something can we?" She looked uncomfortable in the room.

I couldn't blame her. The mats on the floor still looked moldy, and for the first time ever, I noticed another door on the other side of the room. I walked over to it but it wouldn't open. Noah came and stood next to me. "That's where they take our stuff away to inspect it. That must be where they store the sphere too."

"That explains why it's locked." I sighed. There were a lot of places that we'd have to explore, and my last expedition hadn't gone well. I wanted to go into the rooms off Doctor Lancing's office and see what they were like now. I wondered if Eliza was already in that hospital room.

"Come on, Adelaide. We have a few more things to deal with." Noah left the room, and Daphne and I followed him back through the examination room and the other return rooms to the hall. We turned left and continued onward.

170 – The Sphere

I stopped Noah again in front of a door that I knew was the boardroom. It had been locked the last time I was here. Noah looked at me in confusion. "I don't want to go in there," I told him. It was not just the fact that I knew the board was dead, it was also the unease from my only memory of being in there.

"That's okay. I'll check it out." Noah squeezed my shoulder and took a deep breath before opening the door. Daphne and I leaned our backs against the wall facing away from the door. Noah went in, and the door closed behind him. He was only in there for half a minute when he reemerged, his face grim.

"Well?" I asked him.

"They're not in there, but I'm pretty sure you still don't want to go in."

"If the bodies aren't in there, how do you know the board is dead?"

"Trust me, nothing that had been in there survived. Come on, let's find Doctor Lancing."

I stopped at a door that was familiar to me, but it took a few moments to remember why. This was the door I had noticed just a few days ago, where the older version of Noah had been kept a prisoner. "Montgomery," I whispered. I stepped towards the door and paused. "Noah, I think you should wait out here."

"What? Why?"

"I have something rather personal to deal with. I can explain it later. Daphne." She stepped up beside me as I made to open the door.

"Wait, she's allowed to go in but I'm not?"

"Noah please, just wait." I opened the door and pulled Daphne in after me.

Montgomery was lying on the bed. He looked weak and exhausted. I ran into the room and knelt by his bed. Daphne lingered by the doorway. "Montgomery, I'm so sorry."

"Adelaide," he said in barely a whisper. "I knew you'd come back for me." He glanced at Daphne in the doorway. "What's going on?"

"It doesn't matter Montgomery, we're sending you home."

"Adelaide," Daphne broke in, "are you sure you can trust him not to talk about this place?"

I looked back at Montgomery. He nodded and I smiled. "Not like anyone would believe you anyway, hey? Okay. Let's get you back home." I took his hand and helped him up. Daphne walked over and handed me the box as I heard the door slam and looked to the sound to see Noah.

"Who the hell is that?" Noah had followed us. I should've known he wouldn't have listened to me.

I looked at Daphne. "His study, a few moments after he disappeared. Can you see it?"

She closed her eyes and was still for a few moments. I watched as the spark of recognition ignited the rage inside Noah.

"Daphne." My voice both pleaded and warned her at the same time.

She held her finger up to silence me. She would be taking us into a split she hadn't yet traveled in herself but could at least see now. "Go."

"Good." I gripped his hand tighter and hit the button. We stood for a moment. I put the box down and let go of his hand, ready to catch him if he should collapse. How long had he been a prisoner in the lab? I tried to remember. Three weeks? "You're home." His frame trembled a little before he collapsed onto the floor and burst into tears. I knelt on the floor beside him, put my arm around him and tried to steady him. "Montgomery I am so sorry for everything that happened to you. I can only promise you that it will never happen to anyone else, and we will never bother you again."

He tried to contain his emotions and pulled a piece of paper out of his shirt pocket while wiping his eyes with his shirt. He handed it to me with a shaking hand. I barely had to open it to realize it was the note I had left for him.

When I wrote it, I had thought for sure it was full of lies. I tried to keep my face pleasant as I stood up. "I have to go."

He nodded. I grabbed the box off the table. I opened it, but following an impulse I didn't quite understand, bent over to kiss his forehead before pushing the button to return to the lab.

"All good?" Daphne asked.

I nodded.

Noah had had a small outburst. A chair was overturned in the room, and he was raging about, yelling about his right to a real life.

I had now seen three different versions of Noah. It was interesting how his experiences and memories had shaped the man he was. "What did you expect?" I yelled at him.

He stopped short. Daphne glanced nervously between us. I could tell she was uncomfortable with this version of Noah. She didn't quite know what to expect from him.

I continued my rant. "Did you think he'd be happy to see you? Like you'd be one of his sons and you could hang out together, and it would make up for him losing his entire family?"

Noah glared at me. "It's not that. I would never want that life. Never. No matter what that man said to you. You should have let him stay."

I glared at Noah, but I didn't want to fight with him. I knew he'd claim that he knew himself better than I did, and there would be no winning that argument for me. I left the room with the calm silence and air of someone with the absolute certainty that they had just done the right thing, Daphne hurrying after me.

Noah barged back into the hall after me, turning to head back to the living dome.

"Noah!" I yelled.

He hesitated and turned back to look at me, a scowl still on his face. "What?"

His anger disarmed me. I needed his support in this. "Please. We still have to deal with Doctor Lancing."

Noah hesitated. He knew he wasn't needed for this part of the plan either, but the desire to see the man who had made his life a living hell was too strong to resist. He also saw the fear in my face and drew himself up to demonstrate his courage. He walked past us and continued on down the hall, leading the way. He stopped short as he rounded a corner. His eyes narrowed. The two of us hurried to him to see what made him stop.

He stood there, at the end of the hall in front of the closed door to his office as though he had been waiting for us. He looked completely calm, yet there was something in his eyes that I found unnerving. The corner of his mouth lifted slightly in a lopsided cross between a vicious smile and a deadly frown. "Adelaide MacDuff." His voice sounded ancient though he looked no more than twenty.

I froze. Though his voice betrayed no trace of a southern drawl, I recognized it, and him, from our conversation on the road. A chill crawled up my spine. He had known who I was even back then. Why didn't he kill me when he had the chance? I realized that was in the future, in a different timeline that no longer included me. This man would never have that chance.

Noah leaned towards me, a bit of smugness in his voice. "He's just a man, Addy."

Daphne moved forward to stand at my side. I glanced at her out of the corner of my eye, took a deep breath and walked forward slowly. "Doctor Lancing."

He stepped forward as well, and we slowly started to cover the length of the hallway. "I knew you'd show up at some point."

My immature side wanted to respond with a chiding remark, but I knew better than to give anything away. I remained as silent as possible and tried to keep my breathing steady.

"It's like a drug, isn't it?" he asked. "The power of the sphere." I still said nothing. "It's how I got you all to obey. Best not ask too many questions, don't make too many waves? Heaven forbid you be denied access to your venerable sphere."

My fear abated slightly at his mocking tone. Now I was just getting annoyed. I felt a renewed confidence and answered his mocking with a slight eye roll. I shouldn't have given away my position. He re-adopted his silent stare and again I was unnerved. It seemed like he knew something I didn't. As though he already knew my plan and had a way to stop it.

We stopped a couple of feet away from each other. He was unarmed, but he gave off the air that he could kill me with a thought. Though he was not a large man, there was an impression of enormous power in his frame. I was struck immobile by my irrational fear and tried to calm my breath. I thought about Eliza and the vision of her torturing Noah. I felt Daphne's presence at my back.

"Who's your little friend?" he asked.

I kept silent still.

His eyes ran over me and paused at my right hand. There was a moment of hesitation in his countenance, and I tried to cling to that. "What's in the box, Addy?"

I inwardly cringed at his use of my nickname. I raised the box with my right hand, opened the lid and glanced in, keeping the opening away from him so he couldn't see inside. My heart rate accelerated, and the corners of my mouth crept up slightly. "Nothing," I breathed.

In an instant, he cleared the distance between us and wrenched my wrist to turn the box around and see inside. His grip was wiry like that of an old man who has worked with his hands all his life, and the fingertips dug painfully into my forearm. He looked at the empty box and looked up into my face, confusion wracking his features.

His eyes widened. He let go of my wrist, but it was too late. Daphne released my shoulder and took a few steps back, keeping the lid to the box in her hands open and cradling it close to her, her thumb poised over the button. I dropped my empty box on the ground and looked around at the circle of people surrounding us. They had torches and were dressed in dark cloaks that hid their faces from us. "Sarah?" I called out. I stepped slightly away from Doctor Lancing, and Daphne followed me. He whirled around, trying to figure out what was going on. I took advantage of his confusion to increase the distance between us.

Sarah moved forward from her place in the circle and pulled her hood down so I could see her face. She held up her left hand and gently waved a wrinkled piece of paper. I recognized it as the note I had tucked into the back of Noah's journal. It crumpled slightly in her hand as her grip tightened in rage. "Is this the man?"

I responded in a raised voice so Doctor Lancing would be sure to hear me as well. "Delivered, as promised. This is the man who will deceive you and kill many of your people. Do with him as you like." I turned to grab Daphne's hand and watched his face twist with rage as the torches closed in on us. He leapt forward to try and grab us, but landed in empty space.

Back in the hallway, Noah saw the pang of guilt on my face. "He may have just been a man, but he was a downright evil one." He walked down the hallway to rejoin Daphne and me and patted me roughly on the back. "You did the right thing." He was always quick to forgive me. "Now let's fix this pigsty up so we can get back to work!"

# Chapter 24

Noah started heading to the entrance, toward the main living dome. "Wait a second, Noah?"

He stopped and turned to look at me again.

"There's something else I want to check out, that was here when I was here in the future." I half expected him to want to come with me again, but he nodded and continued back down the hall.

"I'll see how the remaining folks are taking the news," he said. Daphne glanced toward him and back at me.

"You can come if you want." I had no idea what to expect, but I didn't want to force her to go with Noah if she wasn't comfortable with him. "Okay then," I said, when she stared at me silently.

I led her through the door at the end of the hall, feeling more confident now that I knew Doctor Lancing was out of the picture. The lights were already on, so nothing changed as we walked through the door. We went over to the dormitory first. Beds were untidy, as though they had recently been slept in and hastily made. There were a few more pictures of children still sitting on bedside desks. "What is this place?" Daphne asked me.

"I'm not sure," I said. "Some sort of dormitory for children. Maybe the children they kidnapped to be programmers."

Daphne shuddered beside me.

"And more." I walked over to the picture of Eliza with the ball and looked at it again. I had thought it had been taken shortly after she had tossed it in the air, but now I knew, she was levitating it. I showed it to Daphne. "This girl—I met her in the future."

Daphne took it in her hands. "How did you recognize her if she was so much older?"

"Well that's the thing, she wasn't older." I let Daphne absorb the information. "Also, I'm pretty sure she's levitating that ball in the picture."

Daphne laughed once. Then quickly quieted and looked at the picture with trepidation. Her breathing accelerated. "Levitating?" She handed the picture back to me.

I nodded. "I don't think time travel was the only abnormal thing going on around here." I placed the picture back on the desk and turned to the door. "Come on, let's see if she's still here."

Daphne didn't move. "Adelaide."

I turned back. "What is it?"

"I'm frightened."

I smiled and thought of my own unnerved feelings from my last trip in here. "There's nothing to be scared of," I said, trying to reassure her. After all, I told myself, she's just a young girl. "Come on." I took Daphne's hand. She let me lead her out of the room and back into the office. We walked over to the door to the hospital room when I turned to her. "You don't have to come in if you don't want to."

"What's in there?"

"I believe that girl in the picture is in there."

Daphne shook her head and backed away, her eyes widening. "No. I don't want to see her."

"Okay. I'll just be a few moments." I tried to give her a courageous smile and opened the door. I quickly entered as I heard the soft beep of machinery and closed the door. Eliza was there. She looked exactly the same as I remembered. "This can't be," I whispered to her. I saw the cable coming out of the back of her head but kept my distance. My eyes fell once again on the helmet. I walked over to the chair and lifted the helmet. I took a deep breath to try and steady my nerves and was about to place it on my head when I heard Daphne scream my name. "Daphne!" I yelled and let the helmet drop back into the chair.

My heart sped as I ran back to the door into Lancing's office. My eyes scanned the room but I couldn't see her anywhere. "Daphne!" I yelled again.

"Adelaide!" Her voice came from the hall.

I ran out into the hall. She stood at the end, torn over where to go. "It's Noah!"

I sprinted to meet her, and the two of us ran through the halls towards the entrance. I heard Noah call my name along the way and called out to him, "Noah!"

We turned the last corner and saw him a few feet from the entrance, a gun in his hand, pointed at the doors. A group of about a dozen people were pressed around them, banging their hands on the glass. "Noah, what's going on?" I asked as we approached.

"They're not happy about this idea, Adelaide. They want in, and they want us out of here." Thankfully the doors were holding, but if a librarian or a scout was out there, they'd be able to get in.

I moved a little closer to the doors, "Listen," I yelled to the crowd outside.

A fist slammed against the glass again, and I jumped back in alarm. "Noah, put that gun away!"

"No way."

"You're not helping," I hissed at him. "Please people, listen to me!"

"Come out here and we'll listen," one of the people yelled. The group echoed their agreement.

"Please, there's no reason to be angry, we're here to help you."

"How do we know you're not with them?" another man shouted.

"You have to trust us," I pleaded.

"Yeah right!" More fists banged against the glass. Someone found a shovel and started banging that against the doors.

"Daphne," I said, backing away. "Get back to Doctor Lancing's office." She turned and ran. "Noah?"

He backed away too, keeping the gun pointed at the group. "Maybe this was a bad idea, Adelaide." He jumped as the shovel made contact again, and a crack formed from where it struck. "Run."

I turned and yelled to him. I heard his footsteps behind me and glanced behind to see him following me with the gun. As we ran past another guard, I grabbed his gun as well. I had no intention of using it, but I didn't want the other people to get their hands on it either. I heard the sound of glass shattering behind us but focused on taking the correct path back to Doctor Lancing's office. I wasn't even sure there were other guards from other parts of the lab, still alive and well armed. "Noah what do we do?" I asked as I ran.

"Just keep going, Addy!"

We turned the last corner. Daphne stood in the doorway to the office, peering out from behind the door. She opened it wide as we approached. I saw her eyes fill with fear as she refocused behind us. I ran through, Noah just behind me, and she slammed the door. Noah threw his weight up against it and scanned for some extra security measures. When the first bang hit the door, he jumped back and re-aimed his gun. "Shit."

Daphne was crying. I pulled her behind me and pointed my gun as well. "Adelaide," she said to me, her voice broken.

"Wait a minute!" I said. I dropped the gun on the desk and ran past her, ignoring what she tried to tell me. "I've got an idea, Noah."

"You better make it quick, Addy!"

"Adelaide," Daphne said again, urgency in her voice this time.

"Just one moment, Daphne!" I waved her off and ran into the hospital room again. I wasted no time in putting the helmet back on my head and sitting in the chair. I saw Daphne follow me into the room and gasp before my mind was assaulted.

I squeezed the arms of the chair and tried to focus the thoughts on the crowd outside the door, but the images I saw kept going back to Noah and Montgomery being tortured. I tried to focus on the office outside, but Doctor Lancing entered my vision, leering down at me, and I was suddenly very afraid. I lost my fight, and my mind was all over the place. Places I didn't recognize, someone's home, other young children, an older man who cowered in a corner. A small bit of consciousness became aware that Daphne had grabbed my wrist. She was going to take us away somewhere. Yes, I thought! She'll take us all out of here! As soon as my mind had registered it though, she let go again. I heard her say something to Noah. Noah was in the room. My body was rigid with pain. My head was pounding. Where did Daphne go?

Noah was yelling something at me, but I couldn't hear it. As soon as I heard his voice, the images in my head went back to those of him being tortured. Suddenly I could tell that he was on the floor, writhing in pain, and it was no longer just in my head. My arms would not move. Noah was pleading with me. I wasn't the one hurting him, why was he pleading with me? "Noah!" I managed to yell. Focus, I yelled at myself. I turned my mind to Eliza, lying in the bed. Noah stopped yelling from the floor. My mind scanned the length of her body, and remembered what the back of her head looked like, the open skull and the claw digging into her brain.

My mind was suddenly freed. I wasted no time in taking the helmet back off. Noah was panting on the floor. "Noah!" I jumped off the chair and went to him on the floor, the sound of pounding on the door outside did not cease. "Are you okay?"

"I think so. What the hell happened, Adelaide?"

"I don't know." I looked around the room wildly. "Where's Daphne?" I exclaimed.

"She left." He shook his head as though trying to clear it and pressed a hand against his right temple. "She told me to wait here."

"As if we could go anywhere."

"She tried to take us somewhere, but she couldn't feel you. She said it was like you weren't here. What is that helmet, Addy?" He looked warily at it.

"Don't worry about that now. We've got…" I was distracted as Daphne entered the room again.

She left the door open. Beyond in the office I could see Jim standing at the desk. "Jim!" I called.

He held a hand up to silence me and pushed a button. I heard a door unlock and a mass of feet padded into the room with him. I tried to get up to defend him, but Daphne and Noah held me back. We could hear confused murmurs through the doorway before one voice spoke up above the rest.

"Jim! You're Doctor Lancing?" I could hear gasps and more murmurs.

"No," Jim said. "Doctor Lancing is dead. I killed him."

# Epilogue

Noah laid in the grass, staring up at the glass of the dome. His eyes automatically went to the spot that had been shattered in the attack. The glass had been repaired months ago, and Jim repeatedly told him that it was exactly the same as the other glass panels now, but Noah swore it looked different. A constant reminder of what had brought him to this state.

He had not anticipated this sort of fear when he and Addy tried to take over the lab. In fact, until the crowd had come after him, he had no fears at all. Now he had nightmares all the time. If it wasn't the lab being attacked again by the Gardians or by Doctor Lancing somehow finding his way back to this time, it was worse: getting stuck back in a time period he couldn't stand and resorting to living a normal life.

He took a deep breath and tried to calm himself. Addy had tried to convince him that if he ever got stuck again, Daphne would recognize it, and they'd come back for him. Daphne, his odd, surrogate daughter. He didn't understand why she clung to him so much. Addy said it had to do with another version of Noah from the future being a father figure to her. Noah laughed once at the idea. The sound disappeared in the massive space.

There she was, running across the open space, calling for him. No, he thought, sitting up. Not calling, yelling. Frantically yelling. Noah was on his feet and sprinting toward her. "Daphne! What is it!" he yelled as he closed the distance.

She stopped and waited for him to approach. "Something's wrong with Addy. When I brought her back, she seemed frightened. She said to get you; she said you'd understand."

The two of them raced across the lawn. Noah tried to work out what would have Adelaide frightened. She made it back, so she must not have gotten stuck. Perhaps she had seen Doctor Lancing. She had sent him back to the early 1600s, and her current mission put her in 1933 and later. Could he be over 300 years old? Adelaide said he looked exactly the same when she saw him in the future as he did just a few months ago.

They went through the glass doors of the entrance to the time travel lab and down the halls to the return chambers. "In here," Daphne said as she stopped in front of a door and opened it.

Adelaide was pacing back and forth, but stopped and ran to Noah when he entered. "Noah! I saw him again, he was there!"

It was just as Noah thought; Doctor Lancing had tracked her down. "What was Doctor Lancing doing in the 1930s? How did he find you?"

She shook her head. "No, not him. Byron!" She whispered the name as though saying it out loud would call him to the present.

The name meant nothing to Noah. "Who's Byron?"

"The man I saw in Shakespeare's time. The one I suspected of not belonging there. I was right, he didn't." She looked at him frantically.

It jogged his memory. He remembered the conversation with Adelaide so many months ago as they ate lunch. He gasped slightly as the implication hit him. "There's another time traveler."

*Special thanks to Sean for introducing me to Nanowrimo and daring me to do it. To PS, who gave me reason to push myself nearly every day in the end. To my sister, Heather, who filled my head with visions of glory after it was over. To my other sister, Nicole, who corrected my grammar and tried her best to point out my plot holes (and who probably has something to say about that sentence). To my mother, who can hunt down a split infinite like a hawk that hasn't eaten in years. To my father, because I had the rest of my family in here and felt bad leaving him out. To St. Elmo's Coffee Pub for providing me with my weekend morning ritual writing space and the best chai lattes in existence. And to Nanowrimo for sending me those motivational emails that I didn't believe until it was actually happening to me.*

Made in the USA
Columbia, SC
24 October 2018